The Love Song of
Miss Queenie Hennessy

The Love Song of Miss Queenie Hennessy

Rachel Joyce

W F HOWES LTD

18926602I

This large print edition published in 2015 by
W F Howes Ltd
Unit 4, Rearsby Business Park, Gaddesby Lane,
Rearsby, Leicester LE7 4YH

1 3 5 7 9 10 8 6 4 2

First published in the United Kingdom in 2014
by Doubleday

RENFREWSHIRE
Dept of
Education
& Leisure
COUNCIL

A CIP catalogue record for this book is available
from the British Library

ISBN 978 1 47129 595 9

Typeset by Palimpsest Book Production Limited,
Falkirk, Stirlingshire

Printed and bound in Great Britain
by TJ International Ltd, Padstow, Cornwall

MIX
Paper from
responsible sources
FSC® C013056
FSC
www.fsc.org

For my sisters, Amy and Emily, and in memory of a garden in Roquecor

All journeys have secret destinations of which the traveller is unaware.

Martin Buber, *The Legend of the Baal-Shem*

THE FIRST LETTER

ST BERNADINE'S HOSPICE
BERWICK-UPON-TWEED

Monday, 11 April

Dear Harold,

This may come to you as some surprise. I know it is a long time since we last met, but recently I have been thinking a lot about the past. Last year I had an operation on a tumour, but the cancer has spread and there is nothing left to be done. I am at peace and comfortable but I would like to thank you for the friendship you showed me all those years ago. Please send my regards to your wife. I still think of David with fondness.

With my best wishes,

Q h

THE SECOND LETTER

ST BERNADINE'S HOSPICE
BERWICK-UPON-TWEED

13 April

SO HERE IT IS

Long ago, Harold, you said to me: 'There are so many things we don't see.' What do you mean? I asked. My heart gave a flip. 'Things that are right in front of us,' you said.

We were in your car. You were driving, as you always did, and I was in the passenger seat. Night was falling, I remember that, so we must have been on our way back to the brewery. In the distance, streetlamps sprinkled the blue velvet skirts of Dartmoor, and the moon was a faint chalk smudge.

It was on the tip of my tongue to tell the truth. I couldn't bear it any longer. Pull over, I almost shouted. Listen to me, Harold Fry—

You pointed ahead with your driving glove. 'You see? How many times have we come this way? And I've never noticed that.' I looked where you were indicating, and you laughed. 'Funny, Queenie, how we miss so much.'

7

While I was on the edge of a full confession, you were admiring a roof extension. I unclipped my bag. I took out a handkerchief.

'Do you have a cold?' said you.

'Do you want a mint?' said I.

Once again, the moment had passed. Once again, I had not told you. We drove on.

This is my second letter to you, Harold, and this time it will be different. No lies. I will confess everything, because you were right that day. There were so many things you didn't see. There are so many things you still don't know. My secrets have been inside me for twenty years, and I must let them go before it is too late. I will tell you everything, and the rest will be silence.

Outside I see the battlements of Berwick-upon-Tweed. A blue thread of the North Sea crosses the horizon. The tree at my window is pointed with pale new buds that glow in the dusk.

Let us go then, you and I.

We don't have long.

ALL YOU HAVE TO DO IS WAIT!

Your letter arrived this morning. We were in the dayroom for morning activities. Everyone was asleep.

Sister Lucy, who is the youngest nun volunteering in the hospice, asked if anyone would like to help with her new jigsaw. Nobody answered. 'Scrabble?' she said.

Nobody stirred.

'How about Mousetrap?' said Sister Lucy. 'That's a lovely game.'

I was in a chair by the window. Outside, the winter evergreens flapped and shivered. One lone seagull balanced in the sky.

'Hangman?' said Sister Lucy. 'Anyone?'

A patient nodded, and Sister Lucy fetched paper. By the time she'd got sorted, pens and a glass of water and so on, he was dozing again.

Life is different for me at the hospice. The colours, the smells, the way a day passes. But I close my eyes and I pretend that the heat of the radiator is the sun on my hands and the smell of lunch is salt in the air. I hear the patients cough, and it is only the wind in my garden by the sea.

I can imagine all sorts of things, Harold, if I put my mind to it.

Sister Catherine strode in with the morning delivery. 'Post!' she sang. Full volume. 'Look what I have here!'

'Oh, oh, oh,' went everyone, sitting up.

Sister Catherine passed several brown envelopes, forwarded, to a Scotsman known as Mr Henderson. There was a card for the new young woman. (She arrived yesterday. I don't know her name.) There is a big man they call the Pearly King, and he had another parcel though I have been here a week and I haven't yet seen him open one. The blind lady, Barbara, received a note from her neighbour – Sister Catherine read it out – spring is coming, it said. The loud woman called Finty opened a letter informing her that if she scratched off the foil window, she would discover that she'd won an exciting prize.

'And, Queenie, something for you.' Sister Catherine crossed the room, holding out an envelope. 'Don't look so frightened.'

I knew your writing. One glance and my pulse was flapping. Great, I thought. I don't hear from the man in twenty years, and then he sends a letter and gives me a heart attack.

I stared at the postmark. Kingsbridge. Straight away I could picture the muddy blue of the estuary, the little boats moored to the quay. I heard the slapping of water against the plastic buoys and the clack of rigging against the masts. I didn't dare open the envelope. I just kept looking and looking and remembering.

Sister Lucy rushed to my aid. She tucked her childlike finger under the flap and wiggled it along the fold to tear the envelope open. 'Shall I read it out for you, Queenie?' I tried to say no, but the no came out as a funny noise she mistook for a yes. She unfolded the page, and her face seeped with pink. Then she began to read. 'It's from someone called Harold Fry.'

She went as slowly as she could, but there were a few words only. '*I am very sorry. Best wishes.* Oh, but there's a PS too,' said Sister Lucy. 'He says, *Wait for me.*' She gave an optimistic shrug. 'Well, that's nice. Wait for him? I suppose he's going to make a visit.'

Sister Lucy folded the letter carefully and tucked it back inside the envelope. Then she placed my post in my lap, as if that were the end of it. A warm tear slipped down the side of my nose. I hadn't heard your name spoken for twenty years. I had held the words only inside my head.

'Aw,' said Sister Lucy. 'Don't be upset, Queenie. It's all right.' She pulled a tissue from the family-size box on the coffee table and carefully wiped the corner of my closed-up eye, my stretched mouth, even the thing that is on the side of my face. She held my hand, and all I could think of was my hand in yours, long ago, in a stationery cupboard.

'Maybe Harold Fry will come tomorrow,' said Sister Lucy.

At the coffee table, Finty still scratched away at the foil window on her letter. 'Come on, you little bugger,' she grunted.

'Did you say "Harold Fry"?' Sister Catherine jumped to her feet and clapped her hands as if she was trapping an insect. It was the loudest thing that had happened all morning, and everyone murmured 'Oh, oh, oh' again. 'How could I have forgotten? He rang yesterday. Yes. He rang from a phone box.' She spoke in small broken sentences, the way you do when you're trying to make sense of something that essentially doesn't. 'The line was bad and he kept laughing. I couldn't understand a word. Now I think about it, he was saying the same thing. About waiting. He said to tell you he was walking.' She slipped a yellow Post-it note from her pocket and quickly unfolded it.

'Walking?' said Sister Lucy, suggesting this was not something she'd tried before.

'I assumed he wanted directions from the bus station. I told him to turn left and keep going.'

A few of the volunteers laughed, and I nodded as if they were right, they were right to laugh, because it was too much, you see, to show the consternation inside me. My body felt both weak and hot.

Sister Catherine studied her yellow note. 'He said to tell you that as long as he walks, you must wait. He also said he's setting off from Kingsbridge.' She turned to the other nuns and volunteers. 'Kingsbridge? Does anyone know where that is?'

12

Sister Lucy said maybe she did but she was pretty sure she didn't. Someone told us he'd had an old aunt who lived there once. And one of the volunteers said, 'Oh, I know Kingsbridge. It's in South Devon.'

'South Devon?' Sister Catherine paled. 'Do you think he meant he's walking to Northumberland from all the way down there?' She was not laughing any more, and neither was anyone else. They were only looking at me and looking at your letter and seeming rather anxious and lost. Sister Catherine folded her Post-it note and disappeared it into the side pocket of her robe.

'Bull's-eye!' shouted Finty. 'I've won a luxury cruise! It's a fourteen-night adventure, all expenses paid, on the *Princess Emerald*!'

'You have not read the small print,' grumbled Mr Henderson. And then, louder: '*The woman has not read the small print.*'

I closed my eyes. A little later I felt the sisters hook their arms beneath me and lift my body into the wheelchair. It was like the way my father carried me when I was a girl and I had fallen asleep in front of the range. '*Stille, stille,*' my mother would say. I held tight on to your envelope, along with my notebook. I saw the dancing of crimson light beyond my eyelids as we passed from the dayroom to the corridor and then past the windows. I kept my eyes shut all the way, even as I was lowered on to the bed, even as the curtains were drawn with a whoosh against the pole, even as I heard the click of the door, afraid that if I opened my eyes the wash of tears would never stop.

Harold Fry is coming, I thought. I have waited twenty years, and now he is coming.

AN UNLIKELY PLAN

'Queenie? Queenie Hennessy?' When I woke, a new volunteer was standing against my window. For a moment he seemed made of light.

'You were crying,' he said. 'In your sleep.' Only now that I looked properly, I found he was not a man after all. He was a tall and big-boned she, dressed in a nun's habit, a wimple and a knitted navy-blue cardigan. I shot up my hand to hide. But the stranger didn't stare and neither did she drop her gaze, as people usually do, to my fingers or my feet or any bit of me that was not my face. She just smiled.

'Are you upset about this man called Harold Fry?' she said.

I remembered your news. That you were walking to see me. But this time I couldn't see the hope in it, I could see only the miles. After all, I'm at one end of England and you're at the other. The wind has a softness in the south, but up here it's so wild it can chuck you off your feet. There's a reason for this distance, Harold. I had to get as far from you as I could bear.

The nun shifted from the window, taking with her a small potted cactus plant from the sill. She said she'd heard about your very exciting message. She knew that you were walking from Kingsbridge to Berwick-upon-Tweed and that all I had to do was wait. She stooped to rescue the cactus from the floor. 'I don't know Mr Fry personally, of course, but it appears you called into the void and an echo came back. What a good man.' She smiled at the cactus as if she had just blessed it. 'By the way, I am Sister Mary Inconnue.' She pronounced it *An-con-noo*, like in the French. 'Pleased to meet you.'

The nun drew up the chair and sat beside my bed. Her hands lay in her lap, large and red. A washing-up set of hands. Her eyes were a sharp, clear green.

'But look at me,' I tried to say. It was no good. Instead, I reached for my notebook and HB pencil. I wrote her a message: **How can I do this? How can I <u>wait</u> for him?** I tossed the pencil aside.

I'd thought I would never see you again. Even though I've spent twenty years in exile, even though I've lived with a piece of my life missing, I thought you had forgotten me. When I sent you my first letter, it was to put my affairs in order. It was to draw a veil for myself over the past. I didn't expect you to post a reply. I certainly didn't expect you to walk with it. There is so much to confess, to atone for, so much to mend, and I can't do it. Why do you think I left Kingsbridge and

16

never came back? If you knew the truth, I'm afraid you'd hate me. And you must know the truth, you see. There cannot be a meeting between us without it.

I remembered the first time I spotted you in the yard of the brewery. Then I pictured your son in my red wool mittens and I saw Maureen too, her eyes blazing, beside a basket of washing in your garden at 13 Fossebridge Road. Don't walk, I thought. The nun with a funny name was right: you're a good man. I had the chance to speak twenty years ago and I failed. Over and over, I failed. I am words without a mouth. Don't come now.

I wrote, **It's too late.**

Sister Mary Inconnue read the message in my notebook and said nothing. For a long time she remained with her hands in her lap, so still that I began to wonder if she'd dropped asleep. Then she rolled up her sleeves like a nun who means business. Her arms were smooth and weather-tanned. 'Too late? It's never too late. It seems to me you have something else to say to Harold Fry. Isn't that why you're upset?'

Well, that did it. I was crying again.

She said, 'I have a plan. We're going to write him a second letter. Don't forget, you opened this can of worms when you sent your first one. So now you need to finish. Only this time, don't give him the sort of message he might expect from a gift card. Tell him the truth, the whole truth. Tell him how it really was.'

I looked to the window. Black gossamer scraps of cloud chased across a weak sky. The sun was a thimble of light, and the dark branches of the tree trembled. I pictured you at one end of England, walking down a country lane. I pictured myself at the other, sitting in a bed in a small room. I thought of the miles between us: the railway tracks, the bus routes, the roads, the rivers. I pictured the steeples and towers, the slate roofs and tin roofs, the stations, the cities, the towns, the villages, the fields. And so many people. People sitting on platforms and passing in cars and staring from buses and trudging down roads. Since I left Kingsbridge, I've remained single. I made my home in a derelict timber beach house, and I tended my heart in a garden by the sea. My life has been small, it has been nothing to speak of. But the past is still inside me, Harold. I have never let it go.

'You don't have to write this letter on your own,' said Sister Mary Inconnue. 'I will help. There's an old portable typewriter in the office.'

I remembered how long it had taken me to spell out my first letter in order for Sister Lucy to copy it on her laptop. And I suppose you noticed the mess I made of both my signature and your address on the envelope. What with all the shenanigans getting that letter in the post, a carrier pigeon might have been quicker.

But Sister Mary Inconnue was still talking. 'Every day we'll do it. You can make notes and I'll type them. I don't suppose you know shorthand?'

I nodded.

'Well, there you are. We will write, you and I, until Harold Fry gets here. I'll do it in the first person, as if I am you. I'll transcribe everything. I won't miss out one word. Your letter will be waiting for Harold Fry when he arrives.'

And you promise he will read it before he sees me?

'I give you my word.'

Already there was something appealing about her idea. Already I was composing the opening sentences. I think I closed my eyes, because when I opened them, Sister Mary Inconnue had moved again and this time she was seated beside the slight bump of my feet. She had put on a pair of blue plastic-framed reading glasses that gave her a goggle-eyed look, and she held up a battered leather carrying bag the size of a briefcase. Its key was tied to the handle with a loop of string.

She laughed. 'You fell asleep. So I nipped to the office and took the liberty of borrowing the type-writer.' She opened my notebook to a fresh page. She replaced it on my lap alongside the pencil.

'You see how it is?' said Sister Mary Inconnue, unlocking the leather bag and removing the type-writer. It was a cream Triumph Tippa. I had the same model once. 'Harold Fry is walking. But in another way, even though you're here, even though you've done your travelling, you're starting a journey too. It's the same and not the same. You see?'

I nodded. **And if I'm not here at least my letter will be.**

Sister Mary Inconnue settled herself and rested the typewriter on her knees. 'Now then,' she said, flexing her red fingers. 'Where's the tab set key?'

We worked for the rest of the morning and then after lunch and into the dusk. Once I'd started, I couldn't stop. I pointed to my writing. **Does it make sense to you?**

'Perfect sense,' she said.

I tore out sheets as I finished, numbering each one, and Sister Mary Inconnue picked them up and typed. I kept telling myself I'd go as far as the next page, and then the next page came and I filled that too. I wrote everything you have read so far, while Sister Mary Inconnue clacked and slapped at her keys. And this is what we are still doing. I am writing and she is typing.

'Good,' she says. 'This is good.'

Tonight the duty nurse performed our evening rituals. She cleaned my mouth with mouthwash and a tiny sponge on a stick. She applied jelly where my lips have cracked, and she changed the dressings. Dr Shah, the palliative care consultant, asked if I had more pain, but I told him no, it was only the same. There was no need for me to be in discomfort, he said. If anything troubled me, a change could be made to my medication. Once the nurse had applied my new pain patch, Sister Lucy massaged my hands. Her smooth, plump fingers travelled my stiff ones, easing the joints and stroking. She fetched her sparkly polish and painted my nails.

In my sleep I saw your son. 'Yes, David,' I said. 'Yes.' I took a blanket and tucked it round him in case he was cold.

SSSH NOW

The night is not good. It's David. David. In my head. I can't sleep.

Every time I close my eyes, I see him. In the armchair beside my electric heater. Black overcoat. Shouting for things.

I ring for help.

SISTER PHILOMENA: *What is it?*

ME: **I have nightmare.**

SISTER P: *Take this. Morphine.*

(Sip, sip.)

SISTER P: *Put down your pencil, Queenie. Put down your notebook. Sleep now.*

THE LAST STOP

After my disturbed night, I slept until midday. When I woke, I had a visitor. She had a grapefruit on her head. She'd also brought her horse. The two of them left only when Sister Mary Inconnue arrived with her typewriter.

I wrote for her that I'd had strange guests who belonged to a circus, not a hospice, and she smiled. 'People pay good money for drugs like yours.' Her eyes went skew-whiff behind her reading glasses.

Do you have a problem with your vision? I spelled out the words.

'Not at all,' she said. 'I was winking at you. How do you feel today?'

The starched cornette on her head shone milk white, as did her habit beneath her belted black tabard apron. She wore sandals over white socks, and the socks bunched a little under the Velcro straps. She pulled a fresh packet of A4 paper from her bag, and also a Tipp-Ex correction pen. 'I see you have another message,' she said, pointing at a postcard propped beside your letter on the bedside table. I had no idea what she was talking about.

I'd gone and forgotten again, you see. I had forgotten in the night about the walking.

'Oh, Queenie. You're not going to cry?' Sister Mary Inconnue laughed, and I knocked back my head to show I wasn't going to make a fool of myself. 'Let's see what Harold Fry has to tell us,' she said.

There was a picture of Bantham Beach. One of the nuns must have left the postcard while I was sleeping. Sister Mary Inconnue showed me the writing on the back. *'Keep faith, Harold Fry.'* You may not know this, Harold, but I'm not a religious person. I hear the nuns pray, their songs from the chapel, but I do not join in. And since when did you know about faith? So far as I remember, you never entered a church. The last time I saw you, well . . . you did not look like a man who'd found God.

So far as I remember, you never walked very far, either. I can think of only one occasion. But maybe now is not the time.

'We'd better get back to your letter,' said Sister Mary Inconnue.

She opened my notebook and passed the pencil. Cramp. I could barely move my right arm. My hand poked solid from the wrist. It must have been all the writing I did yesterday. I'm not used to working with my hands any more. My fingers trembled like anemones in the

24

rock pools of my garden in Embleton Bay. I made it on a clifftop by the sea, and so I called it a sea garden.

'Help me,' I honked. 'I can't write.'

Sister Mary Inconnue put down her typewriter and took my hands in hers. She rubbed my fingers and lifted them to her mouth. Then she blew on them as if she expected them to inflate. 'Look at you, Queenie,' she said. 'With your nails all sparkly now.' She laughed.

Sometimes a person can smile when you are feeling only the difficulty of a thing and the problem unravels before your eyes and becomes straightforward.

'Let's try again,' she said.

She slotted the pencil into my hand. She curled my fingers round it, one by one.

'What do you want to tell Harold Fry?'

I remember Bantham Beach. I went there when I first arrived in Devon. This was nearly twenty-four years ago. It was before you and I met. It was also Christmas, and I had a lot to think about.

I hadn't intended to come to Kingsbridge. All I knew was that I couldn't stay in Corby. Things had gone wrong for me there, and so I was doing what I always did when something went wrong. I was running away.

'Once a thing is kaput,' my mother used to say as she snatched up a cracked piece of china and dumped it in the bin, 'it can never look the same. Get rid of it.' I can still hear the words, her throaty accent. Chipped plates and glassware, ripped stockings, buttonless cardigans, plaster ornaments lacking heads or feet – nothing met her mercy. My parents were never wealthy – we lived on my father's salary as a carpenter in a small rented house at the end of a Kent village – and my mother was a large Austrian woman with chunky hands that seemed permanently smeared with goose fat. She was constantly dropping things. It was a wonder we had anything left. My father checked the bin when she wasn't looking, retrieving what could be fixed and slipping the pieces out to his workshop. Somehow it rarely happened, the fixing, and when it did my mother would only gaze accusingly at a glued-back-together plate as if to say, 'You? I thought I was done with you.'

Perhaps I took my mother more literally than she intended, but I applied her rule to my life; after all, we are all searching for them, the rules. We pick them up from the strangest places, and if they appear to work once we can live a whole lifetime by them, regardless of the unhappiness and difficulty they may later bring. So when I failed a dance exam, I refused to continue. It was simpler to walk away than face my teacher's disappointment. When a friend badly hurt my feelings at holiday camp, I did the same: I insisted on returning home. Years later I applied for Oxford

University, and I suppose you could say that in this way I escaped from my parents. Being their sole child had become too complicated.

Since Corby, I'd been travelling for days. A night here. A night there. Sometimes only hours. Nowhere long enough to know anyone. Nowhere long enough to become known. I barely unpacked my suitcase. I just kept moving and moving until the little bus stopped and I saw the sea. It was the last stop, said the driver. He switched off the lights. He switched off the engine.

And what happens at the last stop? I thought.

I made my way past the sand dunes and tall spikes of marram grass. A battering wind blew up from the Channel, and I had to bow my head in order to push forward, gripping my collar to my throat with one hand and dragging my tartan suitcase with the other. The case contained everything I owned. My books, my clothes. My dance shoes. I reached the water's edge and I felt the terrible despair of someone who is used to running because that is what she has always done, and now she faces a brick wall.

I still remember the winter sky that evening. Whenever I worked in my sea garden and I saw a sunset like that, I'd think back to Bantham Beach. It was as if the sun had been torn open. Everything was scarlet. The clouds were flames, so wild and vibrant that blue didn't look like a colour any more. The sea and land served as a mirror. The ribbed sand was on fire. So were the stones and maroon rock pools. The pink crests of the waves. The burning hump of Burgh Island. The red even shone in my hands.

Why didn't I keep walking forward? I had little money. No job. No place to stay. The water tipped my toes. In very little time it could be as high as my ankles. Once a thing is broken—

And then I felt a small flutter in my belly.

I turned my back on the sea and dragged my suitcase towards the sand dunes. By the time I was up at the road, the wind had dropped and the sun was gone. The sky was a chalky mauve, almost silver, and so was the land. The first of the evening stars pierced the dusk.

I am starting again, I thought. Because that is what you do when you reach the last stop. You make a new beginning.

Sister Mary Inconnue clasps her fingertips above her head and performs a short series of stretches for her neck. My pages are spread at her feet. The light has gone from the window, and the moon is back, a white cuticle.

'Look how much you've done, Queenie. It's only your second day of writing, and see how many pages you've filled. There is so much to tell. You remember so much.'

Of course I remember. Songs from the past fill my head. I will confess everything. I will not be afraid.

'How's the hand?' asks Sister Mary Inconnue. 'Not too sore?'

I try to smile, only it comes out as something else and I need a tissue.

I turn to a fresh page.

LET'S GET THIS BIT OVER AND DONE WITH, SHALL WE?

*S*t *Bernadine's Hospice is a charitable nursing home that offers skilled and compassionate care to patients with any life-limiting illness,* said the leaflet. *The nuns who live and work here are trained nurses and volunteers. A medical team from the hospital is on hand to offer further support.*

'But I don't want to go there,' I tried to say to the GP. This was after my last operation, when I could still manage a few sounds that people recognized as words. I returned the leaflet to his desk.

I knew St Bernadine's. It was a low black flint building on the edge of town. I passed the hospice on the bus if I had to mend tools for my garden and needed the large hardware store in Berwick-upon-Tweed. I always felt a tenderness for my tools and treated them like friends. But passing the hospice, I'd turn my back on the building to look at the sea instead. I pulled out my notebook. **I want to stay in my home**, I wrote.

The GP nodded. He picked up a pen and rolled it between his fingers. 'Of course you don't have to go to St Bernadine's if you don't want to, Queenie.'

He kept his eyes fixed on that pen of his, and every once in a while a sigh slipped from his mouth as if an explosion had gone on somewhere deep inside his chest. 'The cancer is advanced. There's no more surgery we can do now. You know the prognosis is not—?' he whispered. 'You do know?'

'Yes,' I said. I reached for my walking sticks, though I wasn't going to leave. I didn't want him to have to say any more, and holding on to my sticks was about the best thing I could think of.

'I'm not forcing you to go to St Bernadine's. Of course I'm not. But they can make sure you're comfortable there. I'm concerned about you in that beach house. No one else spends the winter on Embleton Bay. I know you have electricity but you don't have proper heating. And the coastal path is almost inaccessible in this weather. We couldn't get an ambulance to you. If we needed one.'

I have Simon. The hospital volunteer. He comes.

'But only three times a week. You need full-time care.'

The air seemed so thick that I had to concentrate in order to breathe. I sort of didn't hear any more, or if I did I heard only select words, like 'complicated' and so on.

Nevertheless, I would have stuck to my guns. I would have stayed in my wooden home, but my whole face began to drop and shift shape. My mouth wouldn't work, and my eye wouldn't open. It was difficult to eat. It was difficult to speak. I stopped my daily walk and I stopped going to the shop. I didn't want people to see me. I was so ashamed. If visitors came, I didn't answer the door. I even avoided working in my sea garden, for fear they'd find me. I thought, *I will sleep now, sleep, sleep*, but it never came, the sleep. I didn't want to trouble anyone. I just wanted to be able to let go. But every time I thought of letting go, I wanted only to hold on. I admit I cried. The rain kept coming, and so did the wind. I watched my sea garden from the door, the gales upending the driftwood figures, the rain drowning the rock pools. Winter seemed to have no end.

When Simon, the volunteer, heard I'd chosen St Bernadine's he said, Oh, his aunt went there. 'It's a very special place,' he promised. 'You don't have to be religious. They do all sorts. Music and art and stuff. And there's a nice garden. You'll like that. My aunt was happy right until the—'

And then he smiled as if he had completely forgotten how to speak.

Simon is a bear of a person, and he wears a duffel coat with toggles that don't quite reach. I sat very still while he packed my nightclothes, slippers, towels. We have been everywhere together, that suitcase and I. Simon asked if there was anything else I would like to take and I couldn't think because it was too strange to think I was

32

leaving. I had lived in that beach house for twenty years, ever since I left you and Kingsbridge. The place was a part of me in the same way that the past was a part of me and you were a part of me and so were my bones. I looked at the painted grey walls, the bare board floors, the second-hand paisley throws I had found in thrift shops and the multi-coloured rag rug I made one winter. The old cooker, the copper pans, the blue wood shutters, the glass bottles and books on the windowsill. The pea-green china cups and saucers with gold rims I'd bought all those years ago in Kingsbridge in case you ever visited and stayed for tea. Already it was so cold without the heat of the woodburner that Simon's breath was a great cloud of smoke above his head. Mine was only a trickle.

Simon carried me down the sand path to his car. All the other beach houses were still shut up for winter. I was like a little bird, Simon laughed, and I knew that if I really were a bird I'd be dead already. I tried not to stay any more with that idea because it frightens me, Harold, when those thoughts come. He carried me past the public golf course and the clubhouse. No one was at the window and I was glad. Simon switched on the car radio to keep me company while he went back to fetch my suitcase, but the solitude and the silence are what I am used to.

As we drove away I turned my head for a glimpse of my sea garden. I saw the flint walls. The coloured flags. The tips of seed heads and the driftwood figures. They were silhouettes up on the cliff against a dense sea mist. In the village we passed the rows of black flint and whitewashed cottages, and the land opened like a winter book. Hedgerows were bare sticks. Last year's leaves clung to the trees like little bats, and a belt of Norwegian spruce swayed in the wind. There was no sign of the Cheviots. Only later did I realize that I'd looked for all these landmarks instead of saying goodbye. But sometimes you don't say the word because you think a thing is ongoing when actually it is already over.

The ten bedrooms here are at the front of the hospice with views towards the battlements, the mouth of the Tweed and the sea. The dayroom, the chapel and the dining room are at the back of the building, with large French windows that open out on to the Well-being Garden. Volunteers like Simon arrive every day to sit with us and tend the grounds, to cut back, to sweep, to dig over. I watch from the window. I watch the nuns, too, their robes blowing in the wind, and they are like white sails on a green sea.

When it came to our goodbyes, Simon said, 'I'm going away. For a few months. But I'll see you when I come back. Yeah?'

I nodded because he is a kind young man and I did not wish to upset things. He stooped to hug me and I felt the great boom of his heart. 'You take care,' he said. His face was wet, but we both smiled as if it wasn't.

Afterwards I watched him bound down the steps to the car park two at a time. I watched him jump into his red car and *peep-peep* the horn as he drove away. Then I turned my head to the double doors that lead to the inpatient unit. They are plain doors, nothing special, but they seemed made of iron and bolts. This is how a prisoner must feel, I thought: as if life is closing down. Sister Philomena, the Mother Superior, took up my suitcase.

From the other side of the door came a hoot of laughter. 'Fuck me. I've won a camper van!' The laughter was followed by a dour Scottish voice: 'You have not read the small print. She has not read the small print.'

Sister Philomena gave a radiant smile. 'Our hospice may not be what you expect,' she said.

THE TALL MAN AND THE SNOW

When I woke this morning, Harold, the dawn sky was the colour of a pearl oyster. A flurry of white blossom passed my window. I remembered snow. I reached for my notebook.

Twenty-four years ago. I'm standing in my new office. This is my first day at the brewery and I'm frightened. Out of my depth. The room is small and intensely cold. There is a desk and boxes of screwed-up invoices but clearly no system. I check my face in my compact mirror and pin up a few brown curls that have slipped free. Lipstick? No lipstick? I am still trying to work out how to look like a trained accountant. The smell of the place, the hops and the cigarettes, makes me want to be sick. Then something catches my eye at the window. A fleck of white. I move closer. I steal a glimpse outside.

The window looks down over the yard and some industrial-size bins. It's hardly picturesque. But the sky is heavy with winter cloud, and snow is beginning to drop like white feathers twisting in the air. I press my face and fingers to the chill of the glass and look up at the dizzying shower of white. No one has forecast snow, so it seems a small miracle, the way it can sometimes when there is a surprise change in the weather. I watch the yard and the bins and they look beautiful, quickly transforming from dark to white, from hard to soft. I forget about feeling ill or cold. I forget about being frightened.

A metal door clunks open and a tall figure in a coat rushes out.

It's you.

Like me, you catch sight of the snowflakes and you seem surprised. You peer upwards, just as I did, with your hand making a tunnel for your eyes. You laugh. Then you glance to your left and right to check that no one is watching and you make your way to the bins. Satisfied that you are alone, you pull out a bag you must have been hiding inside your coat. Quickly lifting the lid on a bin, you place several empty beer cans inside it. All the lights are on in the brewery and you are caught in a bluish inky glow, with your shadow resting beside you on the thin layer of new snow. I wonder why you have to get rid of the cans so secretly. This is a brewery, after all. It is midmorning, and already I've noticed several of the reps are half-cut.

Whatever the reason, you seem relieved to be rid of those cans. You replace the bin lid and rub your hands the way my mother used to when a chore was done to her satisfaction.

You turn to go inside and then you seem to sense someone close by. You check the yard again. No, I think, he's spotted me up here. Discovering it is only your shadow in the snow, you give another laugh. So do I. Your shadow lets us both off the hook.

Caught in a square of light from the window, you lift one arm and your shadow does the same. You wave and your shadow waves back. Then you raise your left foot and shake it a little and so does your Harold double; he shakes his foot too. Once again you check carefully that no one is in the yard, no one is watching, and then you strike a new pose. What are you up to? I'm hooked. With your left shoulder lifted, your elbows tucked into your waist and your hands poised, you begin a soft shoe shuffle in the powdery snow. You glide a little to the left, a little to the right, sashaying your body this way and that, balancing gently on one foot, then on the other. Once, you even twist your heels and give a full turn. All the time you dance, you keep an eye on your shadow and you're grinning, as if you can't quite believe it has the energy to keep up with you.

I'm laughing. I've been a ballroom dancer for years – never professionally, just as a secret pastime. Wherever I've travelled, I've found a dance hall. But I've rarely seen a man move with such light-ness. Mostly the strangers who partner me have two left feet, the medicinal whiff of camphor soap and a clammy hand on my lower back. All around you, soft flecks of white are curling through the air, and they are like music falling, little soft notes of it.

Please keep dancing, tall man. You make me happy. And it's a long time, what with Corby and the Shit and all the travelling, all the loneliness, it's a long time since I've laughed. Remaining at the window, I begin to move too. You mooch to the left. I glide to the right. You give a side step. I make a turn.

Then you glance straight up at my window, and once again I think you've spotted me. But this time I don't care. You look up. I look down. We are joined, you and I. I wave. You lift your hand too. But you don't wave. You catch a snowflake instead. Of course. You haven't seen me at all.

A clunk. A yelp. The metal door springs open, and a young rep is shoved into the yard. Our boss, Napier, is behind the rep, and he's spitting something into the rep's ear. He holds the rep's arm pinned behind his back and pushes him forward on his toes so that the poor man's shoes drag tramlines through the thin new layer of white. I wonder if I should shift from the window, not watch any more, but I can't move.

Other men burst through the door after Napier. They're all shouting. One has a plank of wood ripped from a crate, and he is swinging it at the flakes. You know how it is when a fight is coming. You can feel it, from the way people are all wired up. No one has spotted you yet, but soon they will. There is no hiding in that yard.

You freeze. I remember my father when my mother was angry, and he'd stand very still, hoping she'd mistake him for something else and lose interest. What are you up to down there? Your forehead bunches into lines as you make up your mind what to do next. And the thing you decide to do takes the wind from me. It takes the wind from everyone. You give a wide buffoonish wave and you stroll right towards the men. The snow has been getting heavier, and their shoulders, their shoes, are caked with white. But you sing out, 'Hello there, chaps! Jolly nice day!' You keep walking straight ahead so that they have to part, and where there has been a gang of bullies there is now only a collection of single men looking rather lost and chilly. You transform yourself into a pantomime version of the dancing man I watched only moments before. But you have changed the course of things. The spell of violence is broken.

The rep goes scampering across the yard, and jumping up at the railings he scrambles over the iron gates. Napier and his men beat the living daylights out of a football. With one last glance up at the snow, you slip through the metal door.

I see it all. But you don't see me.

A HARSH REMINDER

Harold, don't take this wrongly, but if you are serious about your journey maybe you should concentrate on the miles and not waste precious time on postcards? Three arrived today. There's one with a picture of Buckfast Abbey, one of 'South Brent by Night' – not a lot happening in that one – and the last a topographical drawing of Devon. You've marked your position with a cross. After three full days of walking the length of England, you seem to be pottering just beyond Kingsbridge.

Have you consulted a map?

I left the cards on my knee. Not wanting a repeat of the attention they brought two days ago, I didn't dare read them. It was Finty who asked what they said. I pointed at my mouth, and mistaking this for a cry for help, Sister Catherine swooped in and read out your messages. She flicked through them like a series of prompts for a wedding speech.

She said, '*Dear Queenie. I have blisters on my blisters but continue to walk.*' She said, '*Dear Queenie. I have come approximately 20 miles. You must keep waiting.*

Harold (Fry).' She said, *'Dear Queenie. Nice day here. Best wishes. Harold.'*

Squashed-up silence again. It was interrupted only by the unsteady breathing of the new young woman.

'Who is this man again?' said Mr Henderson at last.

'He's called Harold Fry,' said Sister Catherine. 'He is a friend of Queenie's.'

'And he says *what*? "Wait for me"?'

'Yes, he seems to be saying that.' Sister Catherine got busy straightening a set of cork coasters on the coffee table.

'While he walks the length of England?'

Sister Catherine made a small *hm hm* noise of affirmation. It was not as impolite as saying nothing, but it was not as big as a yes.

'What a tosser.' Mr Henderson went back to his newspaper. Sometimes Sister Lucy asks if he'd like to do the crossword, since he was an English teacher, but what is the point? he snaps. He may not be here for the answers.

'So is yer man really coming?' said Finty. If you want to picture her you need to imagine a stick-thin scarecrow in elasticated purple slacks, a brightly coloured sweatshirt and a green terrycloth turban. She wears scarlet lipstick, and asks Sister Lucy to paint her nails to match. Her eyebrows she draws in, two high orange arches, so she looks permanently surprised. One of the pluses of chemotherapy, she tells the volunteers, is that all

42

her facial and body hair has gone. It's like a perma-
nent Brazilian for free, she says. One of the minuses
of chemotherapy is that all the stuff on top of her
head has gone too. ('What is a Brazilian?' Sister
Lucy asked the other day. Finty gulped and looked
for help, but the Pearly King was studying a parcel
and Barbara had lost one of her glass eyes again
in her lap. 'It's a sort of haircut,' said Finty. 'Quite
short.')

'Perhaps Queenie's friend is just going for a long
walk,' said Sister Lucy, 'and sending nice postcards
to tell her about it.' She was back with her new
jigsaw. It is an illustration of the British Isles and
it has a thousand pieces. So far she has managed
a thin strip of Cornwall and a small section of the
Norfolk coast. The British Isles are the shape of
an open-toed sandal.

'But why would Harold Fry say he was coming
all the way to Berwick-upon-Tweed?' asked Finty.
'And why would he tell Queenie to wait?'

Mr Henderson scowled at his newspaper. 'Exactly
how old is this man?'

I pretended I hadn't heard, and he repeated the
question, much louder. I held up my fingers very
quickly to show a six and then a five. Sixty-five.
Mr Henderson gave a laugh. 'Oh. Just retired, is
he? Fed up sitting at home? Harold Fry should
try a Saga holiday.' I felt myself disappear in a
blush. It was even in my toes.

Barbara said she had a man who loved her once.
His name was Albert Bates. The Pearly King said

43

he had a lot of women who'd loved him several times and he hoped they didn't get funny ideas and start walking as well. He is a large man, almost a giant, and the buttons on his jacket glitter like a hundred scales. He doesn't talk so much as growl. The first time I heard him, I mistook him for a tractor.

But Harold Fry didn't love me, I wrote. I hoped that would be the end of it. I hoped they would leave me alone again.

'Maybe Harold Fry is doing a sort of modern-day pilgrimage,' said Sister Philomena.

'To Berwick-upon-Tweed?' laughed one of the volunteers.

Sister Philomena laughed too. 'Oh, I don't know,' she said. 'Maybe this is something he needs to do.'

'I see,' said Barbara. 'I see.'

'That's not strictly true,' pointed out Mr Henderson.

'Well, I wish some old geezer would walk for me,' said Finty. 'Even a stroll to the offy and back would be nice.'

Suddenly the new young woman let out a startled gasp, followed by a series of tiny squeaks. It was as if she'd eaten something and it was stuck in her throat. Her face opened – her eyes, her mouth, her nostrils. Her hands flew out, the fingers splayed. For a moment no one moved, no one knew what was happening, and then the penny dropped and everything was movement. All I could hear was the dreadful curdling sound of her choking, and all I could see beyond the crowd of white and black surplices was the flapping of the young woman's slipper as she fought to keep the life inside her. The nuns lifted her to help her breathe. Someone called for oxygen. Then the slipper stopped flapping and hung limp. There was a beat of silence. It was all so quick.

Sister Lucy scooped me up in her arms and carried me away. She had no time for the wheel-chair. She said nothing, but her face was set, like a milk jelly.

I didn't even know the young woman's name. She must have been in her twenties. The under-taker's black van was here this afternoon.

'Lightweight,' said Mr Henderson at tea.

On each table the nuns had placed linen napkins, and grape hyacinths from the garden.

THE DOING OF SMALL THINGS

'I am sorry I am late this morning,' said Sister Mary Inconnue, 'but I was delivering a plant to a friend. I had several difficulties getting it on and off the bus.' She unzipped her anorak and hung it over the back of the chair.

I gave an impatient shake of my head but she interrupted. 'It was rush hour. Imagine. A nun on a bus and a potted myrtle shrub.' Sister Mary Inconnue unlocked her leather bag and set the typewriter on her lap. 'What shall we write about today?' she said.

I thought of all the things she must have done in the time I'd only lain here and been attended to. The light at the window was a clear iced blue. There would be a late frost outside, perhaps the last of the year. I pictured my driftwood figures glinting with sequins. I thought of the crystallized leaves and grasses. The clifftop shining as blue as the bay below. I was overcome with sorrow. I will never get to the end of my letter, I thought. There is a huge story ahead of me, and the truth is so complicated. When a thing is broken, throw it away.

I don't want to be here, I scribbled. **I want to be in my sea garden.**

Sister Mary Inconnue read my comment and sat still. She cocked her head as though she were listening to something a little beyond my range. Then she said, 'I find it helps to start the day by practising one small, regular thing. I knew a businessman once, a very wealthy person, and he went out to collect kindling sticks each morning. He said it helped him to avoid all sorts of conflict later in the day. I have another friend who walks his dog by the sea. Now, I realize sticks and dog walks are out of the question, but you might memorize a poem. Or do some spine exercises. It is good to practise these small daily rituals. What will be yours, Queenie?' Sister Mary Inconnue cast a glance over the room.

It was hardly inspiring. The wheelchair. A sink. A framed print of two blue birds. Yellow curtains. A window. The branches of the tree outside, with only the flimsiest shawl of leaves. There is a television, but I have lived for twenty years without one of those. I lifted my hands in a helpless gesture.

'Oh, very good,' said Sister Mary Inconnue. I had no idea what she was talking about. 'We will do finger stretches.'

So that is what we did. I copied her as she rotated her hands like wheels and placed them gently palm against palm. I copied as she pointed first her thumb, then the index finger, and so on. I remembered how you used to wind down your car

47

window and give careful signals with your hand. From outside the hospice I heard the gulls in the sky, the wind in the tree. I heard the nuns talking with the medical team in the corridor. But they were gentle sounds that ebbed and flowed. I heard them and I let them go. Only the picture of you in the driving seat of your car stayed with me. I smiled.

'That's better,' said Sister Mary Inconnue. 'Are you ready for your letter now? One word in front of the other.'

TIN-POT TYRANT

The irony is, Harold, that I wasn't even a trained accountant. I'd graduated in classics. The nearest I had come to an account book was when I got my first job as a researcher for a politician. He liked me to fiddle his chequebook stubs so that his wife wouldn't get suspicious. He asked me to fiddle other things as well, but I drew the line at those.

After my decision on Bantham Beach to start again, I had taken the cheapest room I could find in a B&B just outside Kingsbridge. The place reeked of gravy and fabric conditioner. The smell was in everything. The woodchip walls, the terylene sheets, the pink bedside lamp and paper shade. Sometimes I'd be halfway down the street and I could still smell it. It seemed to crawl into my skin, my hair, and cling there. I had to find somewhere new.

I saw the brewery job advertised in a local paper and went to the interview. The work was beneath me, but I was desperate. The job would be a stopgap. I'd give Kingsbridge a few months, then

I'd move on. I thought my life would be very different by late summer.

'I'm here to be your new accountant.'

'You?' said a scrappy figure in a shiny three-piece suit. It was Napier. He stopped at the door to his office and stared at me across the anteroom. 'But you're a woman.'

I studied myself, the bump of my breasts, the neatness of my hands, as if I hadn't noticed these things before. 'My God,' I said. 'So I am.'

My remark was supposed to be funny. I liked to laugh. Apparently Napier didn't. He looked appalled, followed by furious. It's a shame short men don't wear heels; it would save the world a lot of trouble. 'Fuck off,' he said. He practically collided with a tinsel Christmas tree in his rush to get away from me.

'You at least have to interview me,' I called out. 'Equal rights and so on.'

This, it seemed, was funny after all. Napier turned and bared his teeth. Then he gave a high-pitched laugh. *Yap, yap, yap.* I could see the gold points of his molars. It was not very festive.

'But you're not the person I want for the job,' he screeched.

It was in me to get up and leave. The smell of the brewery was so nauseating I had to keep pinching the colour into my cheeks. But something about the way that man stared at me and laughed, as if I weren't good enough, as if I never would be, brought out the stubbornness in me. 'That's all right,' I said. 'I'll wait until you change your mind.' Now it was my turn to produce a smile. Only, mine hurt.

I waited all morning. Every time Napier opened his office door, I was still there. 'Any applicants?' he'd call to his secretary.

'Miss Hennessy,' she'd say. The door would slam again.

Around lunchtime, Napier went slinking along the corridor, almost appended to the polished wood panelling. His secretary asked if I was all right, if I wanted water, but I said no. 'Maybe this job is not for you,' she said softly. We listened to him scream at someone in another part of the building before he reappeared, casting round anxiously to check if my chair was empty yet. I stood and waved. 'Here I am, Mr Napier.' I was weak with the lack of food.

'Do you like sex and travel, Miss Hennessy?'

At last. An interview, albeit unconventional. I blushed, but I wasn't going to be bullied. 'I do, actually.'

'Then fuck off.' The door slammed.

I asked the secretary if her boss liked women, and she said he did, but mainly in the back of his car. Also Margaret Thatcher, along with the Queen, though not in the back of the car. Those two were in silver frames. I said something like 'Well, never mind,' but the irony was possibly lost on her.

By five o'clock, no one else had turned up.

Napier's secretary put on her coat and turned off the lights. 'There will be other work,' she said. 'When the tourist season starts in Kingsbridge, there will be waitressing and stuff.' I explained to her that I needed an office job, one that didn't involve lifting, and that I was almost penniless. I had no time to wait. 'Well, good luck,' she said. I sat in silence for another half-hour. The brewery was quiet in the way an old building can be, as if silence is made up of creaks and ticks that are no longer to do with people but only with the things they've left behind.

I knocked on Napier's door and waited. Had he leapt out of the window to escape me? Had I spent all day waiting only to be tricked at the last minute? It was too much. I swung open the door and walked through the gloom of smoke. I took in a collection of Murano glass clowns glowing dimly on his desk, about twenty in all, blue and orange and yellow, like a band of melting musicians in smog. And there was Napier behind them. Swivelling anxiously from side to side on a leather and mahogany desk chair.

'Don't touch the glass clowns,' he snarled. (As if I was going to.) I'm sorry to have to remind you of those things, Harold.

I said, 'It appears you're going to have to employ me, Mr Napier.'

'I told you. This is not a woman's job.' He lit one cigarette from the one he'd been smoking and screwed the spent butt into an ashtray.

'I don't want a woman's job. I want a man's one. I can save you five hundred pounds in six months.' At this point I had no idea how. 'I've sat here all day. If I set my mind on something, I don't waver. What have you got to lose?'

And that is how I got my job in accounts. I bought a cheap brown wool suit, slightly roomy at the waist, from a thrift shop in Kingsbridge. I also bought a black handbag and a pair of sensible brown lace-up shoes – small heel, square toe. I spent every day at the library, reading up about bookkeeping and finances, and sometimes I thought of the one I had left behind, the man in Corby, and I might have cried, but I'd done so much of that already there was no room left for it.

I returned to the brewery in the New Year, half expecting to be turned away, half expecting to be on another bus that same evening, but Napier's secretary said, 'Ah, Miss Hennessy. Your office is on the first floor, three doors to the right.' I could have fallen out of my plain brown shoes.

Word had clearly gone round the brewery that a female was starting in accounts. Several of the reps lingered outside my office to get a look. Woman. Maths. Brown suit. They assumed one thing. This was twenty-four years ago, remember. Behind those Victorian brewery walls, nothing had changed in decades.

'You're the first lesbian we've had,' said Napier's secretary brightly.

'But I'm not,' I said. 'I like men. I mean, I really like them.'

'It's a free country!' she sang, still in the upper register. She smiled, but she didn't shake hands.

Tonight Sister Philomena delivers meds, and the duty nurse changes my dressing and gives me a fresh pain patch. They look surprised to find me still sitting up with my pencil and notebook. 'Are you all right?' says Sister Philomena. 'You look very busy there.'

'I am good,' I grunt. I even smile.

'We're both good,' says Sister Mary Inconnue. She slots her typed pages in order. 'It has been a good day.'

'Good,' says Sister Philomena.

'Good,' says the duty nurse.

We all laugh, as if that is the only word.

SUNDAY SONG

The horse is visiting again, but it must be Sister Mary Inconnue's day off. The horse keeps shifting her hindquarters and bumping into the armchair. Also, she has turned up in a hat and four dancing shoes. The shoes look like mine. The hat is twisted straw, trimmed with a nest of plastic blossom and cherries; it's not dissimilar to the one my mother bought to wear for my graduation. She was a masculine-looking woman, and the hat proved a challenge. To her profound irritation, it kept shooting from her head. '*Scheisse, Scheisse*,' she growled. In the end my father carried it on her behalf, slightly aloft and careful not to tip it, as though he were bearing an actual fruit salad.

There is no sign of the horse's owner, the woman with the grapefruit. Perhaps she is off buying hay.

Before I began writing to you today, I practised my finger stretches. Then Sister Lucy washed what is left of my hair and fetched her blow-dryer. 'You have nice ears,' she said. She picked up some of my pages lying on the floor. She frowned and then she turned them upside down as if that might help.

I pointed to my suitcase, where she could store them.

'I'm writing a letter for Harold Fry,' I told her. 'Sister Mary Inconnue has been helping.' I should have scribbled this sentence in my notebook because the poor girl never understands, but I was tired. Once I'd finished trying to speak, a look of panic swallowed her face. Her small eyes twitched, in an effort to comprehend.

'I'm not sure I got that,' she said slowly.

I reached for my pencil and notebook but she said, 'No, no. Say it again. It's my fault. I am sure I will get it this time.'

'I'm writing a letter,' I managed. I made each sound stand apart, like I used to do at the post office store in Embleton before things got too difficult and I gave up going there.

Her pink mouth broke into a triumphant peal of laughter. 'Oh, I understand, Queenie! I know what you said!'

Sister Lucy got up with gusto. At the door she turned. 'Would you like one sugar in that or two?'

MONDAY BLUES

No postcard.

I expect you've gone home.

'Oh, enough of that,' says Sister Mary Inconnue. 'Let's get back to our letter.'

Another patient has arrived. A man. Probably in his mid-thirties. He wears satin pyjamas, large blue slippers like monster feet and a dressing around his head. From the way the bandage sags over the crown you'd think his skull was a boiled egg, with the top sliced clean away.

His family came with him. Two little girls, a young wife dressed for work in a white uniform, his mother and father, and another woman who looks like his sister; she shares his dark eyes. That man looked the centre of so many lives. They all sat alongside him with tall backs, very stiff, on a bank of chairs beneath the cork noticeboard in the dayroom. You could see them glancing at him and glancing at us and holding tight on to their cups of tea and wafer biscuits, as if dying were contagious and only the everyday things might save them.

'My daddy has new slippers,' said one of the little girls.

'They're nice,' said the Pearly King.

'Also, new pyjamas.'

'Nice one.'

The mother shot her daughter a warning look. Don't talk to strangers. Especially not ones with a sell-by date. The grandmother slipped a colouring book out of her handbag. 'Come here, Alice,' she called.

'What is wrong with that lady?' said the little girl. The young mother pursed her mouth to suggest she was busy thinking of something important and hadn't heard. So the girl spoke again. But this time she stood up. She pointed. 'WHY DOES THE OLD LADY LOOK LIKE THAT?'

'Oh, that's Barbara,' said Finty. 'She's got no eyes. The NHS gave her two prosthetics, but one of them keeps popping out. Doesn't it, Babs?'

Barbara laughed. So did the little girl called Alice.

The family didn't.

'You can do my colouring book, if you like,' said Alice.

'Fab,' said Finty. 'I love colouring.'

A NICE PAIR OF SANDWICHES

'This is Miss Hennessy. She's our new accountant. Did you hear how we first met?'

If I am honest, and after all that is the point this time, one of the things that used to annoy me was when you got out of the car and told pub landlords about our first meeting. Every time you said it, every time it made you laugh, I thought, *Good grief, here we go again.* Listening to you get the detail wrong, over and over, was like being married to you without the happy bits.

'Yes. It's a funny story, actually. Very funny. We met in the stationery cupboard.'

We didn't.

Prior to my unaccustomed display of feeling in that particular repository, we had been introduced. In the canteen. I know this because I'd spotted you every day from my office window. I wanted to know more about the tall man who hid his empty cans in the bins and danced with his shadow and stood up to a bully.

It was lunchtime. I'd had my job at the brewery for almost two weeks, and I was sitting with

Napier's secretary. I have it now – Sheila was her name. She was a slight person, quietly spoken, but her breasts were so disproportionately gigantic that no matter how much one tried to appreciate something else about her, her rather ordinary mouth, for instance, or her thin curtain of hair, your eyes kept forgetting about those bits and landing slap bang back on her bosom. It was the same for everyone. The men had full-on conversations with them. I watched her, her look of patient embarrassment, as if she were waiting for people to lift their faces and realize that she had one of those as well.

I remember asking some sort of polite question about how she was and her giving some sort of polite answer about the weather, when you stopped by our table. I didn't even look up. I just saw yachting shoes and the way the cuffs of your trousers didn't hang quite long enough to cover the zigzag pattern in your socks. If anything, I was struck by the overwhelming ordinariness of your lower half.

That was when I raised my eyes and found it was you. The man I'd been looking for. I blushed.

To my surprise, you did the same. But you were not embarrassed because you had been secretly spying from a first-floor window. Oh, no. You were openly gawping straight down Sheila's cleavage. You couldn't seem to budge your eyes. 'Gosh,' you said out loud.

'Oh, hello there, Mr Fry,' said Sheila.

You looked devastated, as if your mouth had come out with the one word you had trusted would remain inside it. Then you tried to make up for your appalling indiscretion. What you came up with was 'Golly.'

'Harold Fry is one of the reps,' said Sheila to me, as if this explained everything. Sheila said to you, 'This is Miss Hennessy. She's new. She's in accounts.'

You adjusted the knot of your tie. (It was not out of place. It never was. But I came to know it was a thing you did, just as other people clear their throats, or just as my father used to say, 'Well, there it was,' when a conversation reached a natural end.)

'Pleased to meet you both,' you said, offering your hand. And once again you seemed to realize what you'd done, and this time you groaned. By now, the other reps were beginning to put down their meat pies and cigarettes and laugh.

'Would you care to join us, Mr Fry?' I asked.

You were in it now. It was clear you wished to flee both the canteen and your mistake, but you put down your sandwiches next to mine on the table. That seemed to be as far as you were willing to go. I had made my sandwiches that morning: ham on brown bread. Yours were in a Tupperware container with the name *David Fry* taped to the lid. I guessed you had a wife who'd made your lunch.

So there were three of us not knowing what to

say where before there had been only two. Sheila and I looked up at you and you remained on your feet, hovering in close proximity to your sandwich box.

In the end Sheila said, 'I'm getting married next week.'

'Well, how nice,' you said.

'Actually, I'm really nervous.'

'Nervous? Why?'

'I don't know. I just am. I can hardly eat. Look.' She showed us her packed lunch and she was right. She'd barely pecked at it.

You shared a quick, anxious glance with me. It linked us briefly as if it were our duty to join forces and help this young woman. Not knowing her or you, of course, and knowing nothing about marriage either, I merely shrugged. Over to you, tall man. Besides, I was thrown by your eyes. The blue of them was so generous, I couldn't quite think of anything else.

You caught your hands behind your back. You placed your feet firmly astride, rooting them to the floor. You bowed your head a moment, thinking something through, so that those lines appeared again and pleated your forehead. Sheila gave me a look as if to say, What's he doing? And I gave her a return smile that said, I haven't a clue but wait.

'Please don't be nervous,' you said slowly. 'I spent most of my wedding night in the bathroom. It was still the best day of my life. You'll be happy.'

Here you lifted your head and gave a benevolent smile. Your whole face looked full of it, out to your ears. Your eyes shone. I knew then that you would always see the positive side because you liked people, and you wanted the best for them. It was intoxicating.

Before my work at the brewery, I'd done many things, seen many places, met many people. I'd got a first in classics. I'd taken a job in a bar to fund a secretarial course. I'd had the job as a researcher, and when that got too much I'd taken another as a tour guide and afterwards a tutor. I'd hung around for a few years with a troupe of female artists in Soho, I'd got involved with a retired high court judge (the Shit) in Corby. All in all, I'd heard people do a lot of things with words. I'd heard them not say what they meant and I'd seen them not do what they said, but I'd never met a person who could speak so simply and still convey so much. Sheila listened in awe. There you stood, feet firm, shoulders set, believing she would be happy with such conviction that right away she began to believe it too. Then you said, 'Well, cheerio, ladies,' and you walked off with my sandwiches.

It turned out yours were turkey and salad cream on white. Your wife had cut off the crusts. I know this because I ate them.

Sheila said to me, 'He's a good man, Mr Fry. He's not like the others. I'll be OK now.'

'He's a dancer, isn't he?'

Sheila laughed. 'Oh, I don't think so. He mostly, you know, he mostly sits.'

Afterwards I asked the other secretaries about you, but no one had much to add. You had already worked at the brewery longer than a lot of people. You'd never missed a day's work, not even when your son was born. Apparently you took a two-week holiday every summer with your family, but there were no photographs on your desk because I checked when I returned your Tupperware and all I found were paperclips, a plastic pencil sharpener and a complimentary Christmas calendar from the Chinese takeaway. It was out of date.

Watching you from a distance, I discovered several new things: on Mondays, Wednesdays and Fridays you wore a brown suit and a selection of golf club ties; on Tuesdays and Thursdays you wore beige corduroys and a beige V-necked sweater. When it came to fashion, it seemed you were mainly interested in blending in with the background.

Your eyes were a deep blue, almost shocking they were so vivid. Years later, I tried to find the same colour in my sea garden, and sometimes I thought the irises had it, sometimes my blue poppies. On an early summer morning, when the sky was reflected in the smooth folds of the sea, it was there I found you. You walked with a straight spine. Your hair was a thick sweep of brown that never quite sat flat. You wore your scarf (fawn stripes) in a tight knot and this made me wonder if your mother had once said you'd get a cold unless you kept your neck warm. It lifted my spirits at the brewery to watch you from a distance and ask myself these things. I assumed you had a drinking habit of which you were ashamed, but there. We all have secrets.

I never saw you without a golf club tie.
I never saw you with a golf club.
I never saw you without yachting shoes.
I never saw you in a yacht.

THE LONELY GENTLEMAN

Well, Harold, you've been walking a full week and now you have passed Exeter. And two postcards in one day! The description of your feet inside your socks was particularly vivid. I hope you managed to buy plasters in Chudleigh. And I like the picture of Exeter. The cathedral and the green. It's strange to think it is twenty years since I was last there. The day I left Devon for good.

'*Dear Queenie,*' read Sister Lucy. '*Do not give up. Best wishes, Harold Fry.*'

'So the fool hasn't gone home yet?' said Mr Henderson.

'Of course not!' shouted Finty. 'He is walking to see Queenie Hennessy.'

In today's post, she received a voucher offering a year's supply of McVitie's crackers if she fills out an online questionnaire. There was nothing for Mr Henderson.

'With post like yours, who needs enemies?' he said.

The Pearly King had two parcels but said he would prefer to open them in his room. Barbara received a knitted glasses case from her nephew.

66

'That's so nice,' she said. 'What a shame I've got no eyes. But I can keep my syringe driver in the knitted case. That will be nice too.'

Another set of patients will arrive this afternoon.

'When you come in those doors, it's a one-way ticket,' said Mr Henderson. 'Whose turn next?'

I pretended to read your cards.

'Did you live in Kingsbridge once, Queenie?' asked Sister Catherine. I gave a fast nod. 'Is that how you made friends with Harold Fry?' Another nod. 'What made you leave?' I felt my nose prickle. Sister Lucy took my hand.

'So when do we suppose Harold Fry will get here?' she said gamely. 'Tomorrow morning or tomorrow afternoon?'

Sister Lucy is one of the kindest young women I've met. When it comes to French manicures and blow-drying, she has no equal. But I don't believe the poor girl has ever seen a map of England.

No wonder she is challenged by her jigsaw.

Yes, I remember Exeter. It was right at the end. I'd gone to your home in Fossebridge Road to say goodbye and I'd met your wife instead. It was the only time we ever spoke, she and I, and it was one of the most devastating conversations of my life. I remember the busy café opposite Exeter station where I sat early the following morning with my tartan suitcase and wondered what to do next. It was clear I had to leave. Maureen's words rang in my ears. Whenever I was still, I heard them. I'd walked and walked after our meeting, but it was no good, I couldn't get away from what she'd told me. I saw her too. In my mind I saw her. Hanging the washing, over and over, as if the sun would never come and the wind would never blow and her task would never finish. Behind her, net curtains now hung at every window. The house had closed its eyes.

I don't know why some of these memories must remain so crystal clear. I recall one sliver and the whole picture comes rushing back, while other things, for instance, other things I would *like* to remember, are completely unavailable. If only memory were a library with everything stored where it should be. If only you could walk to the desk and say to the assistant, I'd like to return the painful memories about David Fry or indeed his mother and take out some happier ones, please. About stickleback fishing with my father. Or picnicking on the banks of the Cherwell when I was a student.

And the assistant would say, Certainly, madam. We have all those. Under F for Fishing. As well as P for Picnicking. You'll find them on your left.

So there my father would be. Tall and smiling in his work overalls, a roll-up in one hand and my fishing net in the other. I'd skip to keep up with him as he strode the broken lane down to the stream. 'Where is that girl? Where are you?' The hedgerow flowers would boil with insects and my father would lift me to his shoulders and then— What?

I haven't a clue. I don't remember the rest.

But I was writing about the café in Exeter. The place was already packed. Suitcases, bags, rucksacks. One could barely move. It was the very end of the school holidays, and there was an early morning fog outside. All around me I saw joined-together people, talking and laughing and looking forward to their joined-together futures. It was an insult, all of it. So much happiness, it had steamed up the windows. I chose a table by the door. Every time it opened, I hoped it would be you. Harold will have heard what I have done for him, I thought. Even if Maureen has failed to give him my message, he will have bumped into someone from the brewery who will have told him. Harold will come to find me and I will tell the truth. All I wanted was to see you one last time.

'Excuse me? Is this seat free?'

My heart gave a swing. I looked up, and it was, of course, another man. Not you. He had thick brown hair, but it didn't give the smallest kink of a curl at the nape of the neck like yours, and neither did it poke out a little above the ears. He pointed at the empty place opposite mine. No, that seat's reserved, I told him. I'm waiting for someone. Now bugger off.

I didn't say that last bit, but my head did.

The man nodded and moved away. There was something so afraid and careful about him, picking his way around the luggage, the noise. He didn't seem to know the place. He looked like a glass animal, too delicate-limbed. Eventually he found a spare seat beside a family and perched himself on the edge. He kept checking his cuffs, his hair, his shoes, the way people do when they're unsure and they need to remind themselves where they stop and the rest of the world begins. He ordered a pot of Ceylon tea (no milk) and a toasted teacake. Then the child next to him tipped her plastic cup upside down and showered him with squash.

Everyone jumped to their feet. The lonely gentleman, the waitresses, the other customers. Don't worry, don't worry, he kept saying, dabbing his suit with his handkerchief. The girl's parents were passing him paper napkins, and they were saying, Just send us the dry-cleaning bill, why don't you have our food instead? And he was blushing and saying, No, no, please. No, no, please. The more attention he got, the more pained he looked. And I sat watching, I am ashamed to say, thinking, Good. Make the lonely man squirm. At least it isn't me.

A young man arrived. He didn't come into the café. He stopped at the doorway. Jeans. T-shirt. New cowboy boots. With his arms folded, he scanned the tables as though he were counting us. The lonely gentleman stood. He mopped his suit again, but his hands were shaking. Excuse me, he said. Excuse me, world. He left money for the bill and followed the young man out of the café.

I wiped the steam from the window with my sleeve. From where I sat, I watched them make their way down the street. The lonely gentleman walked alongside the young man, hands in pockets, until the young man reached his arm around the lonely gentleman and pulled him close. Other people noticed, skirted them, but the young man kept his arm around the gentleman and steered him forward. I watched them against the fog. Then they were gone.

You see, even the only other single person in the café was not a single person. It was the final straw. Harold Fry is not coming, I thought. You can wait a whole lifetime and he will not come. For what I had done, there could never be forgiveness. I grasped the handle of my tartan suitcase and yanked it through the crowd, in the way I have seen an exasperated mother tug a screaming child out of the way of strangers. 'Mind where you're going,' people muttered at me. I hated them, but really the person I hated was myself. I fled.

At the train station, I scanned the departures board, trying to find the farthest destination. I'd have gone to Mars if it had been listed. As it was, I had to settle for Newcastle.

'Single, madam?'

Ha ha. Very funny. Thank you for pointing that out. 'Yes, I am all alone.'

'No, I mean, are you planning to come back, madam? Do you want a return ticket?'

The truth dawned on me. I didn't want to go.

Please, let me not go. This is not what I want. I am in love with Harold Fry. My life will be nothing if I leave. And then I remembered Maureen's words and I felt again the hollowing punch of them.

'A single, please,' I said. 'I'm never coming back.'

IN WHICH NOT MUCH HAPPENS

I heard that the Pearly King felt too unwell to visit the dayroom today and so did Mr Henderson. There was a patient who sat with her family in a circle around her, all holding hands. Sister Philomena asked if they would like to join her for prayers and they said yes, they would. They closed their eyes as Sister Philomena whispered the words and I thought this must be the nearest humans get to whatever God is, when they hold hands and listen.

A volunteer showed Finty how to make a tissue-paper flower. They made one for Barbara too, but she mistook it for a hat and put it on her head.

She wore it all morning.

The buds on the tree outside my window have popped open to leaves. The tree shakes them every now and then, as if to say, Are you happy up there?

So I was wrong. Something has happened, after all.

Do you see leaves too?

HANG ON, WOULD YOU LIKE MY HANDKERCHIEF?

When you found me in the stationery cupboard, Harold, I'd been at the brewery a full month. It was early February. I'd eaten your sandwiches and sniffed around your desk, but we hadn't spoken since the canteen. I waited for you at my window, though. Nearly every day you were there with your empties, and sometimes I willed you to dance but you never obliged me. Maybe snow was your thing. We never had that weather again, not in all the time we worked together.

So picture this. I'm crying in a cupboard. I hear someone approach and pull at the door, and I try to hide. Or, more specifically, I behave like my father and I try to not be there. But it is difficult to not be somewhere when you are a small woman in a brown wool suit and you have nothing around you but typing paper and manila envelopes.

'I do beg your pardon,' you said. You clearly had no idea where to look. You chose my feet.

I didn't know how to explain. I straightened my skirt and lowered my head. I blamed my anguish on the way Napier and the other reps laughed at me. I said I couldn't take any more, I was going to hand in my notice. I was saying anything that came into my head. What I didn't mention was that I'd been pregnant when I came to Kingsbridge. What I didn't mention was that I'd lost my baby only the previous weekend. What with the stomach cramps and my grief, I could barely stand.

You clearly wished two things: that you hadn't opened the door to the stationery cupboard and that you hadn't found me inside it. I also wished two things: that you would close the door to the stationery cupboard and that I'd never see you again. It seemed best all round. You kept glancing up and down the corridor. Left. Right. Left.

Help didn't come from either direction.

And so you made another small decision. I read it in your face and body. You carefully placed your feet a little apart, just as you had done with Sheila. You caught your hands behind your back and your brow crumpled with concentration while you shifted your weight from side to side, finding your correct balance. It was like watching a tree take root. You were not going to move until you had helped me. And then you spoke.

'Don't resign.' Your voice was soft. I looked up at you and found you were shining your eyes straight into mine. 'I found it hard at the beginning too. I felt out of place. But it will get better.'

It was like another spell of yours. I couldn't reply. For a moment I believed everything would turn out all right for me because you clearly desired that too. It was simple. And I had lost a lot at this point, Harold. More than anything, I'd wanted to keep my baby.

You said, 'Hang on a mo, would you like my handkerchief?' I said no, no, I couldn't possibly, but you didn't hear. You tugged it from your pocket like a magician's scarf and you folded it several times over, very carefully, until it was the size of a small pincushion. 'Please,' you said gently. 'Take it.' I lifted it to my face, and the smell of you tipped me sideways.

Perhaps it was the hormones. I don't know. I still get that smell sometimes. Imperial Leather soap, milky coffee and lemon-scented aftershave. The mix has to be just right. A stranger could pass my sea garden and I'd want to drop my tools and run after him along the coastal path. I wouldn't even wish to speak or touch. I'd need the scent, the feeling of stomach-fluttering warmth that accompanied it. I have tried to find the smell in a plant, but I have never been able to get it. I grew lemon thyme once. When the sun shone, that came close. I'd sit beside it with my mug of coffee, although I had to shut my eyes to imagine the Imperial Leather part.

We were in the stationery cupboard. You asked if I would care to come out and I said, 'Thank you,' and really I could have been saying anything. I wobbled a little with the pain inside me and you held out your hand.

'Steady on,' you told me. 'No need to rush.'

It was the first time a man had touched me since the Shit in Corby. (I don't include the young doctor who examined me while I lay on a stretcher in A&E.) The thrill of your fingers round mine sent prickles of electricity shooting up my spine and towards my hairline. Your hand was large and warm and unwavering. If only I could have stayed like that, my hand in yours. Another time, another place, another life, I might have made a small sashay to the left and swung into your arms. But you were Harold Fry. I was Queenie Hennessy. I pulled myself free and walked away from you as fast as I could. I was almost running.

If only I'd kept going, you might say. I could have saved us all a lot of sorrow.

That night I compiled a letter to the Shit. I enclosed the money he'd pressed on me to have an abortion. There was no child, I wrote. His reputation was safe. ('Come back,' he'd moaned. He was slippery-faced with tears. 'Come back when it's all sorted. I can't live without you, dearest.') I added that I never wanted to see him again. He would probably discover that he could live after all.

I lifted your handkerchief to my face and breathed in the smell of you. I felt healed again.

Can't write any more. Hand tired. Head too. The night nurse asked if I was in pain and fetched liquid morphine in a shot glass to help me sleep.

The two blue birds wake up and take flight out of the framed print. I watch the sky at the window fill with ink. Then I see the stars and they are fizzing out there. Even the slim moon keeps shattering into splinters.

Sister Mary Inconnue says, 'I need to replace my ribbon spool, dear one.'

That is enough for one ni—

AN ULTIMATUM

There was no post for me again today. I confess I was a little downhearted. The Pearly King had another of his parcels, but he didn't open it.

'Maybe you will get a card from Harold Fry tomorrow?' said Sister Catherine.

'There is no such word as tomorrow,' said Mr Henderson.

I felt hot and weak.

Could you really walk? From Kingsbridge to Berwick-upon-Tweed? I tried to picture you strolling down a country lane, and all I could get was a man in fawn, giving hand signals to passing cars.

'Do you have to do that?' I asked once. You looked confused. 'Do what?' you said. 'Winding down your window and waving your hand whenever you turn left or right. Isn't that what indicators are for?' 'Are you suggesting I'm an old-fashioned driver?' you said. And I did think that, only not in a critical way, so I dressed the thought up as something more anodyne and said no, you were just a very thorough driver. 'I thought that was what Napier required,' you said. 'He wants me to take care of you. You're a good accountant.' And I felt a little burst of pleasure, because when you said those things I believed you, in the same way I felt safe when you put on your driving gloves and turned the key in the ignition. 'Also,' you said, still flapping your hand at oncoming traffic, 'it helps us go faster. To be honest, Miss Hennessy, I wish you would stop sitting there like a lemon and help.' When I stuck my hand out of the window and laughed, you suddenly smiled and I got the impression it gave you happiness, to make another person laugh. I remember wondering whether it was the same with your wife.

But that was long ago.

In the dayroom, I imagined your arrival at the hospice. I imagined you approaching the inpatient doors. (Don't be scared of them, Harold. It turns out they are only ordinary doors.) I imagined the nuns fetching you tea and asking about your journey. I imagined you reading my letter. But when I got to the part where you walked into the room, where I saw your face and you saw mine, I turned to the window. I had to concentrate very hard on the sky or the evergreens or anything that was not inside my mind.

I have searched for you, Harold, in the years I have lived without you. Not a day has gone by when I have not thought of you. There was a time when I wished it would stop, when I tried to forget, but forgetting took such strength it was easier to accept you were a missing part of me and get on with life. Sometimes, yes, I have spotted a tall man down by the sea, throwing stones, and with a jolt of excitement that leaves me trembling I have said to myself, That's him. That's Harold Fry. Other times I have heard a car draw up behind me as I walk to the village, or I have passed a man heading towards the castle ruins, a hiker perhaps, or I have stood behind a stranger at the shop. And something about the rumbling of the car engine, or the way the man carries his shoulders, or asks for stamps at the counter with a southern softness to his voice, has allowed me for one moment to pretend it is you. It is a fantasy, a daydream. Even as I indulge the idea, I know it cannot be true. Embleton Bay is a sprinkling of clifftop summer beach houses in the north-east of England, and I never sent you my address. But pretending you are near, for a few moments, I have felt complete again. Only when my illness came did I give up looking for you.

You must have changed, just as I have changed. Where my skin once showed the faintest of lines, there are now ridges and indentations. Where my hair was thick and brown and shoulder-length, it is soft and white as the tufts of old man's beard that fleck my sea garden in winter. My waist that was once plump and beskirted is a hollowing curve between the knobs of my hipbones. Maybe you don't even wear fawn any more. Maybe you have moved on to blue.

I laid aside my notebook and tried to picture you in blue. You looked made of water. I had to dress you quickly back in fawn again. And then I remembered there was no postcard and I felt stupid for thinking all this.

Sister Lucy asked if I'd like to help with her British Isles jigsaw, but I only shrugged. Sister Catherine suggested a visit to the Well-being Garden. 'It's a nice day. A spell outside might do you good. You like plants and things, don't you, Queenie?' I shook my head.

When Sister Philomena came in with the trolley of nutritional milkshakes, I said no to those as well.

'Listen here,' said Finty. 'I've been watching you, missy. You sit in that chair over there and you write away in your notebook. Then it comes to meal-times and you hardly eat. Sometimes you don't even show your face in the dining room. If you're going to keep living, you have to come here and take the nutritional milkshakes with the rest of us.'

'No,' I groaned. 'Please.' I had them in hospital. They made me sick.

'It seems like you've got a man walking the length of England. There are some of us here that haven't even had a visitor. So the least you can do is not kick the bucket. Now, I know you think you look like a monster, but this is hardly a beauty pageant. Look at Barbara here. The Pearly King has a plastic arm, and I'm carrying the contents of my bowel in my handbag. Either you take the drinks like we do or you'll end up on a drip feed. Which is it going be?'

'Don't push her,' said Sister Catherine. 'It's different for everyone.'

'Excuse me, sister, but I'm talking to Queenie Hennessy.' Finty fixed me with a look that was like being pinned to the wall by two orange eyebrows.

I opened my mouth. I could sense them all watching, the patients, the nuns. I didn't think for a moment they'd understand. 'The drinks,' I grunted.

'Excellent,' said Finty. 'Come on, everyone. Gather up. We'll get in a round.'

Sister Catherine helped me out of my chair by the window. It was only a small distance to the other patients, but I was so slow, it was like climbing a hill. She settled me in a reclining chair by the coffee table. I couldn't lift my head. I couldn't look at anyone. I just had to pretend I was very preoccupied by the swirly pattern of the dayroom carpet.

Sister Lucy offered a choice of flavours. Barbara and Finty chose strawberry. Mr Henderson asked for vanilla. The patient with the monster slippers pointed at butterscotch. The Pearly King went for chocolate. I put my hand up for vanilla.

'It makes no difference anyway,' said Finty. 'They all taste like wet cardboard.'

Sister Lucy unscrewed the lids from the bottles and served the shakes in glasses with straws. They were all a colour halfway between beige and pink that has no name except possibly 'blush taupe'.

We drank slowly. Half mine spilled out the side of my mouth. Nobody spoke or moved until the glasses were empty. I was the last to finish. Mr Henderson got up to hand out tissues.

'Thank fuck that's over,' said Finty, rubbing at her mouth and her sweatshirt. 'Let's have a game of Scrabble.'

'Are you laughing?' asks Sister Mary Inconnue.

I am happy. I had a nice time in the dayroom. And also at tea.

She laughs. Her sandals swing, she is laughing so much. 'Good,' she says. 'That's good.'

She murmurs something and it sounds like a blessing until I hear the words 'tuna fish' and wonder whether she's recounting her shopping list.

I will not give up hope.

I will wait for you, Harold Fry.

A DIFFERENT PERSPECTIVE

This morning I asked Sister Lucy if I could borrow a dictionary and a thesaurus. She fetched Pictionary and a throat lozenge.

'Also a glass of water,' she said helpfully.

There is a postcard from you with a picture of the Bluebell steam train. No message. You seem to have forgotten that bit.

'Why doesn't Harold Fry take a hint and spare us the agony?' said Mr Henderson from his chair. He stared at his playing cards as if he suspected them of cheating.

'Is your friend a keen walker?' said Sister Catherine.

I doubt it, I thought. You and I walked only once. I tried to draw a picture in my notebook of you driving your Morris 1100. I don't know if you remember, but art was never my strong point. When I hung out in the late seventies with the female artists in Soho, I used to do their shopping and compose their letters, but I could never draw. I'd sit for them while I read, and they'd paint me naked with my book. They were a delicious bunch but always forgetting the sensible things like food and daylight and only remembering the more intoxicating ones like love and gin. So when Sister Catherine laughed at my picture, it's possible she mistook my drawing of you in a car for one of a man inside a giant rabbit. I didn't mind her laughing, though. She was right. You looked funny.

But Mr Henderson hadn't finished with the postcard. 'If Harold Fry got on a train he could be here tonight. We could have this whole stupid business over and done with.'

'That is not the point, you old bat,' said Finty. 'Any fool can sit on a train.'

'Fool?' he repeated. 'You know who's the fool here?' Mr Henderson's hands began to shake. They look stripped to the bone. The knuckles poked out and his sleeves hung loose as if Mr Henderson had no more substance than a coat hanger inside a dogtooth jacket. His mouth was so blue, the lips looked bruised. 'Have you any idea how far it is from Kingsbridge to Berwick?' Mr Henderson tried to get up, but the effort was too much. His knees buckled and he slumped to his seat again. 'Have you any idea how many miles?'

'Of course I do,' said Finty. 'I'm not stupid. It's a fuck of a lot.'

'There are over six hundred of them!'

I know, of course. I've travelled the distance by bus and train and bus again. Every new mile that passed between us was like shearing off another piece of me. Sister Lucy reddened. 'Is it really that far?' She removed several pieces from her jigsaw.

'Six hundred miles, and the man isn't even a walker!'

'I couldn't do it,' said Sister Catherine, and another volunteer agreed that he couldn't do it either.

'I suppose it's a question of faith,' piped up Sister Lucy, only I knew she wasn't sure. She barely gave voice to that last word. It came out with no middle, sounding more like *fth*.

Mr Henderson slammed his hands down on his playing cards. The cards sprang up in the air and scattered to the carpet. 'It's ridiculous! It's not fair! It's an insult! Has the man no idea what this place is? He's making fools of us all!' He shook so hard he began to cough.

'Need a hand, old man?' growled the Pearly King.

'Ha ha!' roared Finty.

'You make me sick, the lot of you,' shouted Mr Henderson, trying to stand and still not managing. Sister Catherine rushed to help, but he kept pushing her away and hanging on to his Zimmer frame and asking did she think he was a cripple, as she tried to clear him a safe path out of the dayroom. We could hear him all the way down the corridor, shouting, 'Fool! Fool! Fool!' and coughing and banging into the walls. Nothing the sisters said made any difference.

I looked at Finty and tried to smile. Her red lipstick bled from her puckered mouth. I thought of the wild poppies in my sea garden that seeded themselves between the stones. 'I guess it *is* a long way,' she murmured.

Nobody contradicted her. Nobody said anything. In the end Barbara asked if anyone would read *Watership Down* to her. She told us her neighbour had started the book before Barbara came to the hospice, and she was keen to know what happened next. Sister Lucy said in a rush that of course she would; it didn't matter if they skipped the beginning. Everyone seemed impatient to be busy.

Mr H is right, I wrote in my notebook later. **It's too far to walk. It's too late.**

Sister Mary Inconnue was experiencing a minor difficulty with her QWERTY keyboard. 'You listen too much to other people,' she said.

I don't, I told her. I was listening mainly to myself.

She took out a bottle of white spirit and cotton wool buds and began to clean her keys. The sharp smell took me straight back to the hospital. I could see the hard floors. The strip lighting. The crêpe-soled shoes, the masks, the hairnets, the green gowns. There were days when I longed to see a muddy boot. Over the last few years I've had four operations. Cut away any more of my throat and neck, and my head will fall off. And that is all I am going to say on the subject.

Sister Mary Inconnue sighed. 'You could try to look at things from a different perspective.'

What perspective? I can't wait for Harold. I am here to die.

Sister Mary Inconnue was still bent over her typewriter. I could see only the starched points of her headdress. It was like talking to a serviette.

She said, 'Pardon me, but you are here to live until you die. There is a significant difference.'

I could have cried. Instead I wrote, **I don't know if you have noticed but Harold Fry still seems to be down in the south-west.**

Sister Mary Inconnue went quiet a moment. 'I do admit that's a problem. But you love Harold Fry, and you believe you let him down. You must do this one last thing. You must confess the truth.' She fed a fresh page through the paper guide and adjusted the platen knob to fix it in place. 'There. All sorted. Now let's get back to your letter.'

MAKING A FRIEND OF BINDWEED

When I was fifteen my mother said to me, 'There is no such thing as love at first sight. People get together because the time is right.'

My parents had met at a dance just before the outbreak of the war and were married within three weeks. I suspect the wedding was an act of kindness on my father's part to save my mother from deportation, though he never said that to me. The only thing he let slip once was that life had been difficult for them at the beginning and so had other things. By 'other things' he meant sex. It was after the war, when he found work as a carpenter, that happiness came. 'And you, Queenie.' He had cried when he said that, and so I made them both a cup of tea.

It was hard to imagine my mother happy. She rarely laughed. English never came easily, perhaps because people were not kind to her during the war. She avoided friendships. Sometimes my father fetched the dictionary, but she said a housewife had no time for books and so I read the dictionary instead.

My mother's view on love appalled me. It suggested love had more in common with the boiling of an egg than the discovery of another person from whom one couldn't bear to live apart. I had started to explore Baudelaire by then as well as the Romantic poets and the Brontës and I liked to think that when I fell in love I would do it with style.

I liked to think I would do most things with more style than my mother. She cooked with offal. I became a vegetarian. Make-up? My mother had no idea about that. I bought liquid eyeliner, mascara and blusher. ('Do I look nice?' I asked my father once. 'You look very purple,' said my father. I took this as a compliment.) Since she was tall like my father, my mother had given up trying to find dresses and shoes to fit; instead she marched around in his trousers and boots. Appalled by that too, I hunted for fitted dresses at jumble sales – I loved a belt tight around my slight waist – and coloured dance shoes with button straps. It mortified me to be seen with my huge parents. I took to losing letters from the school about concerts or prizegivings. If my father ever tried to hold my hand on the road – he did frequently; my small-ness made him anxious – I did everything I could to swing him off.

So when my mother told me that love was only about timing, I shrugged. I didn't ask why she'd said it, because I was young then; I thought the world centred on me. But now I look back to that day and I see my mother sitting on the back step, with her chin in her hands, and her elbows on the canvas knees of the blue trousers that were not her own. At the end of our small overgrown garden I see my father's profile at the dusty window of his workshop. I see the weeds that grow between my father and my mother, the grass that is the height of wheat, the nettles, the wild buddleia. I see the pain in her eyes, the solitude. And it occurs to me she was saying the words not for my benefit but because she couldn't bear to keep silent. Now I understand what it was like for her, to be a stranger in a foreign country. I know how it is to live in exile from your past.

I wish I had not been so hard on my mother. I wish I had given her my time.

It is many years since she died, but I have come to understand her point about love too. When I first met you, I was ready. I had a space for you. It was because of my baby, you see, or rather the loss of it. The baby opened my heart to you.

The world is full of women who have children, and women who don't, but there is also a silent band of women who almost had them. I am one of those. I was a mother. And then I wasn't.

I never saw the baby. I was only sixteen weeks pregnant when I lost it, and I was discouraged from giving it a name. My loss was nothing compared to the one you and Maureen would later suffer. I tell you only because in my pregnancy I had discovered a new way to love, freely and joyfully and without expectation. Until that point my love was mainly for people who let me down. Now I was part of a club I hadn't even known existed, a club of women whose lives had fresh purpose, whose bellies were home for a life that was not their own. Who'd have thought my little body could become so important? I'd sit daydreaming of the things we would do together, my child and I. I had my new love all set up, you might say, all on tap, ready to go, generous and beautiful, and then in the tick of a moment its heartbeat was gone. Everywhere I looked I saw mothers and babies. I could have hated them, but I had hated life when I left Corby and I didn't want that any more.

I never lost the thick ring of flesh I gained at my waist when I was pregnant. It's because I'm small. As an adult, it's never been easy for me to appear slim. Or perhaps I kept the extra weight because it was all I had left to remind me of my baby. I don't know. I could tell that the reps at the brewery made jokes with Napier about me. But I was recovering from a miscarriage. I heard them call me names and imitate my walk, and I put up my chin and I waddled more. If they were going to laugh, they might as well do it properly.

I had no child and so I gave my love to you. After all, I observed you most days, depositing your beer cans in the bin below my office window. Giving my love to you was like finding a convenient vessel into which to pour the thing I had no use for, just as you had found a bin in the yard for your unwanted empties. Since the stationery cupboard we hadn't spoken, you and I, although I was aware of you, sometimes glancing in at my door to check that I was still working at the brewery, maybe even looking for me in the canteen. I found myself listening for your voice, and if someone mentioned you by name the heat came to my face and my pulse quickened. I still had your handkerchief. But I took care to avoid you, and so giving you my love felt a safe option. It kept me warm, it gave me pleasure, but I expected nothing more.

It was time to pack my suitcase and move on. 'You never rest,' my father said one of the last times I saw him. 'You never stay long enough for a cup of tea.' There was no anger in his voice. Only the habitual moist-eyed wonder.

I hope you are hearing this, Harold. I hope you are taking it in. I confess my part in your tragedy, but you must understand that I tried to remove myself from Kingsbridge, even at the beginning. And this was before I'd got in your car and come to know you. This was way before I'd met David.

At the beginning of March, I went to Napier. I'd finished working through the boxes of loose accounts. I'd put them in order, and in only two months I'd found a way to save him six hundred pounds. I'd achieved more than I promised. It seemed fair to hand in my notice.

Some things in life are a law unto themselves. Napier was one. Bindweed is another. One summer it grew all over my sea garden. It coiled itself round the tender stems of my Mrs Sinkins pinks and strangled the living sap out of them. I tugged it up by the armful, but a few days later it was back. You have to leave only a small piece of bindweed in the ground and it will regrow itself, leaves and roots and everything.

So I said to the bindweed, You want to be in my garden and I don't want you. I can't dig you out. If I poison you, I run the risk of poisoning the plants I want to keep. We have a problem that will not go away. Something needs to change.

Beside every bindweed stem, I pushed in a hazel pea stick. About twenty in all. The bindweed shot up these supports and rewarded me with lilac trumpets of flowers striped with white. I wouldn't say I loved the bindweed. I certainly didn't trust it. It would have scrambled all over my pinks the moment I stopped offering new sticks. But sometimes you have to respect the fact that even though you don't want bindweed you have it, and you'd better get along side by side. It was the same with Napier.

When I told him I was leaving the brewery, he went very quiet. Then he screamed. I've never seen a man fly so quickly from composed to hysterical, missing out the progressive stages in between.

'What do you mean, you want to go?' He slammed his fist down on the desk, and his Murano glass clowns trembled like frightened girls.

'I need to travel,' I said.

'You're not a student,' he said.

I said I was thirty-nine, but I could still purchase a bus ticket.

Napier lifted his fingers to his teeth and ripped the ends off three poor nails. 'You have a good job. Good pay. What exactly is your problem here?' His voice was getting higher and higher. 'Just because you went to Oxford, you think we aren't good enough?'

This last sentence began as a statement but had an identity crisis halfway and became a question. I'd said nothing about him not being good enough. Clearly the person who feared he was not good enough was Napier. But it is easier to argue with another person, especially an employee, than it is to argue with the darker recesses of oneself.

You see how complicated life gets. Even something as simple as a resignation.

I didn't want to make things worse with Napier, so I made an excuse. I said, 'You need to get an accountant into the pubs if he's going to catch the landlords fiddling the books. And I can't do that. You were right. You do need a man. One with a driving licence.'

'You want a driver?' He pulled that face again, and I remembered it was his laugh.

'I realize a driver's out of the question,' I said quietly. 'Which is why I have to leave.' At this point I believed I had the upper hand. In my head I was already on the bus. Goodbye, Kingsbridge. Goodbye, Harold Fry.

Then Napier did the thing he did best. He came

up with the one solution that would cause the most damage. It wasn't even intentional. It was an instinct he had, just as some people have an instinct for the weather or the piano. You would be my driver, he said. All sorted. Bingo.

I think I got as far as 'But—' and I ran out of words.

'You'll have no problem with Harold Fry,' he said. 'The man is married. Straight as a gate. Dull as fuck.' He clenched his right fist and punched it into his left palm. I had no idea what he was trying to suggest. It looked as if he were squashing you.

You as my driver? You and me in a car several times a week? Me, already in love with you from a safe distance, and you married?

'I can't,' I said. 'I get carsick.' I admit that wasn't very clever, but I was beginning to feel cornered.

'I'm about to fire him anyway,' he said.

It was like being hit. I went hot. My skin burned. And then I was so cold I needed a jumper. 'You're going to fire Mr Fry? What for?'

'He's a joke. He's old-fashioned.'

'But this is his job,' I stammered. 'He has a wife and son, doesn't he?'

'His son's a screwball. Have you seen the way he struts round Kingsbridge? Like he owns the place?' Napier shot out a puff of smoke. It went straight up my nose.

'I don't know about his son, but Mr Fry is a good man.'

Napier did the laugh thing. Pointy gold teeth, et cetera. 'Do you think I care?'

No, I thought. Of course you don't. It was time to try a new tactic. I took a deep breath.

'So let me get this straight. If I stay, will Mr Fry keep his job?'

'I'm not saying I like you, but it turns out you're a good accountant. You stay. He stays too.'

'It's a deal.' I held out my hand. 'Now shake on it.'

Napier seemed to get very busy with his smoking habit. Stubbing out his cigarette. Groping for a new one.

'Let's do this like men,' I said. 'Come along.'

He slipped his palm inside mine. It was warm and slight and disconcertingly squishy. Like grabbing hold of a tongue.

'Deal,' I said.

'Deal,' he repeated.

How many times I wanted to tell you all this, Harold. That I had saved your job, that I had stood up to Napier. Months later I sat beside you in your car and my head buzzed with all the things I wanted to share with you. But I had to be so careful not to give myself away and instead I said, 'Another mint?'

Don't be fooled. Napier didn't wish to keep me any more than he wished to keep you. But he wanted to fire me in his own time because otherwise I had control and it would be too frightening for Napier to find himself dependent on me. As with the bindweed, I had to be clever. I had to play his game. I had to offer Napier pea sticks until I came up with something so terrible he had no choice but to do the thing I wanted and get rid of me. Only here was the complication: I also had to save your job.

You see, there *were* some good bits to me.

Little did I realize that a few years later you would do all this yourself. You would provide the opportunity to get me in real trouble with Napier. And little did I realize how much leaving would hurt, when it finally came.

We took our first trip, you and I, a few days later. And I'm sorry to break this to you, Harold: I was dreading it.

A low grey cloud pleats the sky from east to west. The garden is colourless in the twilight. There is a stillness, but it is a Napier stillness. It harbours chaos. Far away, the sea boils.

Rain is coming.

I hope you have an umbrella, my friend.

Or, at the very least, a waterproof hat.

WHERE IS SISTER MARY INCONNUE?

Rain. All night. I hear it thrash the leaves of the Well-being Garden. I hear it smash against the battlements and cobblestones. It hits the windows like gravel and tumbles from the gutters in gushloads. When lightning cuts the sky, everything in my room snaps to life – the bed, the wheelchair, the sink, the bird picture, the cupboard, the television – and is caught in an ice-blue photograph. Once the rain stops, I still hear it. The drip, the tap, the creak, of a world soaked in rain.

I wonder if you hear it too.

My head whirs. Words, words, words. Even when I sleep they wake me. Everything is words. In my dream my pencil races across the page. I'll never get the words out fast enough. My right hand burns.

Sister Mary Inconnue is not here again, and I have torn out so many pages that my notebook will soon be empty.

'You have a temperature,' says the night nurse. 'You must put down that pen now.' She changes the dressings on my face and neck. She examines my eye and then she fetches medication.

As I sip slowly, slowly, her face snaps on and off, on and off, like the lighthouse at Inner Farne Island, blinking through the dark.

The moment she's gone, I am writing again.

THE LONG ROAD HOME

I am standing on one side of your Morris 1100. You are hovering on the other. It's the very end of March.

I say, 'I've heard you're driving me,' because I don't want you to see I'm nervous, but it's a stupid thing to say because why else would I be waiting by your car with my coat and handbag? I hold my bag out in front of me, gripped tight, like a float.

'Hey, Mr Fry!' yells one of the reps from a window. 'Don't do anything I wouldn't!'

I am so flustered I feel plunged in heat.

You go, 'Hr-hrm.' You seem to have no idea what else to do.

You unlock and open the passenger door for me and then glance away while I get in, as if establishing oneself in a car is an act of intense privacy and you are concerned I might embarrass myself and get it wrong. Once you are in your seat, you put on your driving gloves and start the engine. You ask if I need anything. A blanket, or a cushion? It is the first time we have been alone since the stationery cupboard. You can't look at me, and I can't look at you.

There are three cassette tapes on the dashboard. *German for Beginners*. Beethoven's Ninth. *Never Mind the Bollocks*. They belong to your son, you tell me hastily, placing them inside the glovebox and snapping it shut. The car smells of you. My son prefers music to having to talk to the father, you say with a laugh.

And I think it is a funny way to talk about yourself. As 'the father', instead of as Harold Fry.

You ask what I would like to listen to and I say, Oh, I don't mind, and you say, No, no, you choose. And I say, Well, how about music, then? Everything that happens is caught in aspic in my mind. But not the Sex Pistols, I add. You put on Radio 2. You seem relieved. Sometimes you hum, and I wonder if you are trying to send a message in code.

Once we have arrived, you get out to open the car door for me. I poke out my shoe, and as I emerge I discover that you are staring at my lower leg, just as you did with Sheila's cleavage. I wish my ankle were a better shape, because inside this brown wool suit my shoulders, you know, are not so bad and I have had men admire my breasts before now. Inwardly I curse my mother for her bovine genes and vow that I will do ankle exercises every morning.

You introduce me to the landlord: 'This is Miss Hennessy. Funny thing. We met in the stationery cupboard.'

'We met in the canteen,' I say.

But you don't hear. You are too busy exchanging glances over my head with the landlord. I am pretty sure the man is laughing because a woman has shown up, and you, in turn, appear anxious on my behalf. It's the way my father used to look when I told him I wanted to do something with my life, something that didn't involve stopping at home. I realize that, like my father, you want to protect me.

As soon as I examine the account books, it's clear they're fraudulent. Anyone who's used to expenses sheets could work this out. But I start to show off. I put the landlord through his paces. I imply he is trying to steal from Napier. He knows the rumours about our boss. Bubbles of sweat burst from his forehead, and he crimsons like someone being squeezed by the neck. He rushes out of the office. I hear him complain to you, but I don't hear your answer. I worry I've pushed it too far. I do that sometimes. I misjudge things.

When I return to your car you are watching me. And I like it. I like the way you study me with a quizzical look, as if I have just appeared in new clothing. I try to walk like a film star (with slim ankles). You open the passenger door for me and close it, and already there is a new bond between us. It is small, I know. It is only to do with our work. Nevertheless I want to keep feeling it. I'm not ready for this to end.

'Can I buy you a beer?' I ask.

You put up your hands as if stopping traffic. 'No, no. I don't.'

But I have seen you with those empties. I know your secret, just as I know that you like to dance. 'One for the road?'

'I'm teetotal, Miss Hennessy.' The gravity with which you make this confession instantly persuades me that you are speaking the truth. I am ashamed of my remark. It was underhand. Maybe you sense my discomfort, because you smile. 'Shall we take the long or the short road home?' you ask.

'Don't you need to get back?'

'My wife cooks for six. It's only five now. We'll take the scenic route.'

In the passenger seat I close my eyes but I am not asleep, I am thinking only of you. I wonder to whom they belong, those empty cans you are so careful to hide. Your wife? A neighbour? I wonder what your wife cooks for tea.

You stop the car and turn off the engine and I am surprised to discover we are not at the brewery. You have driven us to the edge of Bolberry Down. You don't say anything. You just look ahead.

The early spring day is on the verge of settling into a cold night. The hills are lilac blue, the horizon tinged with purple, the sea and rocks already indigo. A flock of birds flies in a close band back and forth above the beach. They swoop to the left, and then they appear to twist their bodies and swing to the right. They keep doing it. In one direction, their bodies are purpled by the sun's rays. In the other, the birds merge, blue-grey, into the blue-grey of the sky, so that I have to concentrate very hard in order to find them. It is such a simple thing to watch those birds, playing with their wings and the setting light, but as you turn the key in the ignition again and drive us back towards Kingsbridge, I think of how you dance in secret, and how I dance in secret too. I think of you alone in the snow. I picture the ball dress hanging in my wardrobe along with my dance shoes. And for a moment, yes, I put those two pictures together and I think: a sashay to the left, a swing to the right. You and me, side by side. It is like the first time I found your scent on your handkerchief. I feel safer than I've done in years.

You park outside the brewery, and even before I open the car door I get that thick, heavy smell of hops, but I don't hate it any more. I breathe it in. By now the building is a dull mass, like a ship with rows of windows that glint silver against the dusk. They are familiar, they are part of you and me, and for the first time I am pleased to see them. The street is empty, so is the yard. Already a frost is pricking the land. The tarmac glitters.

It is ten to six. Your wife will be waiting at home. Pinny, maybe. Casserole in the oven.

'I need to sort a few things in my office,' I mumble. And before I can stop myself, I add, 'Thank you.'

'It's a pleasure.'

'I mean, thank you for a few weeks ago. The time in the stationery cupboard.'

You turn pale. 'Don't mention it.' And I get the impression you mean exactly that.

But I can't be silent. Now that I've started, I need you to know the truth about me, even if it is only a fraction, so I tell you that I was upset and that you were kind and that I should have thanked you before. I wish I could also confess that you changed my life in the stationery cupboard, but this is too much for both of us. In your embarrassment you are popping and unpopping the fastening on your driving gloves. I leap out of the car before you can see my face. As my parting shot, I tell you that you are a gentleman. And I mean exactly that. You're a gentle man.

I pick my way across the yard, but I am shaking so much it is hard to keep walking forwards. Tears stream from my eyes. I am happy, I am happy, but I want to howl. It is your decency that moves me. Apart from my father, I have never met such a plain-good man.

Without turning, I know you are still there, in your car. I know you will wait until I am safely at the door of the brewery. There are women who might hate a man who will never love her. But how can I? And I can't move on without you losing your job. I am someone who has always run from difficulty, and it dawns on me that I don't have to go on that way. We write ourselves certain parts and then keep playing them as if we have no choice.

But a tardy person can become a punctual one, if she chooses. You don't have to keep being the thing you have become. It is never too late.

So I make a promise. For once in my life, I will stay in the same place and see something through. You will keep your job, and I will try to bring you happiness. I will not ask for anything more.

Oh, Harold. How did I get that so wrong?

WE'RE ALL GOING ONE WAY

The patient in monster slippers was not in the dayroom when we assembled for morning activities.

Shortly afterwards his family began to arrive. As they rushed past the door of the dayroom, where we sat with Sister Catherine, they looked in briefly and then flew their eyes away, as if seeing us were a mistake, a bad omen. They were dressed in smart, dark clothes, even the little girls. Maybe the family had changed when they got the news. Maybe they felt the need to inhabit their grief. After my father's death, my mother gave up eating meat. But why? I asked. She'd always loved meat. Because her life was torn in half, she said. I took her favourite cuts, slices of pink ham, tender roast beef, when I went to visit her in hospital. '*Schön, schön*,' she would murmur, but they stayed wrapped in paper. She never touched meat again. 'I am like you now, *Liebling*.' It was almost the last thing she told me.

From my chair in the dayroom I overheard a woman in the corridor. My hearing is not what it was, but emotion had made her less careful. 'Why didn't he wait for me?' she cried. 'I was only making breakfast for the girls.' It must have been the patient's wife. Then someone asked if she needed anything, and the woman began to howl, big wrenching sobs.

'Why couldn't it be one of those old people?' she wept. 'They just sit there.'

A little while later we watched a small group of mourners gathering in the Well-being Garden. They stood beneath the pagoda, sheltering from the weather. The wind and rain tossed the branches of the cherry tree so that the grass was dashed with pink petals. The older woman, the man's mother, made a batting gesture with her hands as if she had something attached to her and couldn't get it off. Then Sister Philomena cradled the woman in her arms, and the woman hung there, very still at last. Sister Philomena kept hold of the woman and spoke to her, and as she did, the woman wiped her eyes. The group reached for one another's hands, and whatever it was that Sister Philomena was saying, the others began to listen. They nodded and joined in until one man said something that made them smile. I wondered if they were talking about the patient. Sharing how much they loved him. Then the man must have asked Sister Philomena if they could smoke, because I saw her nod before he took out cigarettes.

'I think I might pop outside,' said the Pearly King, rising from his chair and heading straight for the garden.

Finty and I watched the two little girls, Alice and her sister, kneeling on the lawn to pick flowers.

'They will be OK,' Finty said. 'The grass keeps growing.'

The undertaker's van turned into the drive.

Sister Mary Inconnue reads through my page. She begins to type. When she sees me – not writing, just gazing out of the window, nursing my fingers – she smiles.

'Penny for your thoughts,' she says.

No, I think. You wouldn't want them.

'Is your right hand all right?'

I hide it so she won't see.

I must keep writing.

I THINK THAT DRESS LOOKS
NICE ON YOU

A long time ago, I met a doctor of philosophy beside my sea garden. I was rehanging some kelp banners where the wind had pulled them free. 'That's a nice job you've done here,' my visitor said, leaning over the wall. 'Have you made this garden yourself?' Yes, I told him. It had taken many, many years, but the work was all mine. We got talking, he and I. While I tended my garden, he passed me his business card and told me a little about himself.

I had grown used to strangers stopping. As word got round about the garden by the sea, visitors began to park their cars at the golf course and walk the coastal path. They brought cameras. Often they returned with pieces of ironwork for my wind chimes or cuttings from their gardens. Despite my original intention to live apart, there was a time when I was something of a local attraction, along with the footpath to Dunstanburgh Castle, and the golf course and ice cream van. 'You must have been here a long time,' said the doctor of philosophy.

'Yes,' I told him. I'd spent every day there since the first morning I arrived.

'You haven't left once?'

'Sometimes I make a day trip along the coast. But there's always something to look after in my sea garden. I couldn't abandon it.'

I pointed back at my beach house. The place was always at its best in the summer, and its wooden slats shone that afternoon as if they were painted not with bitumen but with gold. The beach house cast a shadow that grew as the light dimmed so that by sunset it almost touched my sea garden. At night, the many stones glowed in the moonlight, and sometimes, when I picked them up, I could still feel and smell the sun in them.

I explained to the doctor of philosophy that when I'd first come across the beach house, it was a wreck. There were other beach houses up on the cliff but no one had lived in this one for a long time. There was certainly no hint of a garden, only swathes of brambles, fern and nettles. I explained that I'd bought the plot from a couple who didn't use it any more. I couldn't make a home up there, everyone had warned. It was too lonely, too out of the way. I'd never survive a winter, they said. No one spent a winter up on Embleton Bay. I replied that was exactly the reason I wanted to buy the place. In order to be alone in the wind and cold.

I spent a whole year making my beach house habitable, and when I began on the garden it was almost by accident. I was trying to clear a path through the nettles, because in places they'd grown as tall as my shoulders. All I found beneath the nettles were boulders, and so I'd begun to pile them, simply as a way to stack them. By the end of the day I was so exhausted, my bones felt so weak, and my skin was so numb from the nettle stings, that I went straight to bed. I lay very still, with only the crashing of the sea below on the rocks, and the wind, and for the first time, I would say, the sounds didn't feel like something I had to fight any more. I slept all night without dreaming or crying. It was only the following morning when I stepped out with a cup of tea to watch the sea and noticed instead the pile of stones, some grey, some blue-black, that it occurred to me I had made a rockery.

And so I got more interested. I began to think carefully about the shape and the size of the stones. My rockery kept me busy even when the rain came so hard that I could barely open my eyes, even when my hands were flayed with sores and cuts. I showed the doctor of philosophy all the things that had followed: the rock pools, the winding paths, the shell beds, the figures, the wind chimes, the flowering gorse topiaries that smelt of coconut when the sun was on them. The wall had come right at the end, along with the picket gate. I put that together from slats of driftwood.

I'd made my sea garden to atone for the terrible wrong I had done to a man I loved, I said. Sometimes you have to do something with your pain because otherwise it will swallow you. I tried to voice your name, and David's too, but already tears were spilling from my eyes. It was always like that. I could never tell the full story.

The doctor of philosophy was very interested in my sea garden until I mentioned the word 'love'. Then he laughed. There was no such thing as love, he told me. Hadn't I heard of Sartre?

Oh, good. A little light debating. I wiped my eyes.

Yes, I said, I'd heard of Sartre. I kept a copy of *Being and Nothingness* next to *The Observer's Book of Sea and Seashore* on the kitchen windowsill.

'We are nothing,' he said. 'At root we know that we're nothing. So when we love, it is only to fool ourselves that we are something.'

Now that I'd stopped my work, I noticed that the doctor of philosophy was dressed in sensible walking gear and a red spotted bow tie. It was as if the walking clothes were saying one thing about him and the tie was shouting another. I liked that.

Nevertheless I said he was wrong on the subject of love. I told him about you, how you danced with your shadow in the snow. I described the way you'd touched my hand in the stationery cupboard, igniting a flurry of sparks and chills that I could still remember if I put my mind to it. I mentioned our drives, how we went out two or three times a week and often made a day of it. While I checked the accounts, you would chat with the landlord and look over the car. I had never asked for your love in return, I said. I had never told you my true feelings.

What I'd described sounded like infatuation, said the doctor of philosophy: a projection of my own needs.

'No, I only wanted him to be happy. That was all I needed.'

'It's easier to tell yourself that you are in love with a person than it is to put up with him day after day. We tell ourselves we are in love in order to stay put.'

'But I didn't stay put. I left. I left, and I still love him.'

I told him that I'd seen the essence of you right from the beginning; I never stopped seeing it all the time we worked together, I only saw deeper versions. My love had even matured since I left you. 'And,' I said, 'Sartre may be right about love in theory, but he takes the fun out of it. Doesn't he?'

'What do you mean?' For the first time, my visitor looked uneasy.

'Sometimes we like to laugh at ourselves. We like to be silly.' I pointed to some of the features in my garden. The figures that wore necklaces of stone. A wind chime made with washed-up keys from the beach. I had put them there to remind myself how we used to laugh, you and I; how I sang backwards and we played daft games like fig ball. 'Or maybe we do something else,' I said. 'Like wearing a fun tie.'

'I should head off now,' said the doctor of philosophy.

I folded his business card into a white bird and fixed it to a branch.

During the course of our drives together, I came to know you better. At the start, we travelled mainly in silence. I'd point out the leaves or I'd say, 'Nice day,' but nothing more. I didn't know the names of trees or flowers in those days. They were only a backdrop to where we were heading. Then after a week or so I began to ask you questions. Small things. Not to intrude or alarm you, just to be polite. The first time I asked about David, you said your son was very clever. That's all. But you cleared your throat, trying to move away from a difficult thought. I remember that I watched you for a little too long, and when you glanced at me you flushed, as if you were afraid I had noticed something odd about you. I hadn't. I was only admiring the blue of your eyes and trying not to smile but wanting to smile because they were so very blue, you see.

I remember too the first time I caught sight of your bare arms. It was a warm day. You unbuttoned your cuffs and rolled back your sleeves. I couldn't stop staring at the softness of your skin. I'd expected your arms to be different, but they were almost boyish. My heart was going cock-a-hoop. I knew I'd give myself away if I wasn't careful, but I couldn't stop drinking you in. I couldn't stop seeing them, your bare arms, even when the air grew cool and you stopped the car to put your jacket on.

So I stuck to my polite questions about David. His intelligence was nothing to do with you, you told me. 'He doesn't get it from me, Miss Hennessy. He doesn't get much from me, actually.' And the way you said this, in a humble way suggesting that no one could get *anything* from you, you'd be lucky if they even noticed you walking into a room, made me want to give you something, you know, a little something to bring you pleasure and show you that you weren't nothing, that for me you were very definitely somebody. I've noticed you, Harold Fry, I wanted to say. I see you. Every day I see you. I spent the weekends in a daze, waiting, waiting for Monday. I bought my groceries, did the washing, but I was thinking only of being with you again.

One day in early May, I produced a Mars bar from my handbag. I didn't tell you, but it was my fortieth birthday and I'd bought the chocolate as a treat for myself. Only once I was at your side, I couldn't think of anything I wanted more than to give it to you. That seemed a better use for it.

'Here you are,' I said.

'Is that for me?'

Your face glowed. Had no one given you a bar of chocolate before?

'Well, I can't see anyone else in the car,' I said.

You gave an embarrassed laugh. 'I'll get fat.'

'You? There's nothing of you.' And then it was

my turn to be embarrassed, because the remark betrayed that I watched you, that I had taken you in, your arms, your eyes, the way your trousers drooped at your waist, and so I urged you to take the chocolate bar before the ruddy thing melted in my hands.

'Thank you, Miss Hennessy.'

'Oh, call me Queenie. Please.'

You twitched your mouth as if you were trying to teach it the new word.

'Do you want me to unwrap the Mars bar for you?'

'Would you mind?'

'Not at all. Let me help.'

So I tore off the corner of the paper and passed you a paper tissue from my handbag, and while you ate I gave you a little story to go with it. I told you that as a child I had hated my name. My father loved 'Queenie', but I found it old-fashioned. I'd always wished I was called 'Stella', I said. And you looked a little perplexed, as if it had never occurred to you that you might be something you weren't.

'I never liked my nose,' you said, taking another bite.

'What's wrong with your nose?'

'It has a bump.'

Now that I looked at your nose I could see this. It did seem to begin as a slim nose and conclude as a big one. You adjusted the rear-view mirror and told me your mother had always promised that your face would grow into your nose, and instead your nose had only grown out of your face. You made me laugh, and then you laughed too. I got the impression you had never laughed about your nose or your mother before.

I bought you chocolate bars regularly after that. I stopped at the newsagent's on the way to work. It became part of what I did, just as some people stop to feed the birds, just as others used to visit my sea garden and throw a penny for good luck into one of the mussel-blue rock pools.

The next time you mentioned David, you told me he was hoping to go to Cambridge after the summer. 'He wants to do the classics.'

'Why didn't you say that before?'

'He doesn't like me to talk about it.'

'But I was at Oxford. St Hilda's. I read classics too.'

'Gosh,' you said. 'Golly.'

'Is that all you can say?' I smiled to show you there was no spike in the comment, I was only being friendly.

'What do you want me to say?'

'I don't know. They're such funny words. It's like "Gor blimey". Or "Blow me down". I thought no one said things like that.'

'Perhaps I say them when I am nervous.'

'Do I make you nervous?'

'A bit.'

You blushed, and I wished I could take your hand but of course I couldn't. I could only sit there with my handbag. Instead I asked if David might like to borrow one of my university text-books; I'd kept a few on my travels. Those books were incredibly precious to me, but I didn't admit that. The truth is, I was trying to find ways of connecting with you, and offering my books to your son was all I could think of.

'Do you think David would be interested?' I asked.

Your reply, when it came, astonished me. 'I think that dress looks nice on you.' I assumed I had misheard. I glanced up and bumped straight into your eyes. I felt my body shower with pleasure.

'It's a brown suit,' I said.

'Well, it's still nice.'

In my bedsit I had a midnight-blue ballroom dress sewn at the bodice with sequin clusters. I had a pair of black velvet dance shoes. But what did you admire? A plain wool suit the colour of a nut.

'Gor blimey,' I said.

By June, it was done. There was no going back for me. I watched you carefully fixing the button on your driving gloves, or chatting with one of the landlords, gentle laugh lines at the corners of your eyes; and me, I wanted to halloo, I wanted to shout. I could barely contain myself. Sometimes I had to give a funny cough or worse – it came out as a snort. Anything rather than tell you my true feelings. It wasn't even because what we said was funny. To an outsider, it might have seemed rather ordinary. But once in a while simply being with a person is enough and so anything he says or does can set you off. I loved your voice, your walk, your marriage, your hands, your zigzag socks, the sensible knot in your scarf, your white bread sandwiches, for God's sake, everything about you. It was the giddying first stage when everything about the person is so new and full of wonder that you have to keep stopping, to watch, to listen, to take him in, and there is nothing else. The rest of the world turns to grey and is obliterated. On a brewery day, we sometimes shared a table in the canteen or you dropped by my office to discuss the next route, but there were always other people close by on those occasions. It was when we were alone in your car that you were mine.

After all I'd been through, I felt human again. I woke in the mornings and the day wasn't something to hide from. I'd sit on the bus, getting nearer and nearer to the brewery, with my heart beating wild in my chest, and that is a gift: it is being alive. I knew you'd never leave Maureen. You were too decent for that. Another reason, of course, to love you.

I began to write poems. Love poems. How else could I express myself? I kept them in the zipped-up compartment of my handbag. I'd reach inside, touch the corners of the pages with my fingertips, and I'd wonder, Will I do it today? Will I tell Harold Fry how I feel? Instead, I'd offer you a boiled sweet.

So when I turned my head away in the passenger seat and said nothing, it wasn't because I was sleeping, Harold. I was picturing you and me. I imagined what it would be like to exist permanently at your side. Or I'd gaze out of the window and look places over, just for fun, to see if we might live in one of them. A nice pink detached house with a bit of lawn for you to mow, handy for shops and the laundrette. Or a cottage by the beach, more remote, but with sea views. Inside my head I put us on dining chairs at a small round table. I put us on an upholstered sofa. And yes, I even put us in a bed. I watched your hands on the steering wheel – and I am sorry to say this but I promised at the beginning you would get the truth – and I imagined those hands on my hands. On my breasts. Between my thighs.

When you are imagining a man naked beside you and actually he is wearing fawn casuals and driving gloves and is married to another woman, you have to do things to throw him off the scent. Once I said I could sing backwards and you looked astounded and said, Can you really? I couldn't, of course I couldn't, what did you take me for? I'd been a classics student. It was my father who could sing backwards. He did it as he planed a piece of wood or rubbed a plank with linseed oil. Nevertheless I went home after you asked that question and I taught myself 'God Save the Queen'.

(The more traditional version.)

Backwards.

What else had I to do?

'Good Lord,' you laughed when I got to the end of it. It was the way my father used to laugh when I was a child, full of wonder that I knew things and he didn't.

Now, I could have said to you, Let me tell you about Socrates. Or I might have asked, What are your views on Bertrand Russell? But we had got ourselves to a place, you and I, that was both unreal and supremely ordinary. We were a tall, married man who was kind and a short, single woman who loved him. It was better to eat sweets and sing backwards than risk unbalancing the small thing that we had. And after a while it became our routine, it became our language, in the way that some people like talking about the weather or driving routes instead of saying the bigger things. There was a boundary.

'I don't have many,' you said to me another time. It must have been early summer, because we were sharing lunch by the side of the road. I was in my suit. You were head to toe in fawn. We looked like two winter shrubs off for a picnic.

'Many what?' I smiled. 'Whatever are you talking about, Harold?'

'Friends,' you said. 'Friends.' You picked the shell from a hard-boiled quail's egg and dipped the egg in celery salt. I'd supplied both items, as well as the spread of carved ham, chutney, grapes, tomatoes, napkins and paper plates. 'I have Maureen. And David. But no one else.' You mentioned your mother. How she'd left just before your thirteenth birthday. You said something about your father too. Drink, it was. I assumed that was the reason you were now teetotal, and I felt a rush of tenderness. It was the most you'd ever confessed about yourself. Your eyes wore a pained expression, as if you'd made a mistake and had no idea what to do next.

It was like the day my father told me that things had not always been good with my mother. You'd let your guard slip, almost by accident, just as my father had, and I wanted to put that right for you.

'You have me,' I said. 'I'm your friend, Harold.' It was important to say those words. I could hear the beat of my blood.

You went back to picking at another egg. You said to your fingers, 'By the way, you know, that dress-thing looks nice on you.'

I realized then it was your way of saying thank you.

Everything had made a place for itself, Harold. You seemed happy. Your job was safe. And I was happy too. I'd got over the loss of my baby. I'd given up the room in the B&B and had rented a ground-floor flat on the edge of Kingsbridge with views towards the estuary. There was no garden, but I was not interested in those days. I found a place to go ballroom dancing on Thursday nights, and sometimes I danced with a stranger, sometimes I didn't. I imagined lifting my hands to your shoulders and taking a waltz.

So long as I could see you every weekday, I was happy to love you from the sidelines.

We would grow old . . . we would grow old. You would wear the bottoms of your trousers rolled. I would keep the truth untold.

And then I met your son.

YES, YES, YES

A bad night. The wind charges at the streets and the sea. It rattles at the window and roars through the tree outside. I see David. All night he is shouting at me. He shakes the framed print, and as the blue birds fly out he snaps off their wings. He asks for all the items he ever stole from me, only he doesn't ask, he screams. I open my mouth, but no sound comes. There is nothing. The words cannot rise beyond my throat.

A tenner! he shouts.

Yes, I grunt.

Another one!

Yes.

A bottle of gin!

Yes.

Another!

Yes, I honk.

Blanket! Beer! Biscuits!

Here. Here.

Your egg whisk!

My egg whisk? Why, David? Why do you need my egg whisk?

I want it! I want your egg whisk!

My throat feels carved with a knife. YES, DAVID. YES, DAVID. YES, YES, YES.

This morning I didn't make it to the dayroom. During the morning rituals, the nurse said she'd heard a volunteer was coming with musical instruments. 'Sometimes people think they can't play music but they can, you know. It's always a good day when the music volunteer comes.' I requested to stay in my room. Later I heard the other patients playing bells and drums, but it was like me being in one land and them being in another. After thirteen days of writing, my hand felt skewered. In the dining room I couldn't pick up my fork to eat. My head throbbed. Twice I was sick. I could not eat. I could not even take my nutritional drink.

Dr Shah examined my neck, mouth and eye. 'There is some swelling in the parotid gland.'

'A little,' said Sister Philomena.

'And what's happened to her hand?'

I tried to pull it away, but I wasn't fast enough. Dr Shah caught my right hand and turned it for a better look. He saw the blister between my thumb and forefinger where I've been holding the pencil. My thumb was hot and inflamed. The palm was pulsing. 'That looks infected. What's she been doing?'

Dr Shah is a good man, but I wish he would talk as if I can hear.

Sister Philomena folded her arms. She smiled at

the pages scattered all over the floor. 'Queenie has been keeping busy. Haven't you, Queenie?'

'You need to take better care of yourself,' said Dr Shah. And he placed my hand very carefully on my lap, as if it were something precious to him, so that I felt wrong for criticizing him in my mind only moments before.

Later the duty nurse came to dress the wound. She punctured the blister and drained it of pus. She dabbed on antibiotic gel and wrapped my hand with a gauze dressing. When she was gone, Sister Lucy sat beside me.

'Why don't I paint your nails?' she said. She concentrated so hard, she breathed through her nose. The room seemed to lift and fall as she sat working.

My nails are now the colour of the dawn sky over the sea at Embleton Bay, when the day is so new it is almost white.

THE NUN AND THE PEACH

'You have been overdoing it, dear heart.'

When Sister Mary Inconnue entered my room this morning, she was bearing her typewriter in its leather bag high above her cornette, like a tray. 'Look,' she said. 'Look what I have for you on this fine Tuesday.' (It was raining.) She lowered the bag. She showed me a plate with one soft, amber peach.

I shook my head to remind her I can't eat. If I am honest, I felt angry. As if she and the letter had become one and the same thing. I showed her my bandaged right hand.

She said, 'Well, what do you expect? You push yourself too hard. You are always writing. On Sunday you hardly stopped. You wrote about Harold and the drives all day.'

But this letter was YOUR IDEA. My pencil stabbed the page.

'I didn't tell you to do it the whole time. Waiting is about being still. You can't keep busy every minute, otherwise you're not waiting. You're just throwing things around to distract yourself.'

Sister Mary Inconnue set her typewriter bag on

the foot of my bed and drew up the chair. 'It's time to concentrate your energy on other things. Like this lovely peach.'

And how exactly was a peach going to help me or Harold Fry? I didn't write that for her. I just thumped the bed.

I shouldn't even think these things, because Sister Mary Inconnue swoops in with an answer as if she's just stepped inside my head and heard me. 'It won't make any difference whatsoever,' she said. 'But it will make you less anxious. The peach is here. It's in the present. Whether you can wait for Harold Fry is not something you will influence by working hard or getting upset. We behave these days as if we can have everything the moment we think of it. But we can't. Sometimes we just have to sit and wait. So take the peach. Don't be so cross. Go on.'

She put it in my hands. Look at the skin, she told me. Look at the colour. The shape. What a beauty. Touch it. The room was very still. Just a peach.

I stroked the velvety red blush of its skin. I felt the give of its flesh as I pressed it with my finger-tips. I traced the well-defined crease. The dimple at its centre where once the fruit was attached to a stem, a tree, and grew there. This may sound strange, but I forgot briefly that you could eat a peach as well as touch it. Sister Mary Inconnue lifted the fruit to my nose, and the smell was so honey-sweet my nostrils began to zing.

'Let's cut it open now,' she said. She took up her knife.

I watched everything. The glint of light on the blade, the nick in the flesh as the knife pierced it, the sudden overspill of sticky amber juice down her fingers and then on to the plate. After she had eased the knife once round, she put it down and held the peach between her two hands in order to prise it open. She twisted the top half away from the lower and pulled her hands apart so that the peach emerged in two glistening halves, one bearing the stone like a wet nut, the other showing a soft naked bed with pulpy ruby strings. My mouth began to flood.

Sister Mary Inconnue cut the flesh into quarters, then into smaller pieces. She mopped her fingers before offering me the plate.

'Have a try,' she said.

I shook my head. I pointed to my throat. **I'll choke.**

'You can spit it out if it's too much.'

I lifted a bit of the peach between my fingers. My chin was already soaked. I slipped the fruit between my lips and felt it nestle on the floor of my mouth. I tipped my head to the left, a little to the right, in order to move the fruit from side to side.

'You don't have to swallow if you don't want to,' said Sister Mary Inconnue.

The thick sweet juice spilt past my larynx and towards my belly. I trembled with hunger. Throwing up my chin, I jumped the fruit into the back of my mouth. If I die choking on a piece of peach, I thought, at least it won't have tasted of cardboard. Then it was gone. I had eaten it.

'You see?' laughed Sister Mary Inconnue. 'You ate some peach. You said you couldn't, but you could.'

I felt happier than if I'd grown wings and learned to fly. We ate another piece and then another. We were the peach and the peach was us and there was nothing more.

'You should rest now,' she said.

When I woke, Sister Mary Inconnue had gone home. I picked up my pencil and held it very carefully so as not to rub the blister. I began to write about the nun and the fruit, taking small breaks in between each paragraph. It has taken me two days.

I hope you are resting too, Harold.

How are your feet?

THREE CHEERS FOR MARTINA

'Oh, I fuckin' love that Slovak gal!' yelled Finty from her chair. 'I want to snog her, I do!'

Sister Catherine had just read out the long message on today's postcard. The one with a picture of the castle and 'Greetings from Taunton'. Did the young woman really rescue you? Did she really offer you a bed for the night and repair your shoes? Did she actually massage your feet?

'I love Harold Fry an' all!' shouted Finty.

Today Finty received a voucher for free dining at thousands of quality restaurants in the UK. She says she is saving the voucher for you. 'I reckon that poor bugger is starving,' she said.

'I'm glad Harold Fry had a day of rest in Taunton,' said Sister Catherine. 'It must have been hard. Walking and walking for two whole weeks. I'd be in agony. It's my flat feet.' She lifted her hem. Her black shoes poked out like two liquorice sticks.

'But if Harold Fry is in Somerset,' said Barbara, 'that means he'll reach the Midlands soon.'

Sister Lucy bit her lip. 'Is Somerset not next to

Newcastle, then?' More pieces were removed from her jigsaw. The Pearly King gave a kiss to his fingertips and blew it into the air.

'A woman washed his feet?' said Mr Henderson. 'Who does Harold Fry think he is? Jesus Christ?'

I smiled, and I am not sure but I think Mr Henderson smiled too. Perhaps it was acid reflux.

I used to take the Taunton bus out of Kingsbridge. I never went as far as Taunton. I got off at Totnes and went dancing every Thursday. For a while, Harold, your son came with me.

I will get to this story. It's especially important and you must know it. The story may bring you pain, and for that I'm sorry. But we are on this path now, Harold. You must hear everything.

There can be no more writing today, however. My hand is sore and I have learned my lesson. You don't get to a place by constantly moving, even if your journey is only one of sitting still and waiting. Every once in a while you have to stop in your tracks and admire the view, a small cloud and a tree outside your window. You have to see what you did not see before. And then you have to sleep.

Soon I will tell you.

A TASTE OF WELL-BEING

'Hat? Shawl? Slippers?' Sister Catherine pulled a baseball cap on to my head and scanned me up and down in my wheelchair as if she had just made me all by herself. She gave a nod of approval. 'It's a beautiful spring day. So here we go. The garden.'

Sister Catherine wheeled me out of my room and along the corridor. There was no one in the dayroom. The doors to the terrace were already open, and the air smelt sweet and sappy. I closed my eyes as we approached the dazzling square of light on the carpet. But then I felt the prickle of sunshine on my hands, my wrists. I gripped my fingers into a ball and dared to look.

The Well-being Garden had exploded. Everywhere I turned, it fizzed with spring. Greenery cracked from the bare branches. In places the growth was so new that the leaves were pale crumbs, and in others they verged on yellowy acidic, as if nature had not yet got the colour mix right. Daisies, buttercups and celandine threaded the grass. There were unfurled white buds on the magnolias and long tassels of leaves drooping from the willow. I thought of the girls I knew at Oxford with their long silky hair. I wonder where they are now? Sunshine flowed through the trees in spangled spokes, and the waxy leaves of the evergreens – the holly, the laurel, the viburnums – blinked where they caught the light.

'Everybody's outside today, Queenie,' said Sister Catherine.

It was true. On the terrace a volunteer was playing cards with Mr Henderson in his wheelchair. Sister Lucy read *Watership Down* to Barbara. The Pearly King was dozing. There were several patients with their friends and family, and children playing hide-and-seek behind the wooden pagoda. Down by the pond, Finty lay spread-eagled on a mattress. When she saw me she sat up. She waved.

'Feel them rays, Queenie Hennessy!' she yelled. 'I'm topless, gal!' No one minded. Her torso was milk white, small as a child's. Her ribs stuck out above and beneath the flat currants that were her breasts.

Sister Catherine showed me the last of the primroses and daffodils. She pointed to the blue haze of forget-me-nots beneath the sycamore trees. Soon the yellows of a spring garden will be replaced by white. There will be blossom on the hawthorn, banks of cow parsley. Peony buds sat tight as marbles. I would love to see them flower.

'Do you want to smell the mint, Queenie?' said Sister Catherine. She snapped off a stem and crushed the leaves between her fingertips. It was as good as drinking summer.

I wanted to describe my sea garden, but I had no notebook. I thought instead of the rock pools and flowerbeds. I remembered the first driftwood figure I made from a bleached branch that I found on the shore; it was tall, you see, about six feet in all, and washed-out fawn in colour. When I erected it at the centre of my garden, it was like bringing something of you into my exile. I made many more of those figures over the years, and sometimes, if they looked sad – by which I mean, I suppose, if I felt sad about them – I hung them with garlands of seaweed or holey stones. When the flowers died back in the summer, the stones and figures took over. A garden should never seem shut down in winter. And all the while I thought these things, Sister Catherine smiled as if she understood.

'I wonder where Harold Fry is today?' she asked the air. And a little later she said, 'One day, I'd like to walk to Santiago de Compostela. But it's my feet, you see. So I don't suppose I will.'

Tonight the Well-being Garden is still. It is not quiet but it is peaceful. From inside I hear Barbara singing in her room. Someone coughs. There's a television, and an exchange between the night staff that ends with laughter. The wind ruffles the North Sea, and a pearl-white moon shines above the tree.

138

I wait.

I remember.

The slant of a smile. The scuff on a shoe. A spilling of sunlight.

REBEL CHILD

It's July in Kingsbridge and there's a sudden downpour. I am walking down Fore Street with my shopping basket. The quay is hidden behind the veil of rain. The water plashes my face and shoulders. It drops in solid sploshes from the shop awnings, and it gushes in rivulets down the street. I bow my head. I have to place my steps carefully in order not to lose my balance and slip. It's a weekend, so I'm wearing sandals, a loose dress, a light cardigan. My hair is soaked and so are my feet.

'Why can't you watch where you drive?' shouts a male voice. 'What's wrong with you?' With my hands to my eyes, I glance up.

The fuss is coming from a young man outside a pub on the other side of the road. He's pointing at a driver in a car. I quickly understand that the motorist has pulled into a parking space beside the young man and splattered him with water from the gutter. It's all over the young man's coat, his big boots. His hair is so wet it sticks flat against his head like black streamers.

'And what are you in a sportscar for, anyway?' the young man shouts. 'What's your problem?'

The driver gets out of his car and locks it in a hurry and tries to pretend the young man is not bothering him. But the young man won't give up. He waves his arms at the grey street, the shopfronts, the rain.

'This is Kingsbridge,' he shouts. 'Not Monaco.'

I am not the only person who's noticed. Other people have stopped too. They tell the young man to calm down. Move away, they say. So he starts shouting at them as well, calling them names, only the ones he chooses make him laugh. Capitalist! Golfer! Bank manager!

'Walker of small dogs!' he shouts. 'Reader of Tory newspapers! Drinker of Rotary Club port!'

Someone calls out that there is no need for this sort of behaviour in a nice place like Kingsbridge, though as I look at the crowd around the young man – the corduroys, the waterproofs, the golfing umbrellas and blazers – I see that he is speaking the truth. I can't help smiling. He laughs too, and then his face falls and he looks nothing except incredibly bored. 'Oh, fuck you,' he says, turning away. Only it isn't as if he is saying it to the passers-by or even the driver. It is as if he is saying it to the whole world.

He has a narrow face, very pale, pointed at the chin. He is tall, too tall; his legs and arms poke out at the ends of his trousers and sleeves. I'd know that profile anywhere.

'What did you say? What did you say to me?' The driver has had enough. He hops from one foot to

141

the other. 'Did you hear him?' he shouts to the crowd. He looks far more out of control than David. In fact David is very still, watching the growing rumpus with amused detachment. The rainwater streams down his face.

Bursting out of the pub comes a thickset man with a bottle in his hand, and behind him is the slight figure of Napier. Our boss keeps to the back, dancing from one foot to the other, but he has several other men with him. David doesn't seem to hear, but they are calling him names. Gay boy. Wanker. It's hardly imaginative. As soon as David turns, they will grab him and shove him down an alleyway. Their hands are already fists. Their chins jut forward. Nobody's going to stop them.

My arm shoots up. I yell, 'Here I am! Here I am!' I am already charging into the road, though I have no idea what I am going to do when I get to the other side. 'David Fry!' I am pushing through the crowd. 'Yes, he's with me!' I am calling. 'Excuse me!' Spotting me, Napier's henchmen slink into the shadows.

The sodden lapels of David's overcoat are pinned all over with coloured badges. FASCIST LEMSIPS. THE SEX PISTOLS. DON'T BLAME ME I VOTED LABOUR! FREE NELSON MANDELA. But also, strangely, a picture of Paddington Bear. David smells of damp and patchouli and cigarettes. 'Come along or we'll be late,' I say, steering him past the crowd. I talk very loudly, as if no one else is present, and then I march him down the street. He doesn't resist. We walk fast though I can feel him looking at me. I think he's even smiling. In a detached way. The way he watched the crowd earlier, as if he likes unexpected adventure.

Once we're down by the quay I slow my pace. We stop under the awning of the newsagent's. The rain *pop-pops* above our heads. It dimples the skin of the estuary and beats at the little boats so that they bob and sway.

'What was that about?' David brushes his wet sleeve. His hands are very fine. He seems to be removing my touch from his coat.

I know your father, I tell him. I work with Harold Fry.

David laughs as if he has just got the punchline to a joke only he knows. 'Oh, right,' he says.

'I don't know why you think it's funny. You were about to get into a lot of trouble back there.'

'Kingsbridge needs some trouble. It needs an enema. That's what it needs.' David grins at me. His face is full of it. 'Do you have any cash?'

'Are you serious?'

'Well, I am, actually. Sorry about that.'

When I open my purse to give him a pound coin, he says the five-pound note will do it. And when I object, he begins to talk. He tells a complicated story about someone stealing his wallet, his grandmother dying, the cat dying, only even as he tells me the story he has had enough of the lie and he starts smiling. The grin erupts into another laugh. He has your eyes. Very deep blue. But they do not have your gentleness, and neither do they have your humility. This boy is smart. His intelligence is like a knife. Nevertheless, the story about the cat is elaborate and wild. It's the sort of thing I would have made up once, though in an exercise book and not with a stranger. I begin to laugh too.

'Are you going to give me this money, or not?' he says.

'What about a cup of tea, David?'

'With you?' He gives a look that is a question mark. I feel ashamed of my suggestion. It is too forward. Then he says, 'You can buy me a can of beer, if you want.'

The cans of beer. Of course. I picture you secretly disposing of those empties in the yard, and once again I feel a flush of such tenderness for you that my throat thickens. 'Isn't it a bit early in the day, David?'

'No one gives a toss in Kingsbridge.' He offers me a cigarette, and when I say no, he shrugs. 'I started drinking in pubs when I was twelve. I was in my school uniform and no one said anything. Nice meeting you, Queenie.' He taps the side of his forehead with his fingertips in a mock salute. Then he turns and strides away. 'See you again some time,' he calls as an afterthought.

I watch him as he strides back through the rain towards the High Street, pushing with his shoulders past strangers, his coat flapping, his Dr Martens boots slapping the wet pavement. He rolls his neck every now and then as if it is a hard thing to carry so much cleverness in that head of his.

Only when he's gone does it occur to me that he is not the only person who stands out in Kingsbridge.

David knew my name.

HOMAGE TO HAROLD FRY

A day of mist. At the window there is nothing. No tree. No sky. It is as if the hospice has been cut from its moorings and we are drifting in a white sea. I hope it is not misty with you, Harold. In my mind, I give you a fluorescent jacket and a lantern.

This morning something unexpected occurred in the dayroom.

'What exactly are those?' enquired Mr Henderson, pointing at the cork noticeboard. Two new pages had been pinned up, above the NHS posters about care in the community and useful contact numbers in Northumberland. I went back to my notebook.

We were all at the table. A volunteer was demonstrating how to make greeting cards. Sometimes it helps, she said, to write a message for a person you love. 'It is another way of voicing the things you find hard to say.' The volunteer had brought a tote bag of glue, folding cards, sequins, foam craft stickers, assorted feathers, self-adhesive stars and metallic pens. Finty had made a card to send to Prince Harry, because he is her favourite royal. Sister Catherine was helping Barbara to make a

146

card for her neighbour. The Pearly King had lifted the glue tube to his nose several times and told us there was nothing like the good old days, but so far he had not used it to stick any foam shapes to his greeting card.

'Is everyone deaf, as well as dying?' shouted Mr Henderson. Surprise, surprise, he had not made a card. He pointed again at the noticeboard. This time we all stopped our work and looked up. Sister Lucy rose from her chair.

'Oh, I did that,' she said. She removed the pictures in order to show us.

They were two calendar pages, for April and May. Each had a glossy photographic illustration, one of yellow primroses and the other of a tortoise-shell kitten. Sister Lucy squinted a little in order to read out the captions.

'The first is "Spring in Berwick-upon-Tweed".' She pointed to the second. 'And this is "A Sweet Kitten".'

'Is the sweet kitten also in Berwick-upon-Tweed?' said Mr Henderson.

Sister Lucy chewed her mouth. 'Well, I suppose. It doesn't say.'

Mr Henderson flapped open the newspaper. 'No comment,' he said.

'But why are there kittens and flowers on the fucking noticeboard?' shouted Finty. I should add that she was wearing a pink cowboy hat. If I knew why I would tell you. But I have no clue. One of the volunteers has a dressing-up box at home for her children. She brings the hats for Finty because Finty likes them.

Sister Lucy explained that she had torn the pages from a spare calendar in the office. She had coloured every day that you have been walking. It is so that we can follow your progress, she said. She also pointed to a photograph she had cut from a celebrity magazine of a man in walking boots.

'But that is John Travolta,' said Finty. 'Fuck me. Is he coming as well?'

Sister Lucy said she didn't know anything about John Travolta. So far as she knew, it was only Harold Fry who was walking. 'I asked Sister Philomena, and she said we can have a Harold Fry corner,' she added.

'Fab!' yelled Finty. 'Can we have a drinks cabinet, and all?'

Mr Henderson made a noise I am not going to describe.

Sister Lucy blushed so hard she looked perman-ently stained. 'Today is—' She interrupted herself in order to point her finger at each date and count under her breath. 'Today is the twentieth day of Harold Fry's journey.' She moved to the second page, with the kitten, and taking a pen from her pocket she carefully coloured the first square. 'It is also the first of May.' She suggested that she might display your postcards beside the calendar pages so that we can all see where you have been. When I agreed, she fetched them from my room and pinned them up. She wheeled me closer to the Harold Fry corner. 'Look,' she said. 'Look, Queenie.'

'Does that mean I've been here more than twenty days?' growled the Pearly King. 'Plenty of life in the old dog yet.'

'What is that funny noise?' asked Barbara.

Finty laughed. 'It's the Pearly King. He's beating his chest. Don't try it, Babs. You'll knock your eye out again.'

'Good grief,' sighed Mr Henderson. 'This is worse than *Huis Clos*.'

'Wee what?' howled Finty.

I returned to your postcards. Kingsbridge. Bantham Beach. Buckfast Abbey. South Brent. The topographical map. Chudleigh and Exeter. The Bluebell steam train. Taunton. Harold Fry is really coming, I thought. And I experienced a little spring in my heart, the way I used to when the spiny burnet rose in my sea garden rewarded me with one white flower.

Then I remembered all the things I still have to tell you. I glanced at the thick mist pressed to the windows. I lowered my head.

'I still don't understand,' Mr Henderson was saying. 'Why is there a *kitten* on the calendar? Will someone explain to me what a *kitten* has to do with Berwick-upon-Tweed? Miss Hennessy?'

But I was back with my notebook.

A ONE-WAY TICKET TO NEWCASTLE

Tiverton Parkway, Taunton, Bristol Temple Meads, Bristol Parkway, Cheltenham Spa, Birmingham New Street . . .

I stood on the platform at Exeter, peering along the track. The line of sleepers stretched a little way and then disappeared in fog. When the train came, it didn't so much arrive as appear. There had been nothing, and suddenly there were eight carriages.

Even as I opened the door to the train, I believed you would rush out and stop me. I lifted my suit-case slowly up the step. I paused. Looked back. I was still hoping for that goodbye, you see. I was still waiting.

In the carriage, I took my seat and pressed my face to the window. I kept my eye on the entrance to the platform. People were rushing through with their luggage. Is this it? Is this the Newcastle train? Plenty of time, madam. No need to rush. Even now it would not be too late for me to jump out. Jump out and run through the station, past the ticket office, through to the car park, where you might just have parked your car. Yes, maybe even

150

now you were rushing past the ticket office, looking for a woman alone, thinking no, it surely was not too late. Glancing at your watch, the platform clock—

Beyond the station, the outlines of the buildings and roofs and windows were smudged by the fog. Nothing looked substantial.

The guard blew his whistle. The train gave a lurch. The familiar landscape began to slide away.

In panic, I stood. No, no. Not yet. I pressed the side of my face flat to the window. My eyes strained with the effort to stay focused on the little platform, the people waving, the absence of you. I watched them grow smaller and smaller until the platform was a dent and the people were specks and still there was no you. They vanished to nothing in the fog and I was the same. I was so small I was nothing. I slunk back to my seat. At least I suppose I must have done. Because after a while I realized I wasn't standing any more.

I couldn't look at a book. I couldn't cry. I couldn't do anything but sit as the train bore me away. It still didn't seem real that I was on the move again. That I was leaving you behind. I stared at the window and the land was shifting hints of autumn: russets and golds and greens on the turn. They were like watercolour paints, bleeding on a wet page, and I didn't know if it was the fog that made them run or my tears.

Taunton.

Did someone say 'Taunton'? It was not too late! I could get off. There was a bus service, I knew that. Even as I fumbled for my coat, even as I wiped my eyes and dug my hands into the sleeves, I thought of what I had done and I remembered my conversation with Maureen. The air was punched out of me. Everything was over in Kingsbridge. I sat again, very neat, not daring to move a muscle in case my body carried me off the train before my head could stop it, waiting for the guard to blow his whistle.

As the train ploughed north, the fog began to lift. The sun poked its way through – a pale, white eye – and touched the clouds with silver. Bristol Temple Meads. Bristol Parkway. Cheltenham Spa. The miles you tread every day, Harold, I witnessed at such speed it was like slicing my way through England. Hedgerows, rosebay willowherb, buddleia, bridges, fields, canals, burnt-out cars, streams, gravel pits, concrete boulders, gardens. They flashed past and they meant nothing, they were broken pictures that held no connection. At Birmingham a wedding party crowded into the carriage: red cheeks, pillbox hats, loosened ties, open bottles. They sang until the next stop and then a woman began to cry so hard her make-up ran and her tiny hat slipped above her ear and her face was streaked like a tiger. I wondered if she loved the bridegroom and no one knew but me. Later I noticed the crooked church spire at Chesterfield, like an askew pointed hat, and I longed to say to you, *Look!* I knew we would have laughed, and laughing at the same thing would have been another way of being together, but you weren't there and so I could only notice that broken steeple and feel your loss. At Sheffield a gang of young women boarded and took up a discussion about door-to-door sales. The young women got off and were replaced by families with suitcases returning home, and shoppers laden with bags. And so it continued. People getting on, travelling a little, talking of the future, while I sat alone, belonging nowhere. Only in motion. Even the upholstery had more colour than I did.

Voices round me grew higher and flatter. Electricity pylons and telephone poles spanned the landscape, carrying cable to places I couldn't see. There were farm buildings, some red-brick, some dirty pinks and then there were housing estates and makeshift warehouses. In the distance, smoke gushed from the chimneys and blew at a sideways angle like giant grey sheets against the sky. Humanity looked so industrious, so busy being what it was, I could no longer find my place in it. After Doncaster the land flattened and spread. Recent rainwater sat on the fields.

By the time we passed York, the day had become a mellow gold and the trees glowed. At Darlington there was more red-brick and then once again there was movement in the earth. Houses were stacked and pitched into the hillsides, fields were yellow with wheat for harvesting, the river snaked alongside the railway line. The black profiles of Durham's cathedral and castle met my eye, their towers and spires cutting into the sky. Down below, the slate roofs of the city shone black. There was already a darkness creeping into the late afternoon. Newcastle would be the last stop.

All change! All change!

I was the last to get off. As I stepped down to the platform, I had to hold on to the door to keep steady. People were pushing past me, impatient to arrive at wherever they were heading. It had been all right, I realized; the journey had been bearable so long as I kept moving. But now that I was still again and the ground was solid beneath my feet, I felt so light-headed I could barely breathe. I tried to fix my eye on the iron girders of the station roof, but even as I found them they unhooked from their rivets and swam free.

My stomach lurched. My knees buckled.

I began to fall.

THE PUZZLE'S PROGRESS

This afternoon, Mr Henderson stopped by Sister Lucy on his way out of the dayroom. Looking over her shoulder at the jigsaw, he frowned a moment as if he were checking it for mistakes.

'I don't think it's quite working,' said Sister Lucy. 'I should probably give up.'

Mr Henderson glanced back at me and my notebook.

He said, 'I hope you don't write about us in there. We would make poor copy.'

I gave what I could of a smile.

With a shaking hand, Mr Henderson took one piece of Sister Lucy's jigsaw from the box and slotted it very carefully beside another.

'That's St Ives,' he said. 'My wife and I used to take a holiday cottage in St Ives.'

Mr Henderson stayed with Sister Lucy all afternoon. They have completed a section of Cornwall and also East Anglia.

And you, my friend? Where are you?

A DANCE LESSON FOR DAVID

August. A Thursday evening. I stood at the bus stop, waiting for the bus to Totnes. I'd changed secretly in the women's toilet at the brewery. Under my summer coat, I wore my ballroom dress. I had my dance shoes in my bag along with a library book. I'd unpinned my hair and sprayed it to give it some curl.

You were on your family holiday and it shocked me how much I missed you. Napier had arranged to replace you for the fortnight with a younger rep. Nibbs, that was his name. Do you remember? Nibbs drove fast and yawned a lot. Often both at the same time. When a thing is taken away, you see more clearly what it brought to your life, and every time I got into Nibbs's car I missed the safety, the companionship, of yours. I made it clear to Napier that Nibbs was not an appropriate replacement, just in case our boss had any funny ideas about sacking you on your return. It was my fourth day without you. I still had another full week to endure. I needed to dance. I needed to stand beside a tall man and lift my arms and pretend, for a few moments, that I was with you again.

At the bus stop I felt a tug at my sleeve. I got that smell. Patchouli, cigarettes, beer. I knew David before I saw him. Were you already home?

I hadn't mentioned to you that I'd met David because I didn't want to embarrass you. He'd almost got into a fight, and then he'd taken my money. Finding me all dressed up, my hair in soft curls, my mouth a coral pink, David twisted his face into a grimace. He cocked his head, as if he were trying to fix me in a new perspective. Apparently the change amused him.

'Where are you going, Queenie Hennessy?'

'Out.'

'Out? Where's out?'

I turned my gaze to the road. I'd never told you that I liked to dance, and I hadn't mentioned that I'd been a few times to the Royal. (I didn't want you to think that I was desperate.) I needed to think straight. Your son looked the sort of young man who might betray a secret, just to see what happened. 'Never you mind where I'm going,' I said.

David took up residence at my side. 'Never you mind? That sounds fun.' He lit a cigarette and wagged the match without looking. 'I'll come too.' He blew out the first plume of smoke.

Wherever I went, wherever I travelled, I found a dance hall. I went alone, even if I didn't always leave that way. When you're alone in a dance hall it's a different kind of loneliness. It's not like sitting in a bedsit and no one knowing a thing about you. In a dance hall you can be defined by your separateness. You can be both a part of something and not a part. Also, my parents loved it. The dancing. It was how I'd first met the Shit in Corby. He asked me to foxtrot and things followed from there.

I said to David, 'You don't want to come with me. It will be full of old people. Go home. Your parents might be worried.'

He laughed. 'It's only half past six. And anyway, they're still on holiday.'

Despite myself, I felt my shoulders slump. 'And you're not with them?'

'You've got to be joking.'

David began scouring the oncoming traffic. He stepped out into the road, and I had to yank him back. 'You can buy me that beer you owe me,' he said.

I refused to sit beside him on the bus. If he wanted to go to Totnes then of course I couldn't stop him, but he wasn't travelling with me and neither was I paying his fare.

'I don't know why you're so touchy, Queenie,' said David, resting his big boots on the seat near mine. I kept trying to read my library book, but I might as well have been holding it upside down. All I was aware of was this slim dark-haired young man staring at me with your eyes. There were no other passengers and the conductor was upstairs. I felt very much on my own with David.

'What are you reading?' Before I could reply, he

had got up and slipped the book out of my hands. 'Proust? Nice.'

He recited the opening sentences: '*For a long time I used to go to bed early. Sometimes, when I had put out my candle, my eyes would close so quickly that I had not even time to say "I'm going to sleep."*' As he spoke, he too closed his eyes so that the words came softly like a song already inside him. Then he returned the copy to my lap. 'I prefer the existentialists myself. Also Blake. Do you know him?'

'William Blake? Yes, I do.' I recited, '*O Rose thou art sick.*'

'Smart,' said David.

The conductor emerged at the foot of the stairs and made his way towards us with the ticket machine. I asked for a ticket to Totnes, please.

'Me too,' David repeated. 'Totnes. A child's ticket.' He didn't say 'please'.

The conductor scanned David up and down. 'You? A kid?' In turn, David folded his long legs and then his long arms and stared straight back up at the conductor. Smiling. I have rarely seen an eighteen-year-old look less childlike.

'I'm fifteen if I'm a day, sir.'

'I could throw you off,' said the conductor.

'Is that a promise?' said David.

For the second time, I ended up coming to his rescue. In order to avoid a scene, I said he was with me and quickly paid for his ticket. When David followed me to the Royal, I ended up paying for

159

him to go there too. Later I also ended up footing the bill for a can of Stella, a whisky chaser and a packet of cigarettes.

The dance was under way when David and I arrived at the Royal. You could hear the band, though the music was muffled as if it were coming from beneath our feet.

We stood on the opposite side of the road, watching the new arrivals climb the concrete steps. It was still light, but the illuminated sign flashed the word DANCING over the glass double doors and there were two pillars of fifties-style boxed window lights glowing on either side of the entrance. Dancers wore coats over their suits and ball dresses. All that marked them apart from other pedestrians were their silver court shoes and shiny polished lace-ups.

'What's the average age here?' said David. 'Sixty?'

'About that.'

'And they just dance, yeah?'

'Ballroom dancing.'

'They should watch it on the telly on Saturday nights.'

'That's not the same as doing it.'

'No?' I felt him gaze down at me with interest. I didn't look back at him.

'No,' I said.

David lit up a new cigarette. Shook the match and dropped it. 'So why do you come here? Couldn't you go dancing in Kingsbridge?'

'If I went in Kingsbridge, people might know me.'

'And you don't want them to know you?'

'No. I like to go by myself.'

Sometimes people judge their happiness by the price they have to pay for it. The more they've spent, the happier they think they will be. I judged mine in those days by how far I had to travel. David seemed to understand. He pressed his lips into a smile and gave several slow nods. It felt strangely pleasurable to gain his approval.

I said, 'Look. You're much younger than everyone else. Why don't you do something different? I'll meet you for the last bus home.' I was already beginning to feel responsible for him.

David threw out his arms and began to sing, 'I've got the music in me.' *Shh*, I went. People were turning to look. He pulled a serious face, but it still had a spark.

'I won't embarrass you in front of your friends,' he said.

'I told you already, I don't have friends here. I dance.'

David gave a shrug. 'Whatever you do, I'll sit quietly.'

I explained that people might think it odd: a woman just turned forty and a boy who was soon to start Cambridge.

'What does it matter what people think?' he said.

His voice was soft but the words were so sharp, it was like being with a you I didn't know. I had to drop my face to hide the blush.

David tossed his cigarette butt at the road. 'So

do you think they'll let me in? Or is there a ban on vitality?' He pulled his fingers through his thick hair, trying to smarten it. I opened my handbag and passed him a comb.

'The Royal is only a dance hall,' I said. 'It's not a club or anything. Mostly it's just a lot of old people and me.'

'Yeah, yeah, you told me all that. How do I look?'

He moved forward a little, and the flood of lights shone on his face. How did he look? Very fine. Ivory-skinned. Long chin, carved cheekbones. Eyes like blue lamps. 'You'll do,' I said.

'Come along, Q.' To my surprise, David took my hand in his and steered me across the road and up the flight of steps. I don't believe he even thought about it. I barely reached his shoulders, and I had to move fast to keep up. I paid for the two of us at the kiosk without looking at the woman behind the window and then we moved through the double doors, hand in hand again. When we reached the area of light and shadow between the foyer and the dance floor, I experienced a shiver of excitement that I had not felt before at the Royal.

I was not yet a regular. I'd gone there only six or seven times. There were a few men I knew better than others, but I was not looking for a relationship because I had you, Harold. My love was already taken. So if a man approached me on the dance floor, I partnered him but didn't offer my address. If he led me up the blue-carpeted stairs to the bar, I paid for my own drink. Generally I straightened my spine and shifted to one side if he reached to place a hand on my shoulder.

'You have the most beautiful mouth,' said a man once. 'Like a rosebud.' His hair was so slick it looked plastic. 'I may not be able to resist kissing you.'

'Well, why don't you try very hard?' I replied.

He gave me his phone number in case I changed my mind and fancied dinner.

I took up ballroom dancing after Oxford. I'd realized I had no wish to be an academic, and I'd headed for London to find work. One afternoon I passed a dance hall in Woolwich, and the sound of that rhythm – slow, slow, quick quick slow, slow – stopped me in my tracks. I had no dancing shoes then. No ballroom dress. But I paid at the kiosk and went inside, sitting in the dark where no one could see me. I stayed all afternoon. Life wasn't so easy then. I was working in a bar to make ends meet. But when I watched the couples dancing, sequinned dresses, white frilled shirts, a swing to the right, a sashay to the left, I saw beauty again. That is how it began, my ballroom dancing. It's a bit like asking a person how he started smoking. The habit suited my need.

And I don't know why Thursday was my evening at the Royal. It happened that it was a Thursday the first time I went, and so it became the way I did things. Like most people who are free-falling, I've always clung to routine.

The dance floor was already crowded when David and I entered the hall. I chose a round table towards the back, away from the yellowy light of the chandeliers. At the opposite end of the hall was a stage with red plush curtains. The band played a midpaced swing. I bought David his beer.

From the way David sat, hunched forward, his knee jigging up and down like a piston, his chin crammed in his hand, I assumed he loathed the Royal. I couldn't help seeing the place through his eyes. It was just a dingy low-ceilinged hall with fake crystal lights and a load of old people shuffling arm in arm. Even I in my blue dress looked dumpy and made of wax. What was I doing? I wouldn't come again.

I reached for my clutch bag. I said we should go.

Now? he said.

Yes, now, David.

But it wasn't finished, he said.

I was tired, I told him.

'I thought we were going to dance?'

'You and me?' I laughed again. Mistake.

'If you don't want to dance with me, I'll do it on my own.' He stood so abruptly that the gold legs of his imitation rococo chair jerked up and the chair flew backwards, landing upturned. He strode towards the dance floor, brushing the shoulders of other onlookers and seeming not even to notice. I followed him at a small distance. I didn't want a scene. Before I could stop him, he'd pushed

164

his way to the centre of the floor. There he was, in the middle of all those lilac ladies and balding men, like the heart of a ghastly pastel-coloured, slow-revolving wheel. I stopped at the very edge, just in the shadows.

I thought of the first time I saw you, swinging your body in the snow. I was so lost in the memory, so very different from the dance hall, that for a moment I forgot about David. I thought only of you.

Then someone said, 'What's that kid doing?'

David stood absolutely still. He seemed to have forgotten where he was. A pair of older ladies in matching taffeta dresses shuffled into him and bounced off again. Then something happened.

David stretched out his arms and pointed his right foot. He started an elaborate tango up and down the length of the dance floor. He glided, he swooped, he twirled. People paused to look and frowned before returning to their more conventional steps. Within moments, David seemed to grow tired of his dance, and he drew his elbows tight at his sides. He began to rumba. And when he'd had enough of that, he started a mock waltz with an invisible partner. He was practically galloping the circumference of the dance floor, dodging other couples. The sides of his greatcoat – he was still wearing it – flapped like giant wings.

Of course people became irritated. How could they not? They stopped, they broke apart, and one by one they peeled away so that there were only

David and a few brave couples left. I still didn't move.

'Who's the wally in the coat?' said the bandleader into his microphone. There was a flutter of laughter.

But David didn't seem to notice. He had abandoned his ballroom steps altogether. He was pogo-jumping. I was on the verge of leaving. That's the truth. If he was capable of bringing a dance to a halt, he was more than capable of getting the last bus. And then I looked again and there was something so unrestrained about him, so singled out and joyful, I couldn't quite move. It was not the way I'd seen you dance, it was not the way I danced, but it was something all the same. Your son was inside it.

A bouncer stopped beside me and flexed his shoulders as if he intended to hit David. Your son seemed to have that effect on people.

So I marched to the centre of the floor. David's eyes were closed. His hair and face shone with sweat. But I took my place beside him and I jumped.

'This is fucking great!' he laughed.

Yes, I said. So is the foxtrot, David. How about trying that instead?

On the bus home David was quiet. In the end he said, 'You won't tell Father that I came with you tonight?'

'Why?' I said. 'Why shouldn't I?'

'Mother would get upset. I promised, you know.

I promised to stay in while they were on holiday. It's best not to mention stuff. She gets headaches.'

I felt a small jolt, as if I had briefly lost my balance. I don't know if it was unease, or something else. Guilt? Why had I not tried harder to get rid of him? He was your son. He wasn't you.

'But I'll see you next Thursday, yeah?' said David. 'I'll come with you again.'

As it turned out, the following week was even worse at the brewery. There were several difficult meetings with landlords. There were complaints to Napier that I was interfering. Meanwhile Nibbs drove so fast I was constantly slamming my feet on invisible pedals. I missed you terribly. I needed to dance.

But I didn't go back to the Royal that Thursday.

THE MAKER OF CHAIRS

Slow, slow, quick quick slow, slow. Two backwards steps followed by two smaller chassé steps to the side. Feet together, like the pause for a new breath, then you start again.

My father taught me to dance. My mother sat astride a kitchen chair and sang the tune. She was too big for dancing, she told us; she'd only break something. I never understood that, because she must have danced when they first met. In my memory my mother is also shelling peas as I dance, though she can't have been doing that throughout my childhood. My father placed my small feet on his big boots so that I could get the hang of the steps. Everything has beauty, he said, on a dance floor. Don't laugh, Queenie. Ask your mother. This is a serious matter.

He was a carpenter. Did I say? He made wooden chairs. Garden seats. He spent his adult life creating places for people to sit, and then he died before he was able to enjoy a rest himself.

My father liked a game. Maybe because my mother was so practical and because language was a problem, he often played the games with me. The ones he liked most were those of his own invention. When I was very little, he'd stand in the sitting room in his overalls, apparently unable to see me. I was smaller than my parents, of course, but I was never thimble-size.

'Where is that girl?' he would say, lifting the plastic mats from the table, the antimacassars from the sofa.

'Here I am! Here! Here!'

He never seemed concerned, never angry, just extremely sure of finding me. I'd be the opposite. Wheeling my arms, pulling at his overalls, sticky and screaming and laughing so hard my insides felt screwed up.

'Where is that girl?'

The game was hilarious because it was safe. I was there and my father was there and even though he appeared to have lost the ability to see – or was it me? Had I acquired the ability to not be seen? – I knew that the game wouldn't end until my father's eyes swooped down to meet mine and he exclaimed, 'Well, *there* you are,' and lifted me on to his shoulders.

'You two,' my mother would say, as if my father and I were strangers from a place she'd never visited. She would go back to shelling peas or dropping things.

When I was older, my father invented a new game. It began with 'I have a serious question.' This became my mother's cue to stand up, although my father was a mild-tempered man and he never took offence. He'd describe a journey on an aeroplane. Suddenly you're told the plane is about to crash. What do you most regret not doing with your life? (Here I'd answer, 'I wish I could play the piano.' 'I wish I had bosoms like Wendy Tiller.' That sort of thing. My mother's answer – if she could be persuaded to play, and unless it was Christmas or my birthday she couldn't – my mother's answer was more pragmatic. She'd roll her eyes and begin to stack plates. *Clash, clash.* We winced. 'I wish a person would make a cup of tea.')

'Good news!' my father would say. 'Your plane has been saved!' He'd look jubilant, as if he were directly responsible. 'But what are you going to do, Queenie, about learning to play the piano?'

All this from a man who had never been on an aeroplane, let alone played a musical instrument. It moved him every time.

As I grew older, I grew less tolerant. I regret this, but I began to follow my mother's line.

Your plane is about to crash. What do you most regret, Queenie?

What do I most regret? Going on holiday.

What do I most regret? Not booking a train ticket.

My mother found these answers disproportionately hilarious. In fact they made her snort.

When I left for Oxford, my father abandoned his games as if they were foolish. I'd come home for holidays, but there was a coldness in the house. My father lined up broken items in his workshop. My mother dropped them and threw them away in the house. I'm not saying it was an unhappy marriage, only that it had become a well-worn one, like an old coat you stop looking after. There were holes during that time. There were thin patches. My mother would have thrown it away, and my father hoped he would one day get round to mending it. Neither thing happened. They just kept wearing it. My presence, when I deigned to visit, seemed to pin the marriage back together. My mother would fetch out what was left of the best glasses. She would try to entice me with pan-fried liver. ('You look pale,' she'd say. 'She looks pale.') My father would watch me with glittering eyes. I think my parents could never quite believe they had a daughter at Oxford. They treated me as a prize, a thing above them, and I, in turn, behaved like someone a little apart. I wrote letters, but they were not regular. I rarely telephoned. After Oxford, I found reasons – good ones, all of them – for not visiting.

I regret now that I did not see my parents more frequently. But I got caught up in my own life. My own mistakes. The last time I saw my father he was pruning an old apple tree. He said he wanted it to see another spring, but from the way he was going at it I'd have been surprised if it made another week. I fetched the ladder and did it for him, though I had no idea in those days about trees. The rest of the weekend we spent mostly in the sun. My father talked about his retirement. He said he would like to take my mother to Austria for a holiday, and she held his hand. It was a happy time, and I remember wondering why I had kept away so long. In my absence they had clearly resolved their differences – or at least they had grown to treasure the kind of love that they had. My father was sixty-two when he died. My mother died only months later. And the rented house? That, of course, went with them. They never made it to Austria.

But it is a noble profession, the making of chairs. I wish I'd shown my parents I could dance. It is what they gave me, after all.

WHAT SHALL WE SING
OF WHEN WE DIE?

'*Dear Queenie,*' read Sister Catherine. '*Visited the Roman Baths and had spa experience. Also met a very famous actor whom I did not recognize and had cream tea with a surgeon. It has been a difficult day. Best wishes, Harold Fry.*'

'It doesn't sound that difficult to me,' laughed Barbara.

Today we were promised a visit from the counselling unit at the hospital. Owing to staff illness and recent cuts, the counselling unit was a single woman in her early thirties who spent a long time trying to negotiate her Fiat into a parking space. From the dayroom we watched her reversing first over the Well-being Garden and then into the sign that says DO NOT PARK HERE. She was dressed head to toe in purple. Purple headscarf, purple dress, purple cardigan, purple shoes. The woman looks like a giant bruise, said Mr Henderson. She ran through the rain with her head bowed. The wind lashed the windows and flattened the plants.

The counselling unit arranged us in a circle and asked if we wanted to talk about dying. We could ask any question we liked, she said. There was only a soundscape of throat-clearing and raspy breath and stomach grumbles. We all got very busy, doing nothing. Steam rose from her wet hair and clothes.

'I'd rather talk about sex, if you don't mind,' said Finty. 'Anyone had it lately?'

The Pearly King laughed so much his arm fell off.

No, it did. He admitted that he hadn't strapped it on to the stump, he'd just propped it inside his jacket sleeve. The straps make him sore. Barbara made a happy humming noise to cover a fart. The counselling unit opened her file and examined her notes.

Perhaps we should talk about music instead, she suggested. Did anyone want to make a request for their funeral? A lot of people die, she explained, without sharing their favourite songs or poems. 'And it is *your* funeral,' she said. 'You must say what *you* would like. It can take enormous pressure off friends and family if they know your favourite songs.'

'None of us has got any friends or family,' said Mr Henderson.

'Speak for yourself,' said the Pearly King. 'Last time I asked, I had twenty grandchildren.'

'And I have my neighbour,' added Barbara. 'She is just too busy to visit.'

'Oh, God,' said Finty. 'My life has been a right

mess. Married at sixteen. Divorced at seventeen. And that was the best bit. No one's gonna shed a tear for me. When I go, you can stick a match under me and turn on the radio.'

This time when the Pearly King laughed, he held on to his shoulder.

Mr Henderson rolled his eyes and stared at his watch. A patient with a tartan dressing gown – he arrived yesterday – had already closed his eyes.

I felt sorry for the counselling unit. I wrote something in my notebook for Sister Catherine to read out.

'Queenie would like a song by Purcell called "O Solitude". And also "Mighty Like a Rose", sung by Paul Robeson.' My heart was pounding.

'That's very lovely,' said the counselling unit with such enthusiasm that the new patient was woken and cried out in alarm. 'Would you like to tell us why?'

I wrote in my notebook that I used to listen to the Purcell on my record player in Kingsbridge. I'd borrowed the record from the public library. I wrote that it reminded me of a friend's son, though I was careful not to name him.

The second song, I wrote, was one of my father's favourites, and so it had become one of mine. He used to sing it from his workshop, and my mother would stop her housework and listen. Sometimes you can love something not because you instinctively connect with it but because another person does, and keeping their things in your heart takes you back to them. It took a while to get all this down in my notebook. No one complained, not even Mr Henderson. It was the first time I had written about my funeral.

I didn't add that I still possess the Purcell record. I've never stolen anything in my life, apart from that. The record department of Kingsbridge library could buy a whole new classical section with my penalty fine.

If there is still a library in which to put the classical section, of course.

But I expressed none of this in the dayroom. 'You're a class act, Queenie,' said Finty. 'I'd be that gal on the *Titanic*. With her arms out and everything. What's that song?'

'Do you mean "My Heart Will Go On" by Céline Dion?' asked the counselling unit. 'That's a popular choice for funerals.'

'My third wife chose it for our wedding,' said the Pearly King.

'Also weddings,' added the counselling unit.

'My third wife's heart didn't go on for very long. She took off with the barman.'

'Céline Dion has a new scent out,' piped up Finty. 'So does Jade Goody.'

'Isn't Jade Goody dead?' asked Mr Henderson.

'She still has a new scent out,' said Finty.

'Shall we get back to our funeral music?' called the counselling unit.

Things livened up after that. Finty told us she'd like everyone to wear bright colours at her funeral and have a bop in the car park. She didn't want us to hang about being sad in the Chapel of Rest. ('No offence, Reverend Mother,' she added. 'But it gets nippy and a bit serious in there.') Everyone laughed, including Sister Philomena, and Finty told the counselling unit she could wear her purple, if she liked. Then the counselling unit went very quiet, very still, as if she'd been touched inside her clothes, and said, 'Do you mean you want me at your funeral, Finty?'

''Course I do. I need all the friends I can get. At the reception I want Cornish pasties and alcopops in all them colours. There can be lemonade for any AA geezers that turn up, and also the nuns.'

Others began to join in. The Pearly King said he hoped there would be no trouble at his funeral. His ex-wives had issues; his daughter's wedding had cost a thousand pounds in damages. Then the new patient said he'd like to be buried in a willow box, and Mr Henderson asked, Willow? What's wrong with the traditional wooden coffin, brass fittings, silk lining? The Pearly King growled, That's fine if you can afford to bury cash, and the new patient said, Some of us have got families to think about, and Mr Henderson shouted, Do you think I like living alone?

As the noise rose, the counselling unit went pale. 'One at a time! One at a time!'

'Oh, shut up,' said Finty. 'We're having a nice time. This is living.'

Well, that did it. Everyone was howling, even the

counselling unit. And Finty was right. We've spent so much time recently, all of us, being examined and cut open and having bits removed. We've spent so much time being the recipients of bad news. It doesn't lend itself to jokes, all that. But here we were, rejects, you might say, or at least at the end of the line, and it was a relief, a blessed relief, to look at the end of the line and stop being so fearful and argue like anyone else. Even if the topic in question was our funeral plans.

'What about you, Queenie?' said the counselling unit. 'What do you want?'

I thought a little and then I wrote, **Please scatter my ashes on my sea garden.**

Barbara began to sing 'My Heart Will Go On'. She sat with her hands in her lap, and also her eye. ('I swear that thing's moving,' said Mr Henderson.) Barbara's voice was thin and pure, like a veil of sea mist when it swirls in with the tide and hangs above the branches of my garden. Then the Pearly King began a deep bass accompaniment, followed by Mr Henderson. The new patient managed a few bars, and Finty nodded at me and said, 'Come on, Queenie. Hum along, gal.'

I'm not saying we were a choir. I'm not saying we got the same words or even a tune. But it felt a small gift, to open my mouth and no longer be one person.

Do you remember? '*Mice blind three*'? I remember. When I sang to you it was like showing you my feet without my shoes.

After the song, the counselling unit blew her nose and apologized. The Pearly King said, 'You cry if you want. God bless you for coming. There's a load of people that wouldn't even cross the threshold. Would you like to take my arm?' But I think by this point she feared he meant without the rest of him attached, so she said she was all right, really. It had just been a strange day, she said. Strange but wonderful.

'That's the bugger with funerals,' said Finty. 'All those nice people singing songs you like and saying stuff about how good you were and you're not even there. I'd rather hear it now.'

'For what it's worth,' murmured the Pearly King, 'I think you are one in a million.'

Finty went the colour of boiled beetroot. 'I bet you say that to all the girls.'

'I do, darlin', but it doesn't mean it's not true.' He gave a soft smile and kept his deep-brown eyes on Finty. He must have been very handsome once.

'Aw, fuck no,' she cackled. 'Get off, will you.' She couldn't speak for smiling after that.

Over tea, Mr Henderson kept looking at me. I thought it was because of the mess I had made down my linen serviette, but he was still doing it when the plates were gone and everyone had left the tables. He stood and limped towards me and stopped his Zimmer frame at my side.

'I like Purcell,' he said.

★　　★　　★

'So is it true?' asks Sister Mary Inconnue once she has finished typing. She is reading through her pages, checking for mistakes. She pulls out her correction pen and amends an error.

I give her a questioning look.

'Was today the first time you have thought about your funeral?'

I nod. Yes.

'And was that OK?'

It was just there. The thought. That's all. It wasn't anything else.

Sister Mary Inconnue smiles. 'Good,' she says. 'That's good.'

PATIENCE ON A MONUMENT

H arold? I said.

It was your first week back at the brewery. Do you remember? I need you to think back, because it is very important that you understand.

You'd caught the sun while you were away. I tend to look sore when I tan, but your skin was honey-coloured. There were little gold flecks in your hair, and your eyes were even bluer than I remembered. It had clearly suited you, the good weather. I would have liked to throw my arms around you, just with relief. The relief of you being at work again, and Nibbs being gone, and the smell of your car, and your hands on the steering wheel. You in the driving seat, me at your side.

'Something tickling you?' you said.

I had to pretend I was thinking of a joke. It wasn't a very good one. Two robbers and a pair of knickers. Oh, ha ha ha, you went. Laugh lines sprang all over your face. 'That's good,' you said. 'That's good.' And so even I began to see the funny side of it.

Later I asked how you'd enjoyed your holiday,

and you said, 'Yes, yes.' Then you said, 'Did you miss me?' Only you said that too in a joke way, as if no one would miss you.

Make me a willow cabin at your gate and call upon my soul within the house. 'I have a life, Harold,' I said with a smile.

'So what did you get up to?'

'Oh, the usual.' I couldn't look at you. I thought of David jumping at the Royal, the bouncer flexing his shoulders. I thought of the concentration on David's face as I taught him to foxtrot.

'You all right there?' you asked. And I told you I needed to stop. I needed to tell you something. Maybe it was the sun, you said. And I said maybe. I just needed air—

'There's something worrying me,' I said.

You pulled the car over at a Little Chef café. Try to remember this, Harold. You found me a table out of the sun and went to the counter to order me a cup of tea. I watched you tugging your wallet from your back pocket and saying something or other – I couldn't hear what it was – to make the till girl smile.

Harold? I began.

But you interrupted. Did I want sugar?

I tried again. Harold? I said.

What about more milk?

No. Thank you. No more milk. My tea is fine as it is. Harold—?

'My wife worries too,' you said. It came out of the blue.

'Oh?'

'She worries about our son.'

'Why?' I felt suffocated.

'Oh, you know. He's just growing up, I guess. She missed him while we were away. I don't think it was her favourite holiday.'

It was my cue to tell you I'd met David. That we'd been dancing. But now you had told me about Maureen worrying, I couldn't find the words. It seemed cruel. And in order to tell you about the dancing, there were so many other things to say too – that, like you, I knew how to dance. That sometimes I went to the Royal in order to pretend that a stranger was you. That I had rescued David once on the High Street. That he'd asked me not to tell you about the Royal. That, yes, Maureen could be right to worry. Your son was a handful.

All in all, this was a lot of things to say in a Little Chef.

Face to face with you across a laminated table, I felt the words dry up. I put my head in my hands.

'Headache?' you said.

'I'll be OK.'

I went to the bathroom to splash my face. Catching myself in the mirror, I was appalled to see how washed out and strained I looked.

We walked back to your car, and already your son had grown like a small dark crack between us.

I wish I had told you the truth that day.

THE BOY WHO WAS
ALLERGIC TO BLUE

In the night, I am woken by footsteps. Up and down the corridor.

'Come to bed, Barbara,' calls a nurse. 'Let me help you.'

I try to rest, but sleep comes on and off. I am woken by three visions of David. Three separate memories. I make a note in my mind. Dancing. Smile. Gloves. I think the words over and over so that I will not forget.

The morning rituals are complicated. The duty nurse spends a long time examining my neck and jaw. 'Do you feel any pain?' she says, but I only point to my notebook. I want to tell you those memories, those snapshots, Harold, that came to me in the night. A father cannot see his son with the eyes of a stranger, and so he misses things. It is one of life's small tragedies.

Come.

This first memory is taken three weeks after David first followed me to the Royal. I haven't been back since then and I think it should be safe now. But David's waiting for me at the bus stop.

'What happened to you?'

I make a limp excuse. He gets on the bus with me. He doesn't even ask. My heart sinks.

He wears his big coat. I wear my ball dress. I have my shoes. He's swapped his Dr Martens boots for a pair of plimsolls. At the Royal, he follows me on to the dance floor and asks if we can do the foxtrot. Slow, slow, quick quick slow, slow. It astonishes me how fast he is to learn. He has only to watch and he can do it.

The usual bandleader is on holiday, and his replacement has a mischievous look. He speeds up the pace. I can't tell whose idea it is to go with the music, mine or David's, but we speed up too. It isn't slow, slow, quick quick slow, slow any more. It's quick quick run run quick quick. David and I are moving around the floor as if we don't have feet. I wonder how it is there hasn't been a collision, and this is when it occurs to me that everyone else has stopped dancing and cleared the floor for us. David swings me away from him. He pulls me back. He spins me hard and grips me in his arms and then he throws me out and catches my hand. I think, Where did you learn all this? But he hasn't. He's making it up as we go. My lungs hurt. My skin is dripping. I've never danced like this in my life. When the music comes to a stop, I am trembling.

David laughs all the way home. 'They clapped, did you see?'

Yes, David. A few did.

'They noticed.'

They certainly did.

'There was this dance competition once. We were on holiday, me and the parents. I wanted to win. But I was a kid. I didn't know how to dance. I just, you know, I threw my body all around. I thought people were laughing because it was good, but then I saw they weren't. They were laughing because I was strange. I searched for the father and guess what? He was laughing too. And Mum. Well, she just had her head in her hands. Like she had no idea what to do. I look at them, Q. And it's like I don't belong.'

The story moves me. I feel for David. I know how bewildering it is as a teenager to watch your parents and find little trace of yourself. But I know too how much you love your son. I want to protect you. 'Maybe your father was laughing at something else. A joke or something.'

'He wasn't,' says David. 'He doesn't know how to deal with me.'

'It gets easier as you grow older,' I tell him.

He scoffs and turns away.

David gazes out of the window at the blackness. His blue thin face sails in the dark. He closes his eyes and falls asleep. I watch him with his forehead against the glass, and I see the two of you in one person. There is David who wants to be noticed, and there is you who wants to disappear. You and your son are polar opposites of the same man, and here am I in the middle. Maybe I can be a bridge. Maybe I can join you and David back together.

There is no need, I tell myself, to mention that your son and I have been dancing. After all, I'm doing repair work here. I will tell you another time.

The next memory is taken on the bus to Totnes. David has turned up a third time, and I am happy to see him. I tell him about you. How you are respected at the brewery. How well you deal with the landlords. To be honest, I'm enjoying myself. I like talking about you – I don't have anyone else to say it to.

'Yeah, yeah, right,' says David. He sticks his feet on the seat opposite.

'Your father likes to give people pleasure.'

'Pleasure?' he repeats. He has a way of making very average words sound inadequate or, at least, in bad taste.

'Yes. He likes to see them smile. He's a good man.'

His face twists.

'That's better,' I say. 'You're smiling too now.'

'I don't know what you mean,' he says.

David clearly keeps thinking about what I have said, though, because on the way home I catch him scowling into the dark window of the bus. He screws up his face, moving his mouth up and down, even nudging it into a half-moon shape with his fingertips. When he notices me watching he says, 'It never looks right.'

'What doesn't look right?'

'When I smile. It never looks like me.'

'And how do you think you look?'

He pulls an odd face. It's childish. He sticks out his tongue and pops his eyes at me, like some sort of ghoul, as if he wants to shock me, and then even as he does so, he laughs. I offer him a mint, and he says, 'Give over with the sweets and crap. Say something real, Q. Do you have a boyfriend?'

The question unbalances me, but I don't flinch. 'I'm in love with a man who doesn't love me.'

There is a small silence.

'That's too bad,' he says softly. He pats my hand. I say nothing. 'Who is he, Q?'

'It doesn't matter.'

'Does he know?'

'God, no.'

'Are you happy?'

'Yes.' I laugh. 'Very.'

David stares at me for a while, trying to see inside my head and find the man I will not name. This time it is me who does the looking away.

Memory number three. We are down by the quay. Your son has beer. We are in coats and I wear gloves because we have just got back from Totnes and it's late. We can't see the water, but we can hear the creak of the boats against their moorings. It is taken, this memory, in October just before

David leaves for Cambridge. Perhaps it's the smell of decay in the night air that makes me sad. We have danced together only four times, but having David in my life has been like looking after another part of you.

And so I am surprised when he asks for my textbooks. He reminds me that I'd told you once that I would lend them. I hadn't realized you had mentioned the idea to David. I wonder what else you have told him about me. Meanwhile, David says he could drop round at the weekend and collect the books before he goes to Cambridge. He asks me for my address. I write it on the back of my bus ticket.

He pockets the address without looking and then he says, 'I think I'm allergic to my gloves.'

I laugh. It's the sort of thing you would do: pop up with a remark that seems little to do with anything that came before. 'How can you be allergic to your gloves? They're not even wool.'

'It's the colour. Blue makes me sneeze. I had a blue scarf once. Mother gave it to me. That made me sneeze as well. It was like having a cold all the time. I had to pretend I'd lost it.'

'But that's ridiculous, David. A colour can't make you sneeze.'

'You mean a colour can't make *you* sneeze. People always assume that just because something is true for them, it must be true for everyone else. It's a very narrow way of looking at life.'

I rip off my red wool mittens and offer them.

David wriggles them over his fingers, although they are so small on him they barely cover his knuckles. He studies his hands with interest, tilting them over and back again, as if he hasn't seen them before. I have to rub my palms against the cold.

'Thanks,' he says. 'I'll keep those, Q.'

And he does. He keeps them.

'Do you think I'll be OK at Cambridge?' he says to the dark.

In the dayroom, Finty interrupts my writing to ask if I heard Barbara in the night. I am focused on finishing the three memories of David, so at first I don't look up.

'Oi, gal,' she says. 'Put down your notebook. I'm talking here.'

When I turn to Finty, she has an anxious look. She comes and takes the chair beside mine and sits with her arms pulled around her, tight, and her knees poked high. She straightens her pink cowboy hat, pulls the cord tight up to her neck. She says, 'It's what happens to some of them. Right at the end. They get restless. They can't let go, see. I've seen it before.' She rubs her nose with her knuckle, and I wonder if she's crying.

We watch Barbara sleeping in her chair. She is pale as a primrose. Sister Philomena holds her hand.

Finty says, 'But she looks better today. I reckon she'll be OK. She'll pull through. I really reckon that. Don't you?'

Outside, the nuns help patients walk in the

morning sun. The wet grass shines silver. The blossom is almost gone. A cobweb hangs from a corner of the window and it is so wet it looks made of felt. Finty shakes my arm. Her face is close to mine. Her eyes brim.

'Fucking shoot me,' she whispers, 'if I get restless.'

A LETTER TO DAVID

'Your son will be OK,' I told you in the car. 'I am sure he will be OK. University is fantastic.'

It was just before David left home. You hadn't told me you were anxious about him going. It was nothing so direct as that. As far as you were concerned, I didn't even know your son. What you'd told me was that your wife had been preparing food parcels for David. Fruitcakes wrapped in greaseproof paper. Bottled fruit. Jars of pickled onions. (His favourite, apparently.) Things that would keep a long time in his room. She was worried that, left to his own devices, David would forget to eat. She had also made a special trip to Plymouth to buy him dress shirts and a jacket because she wasn't sure that students at Cambridge could wear black T-shirts.

'But students can be very scruffy,' I said.

'Really?'

'Yes, Harold. They don't wear golf club ties.' I laughed, and you laughed too.

'I hope he writes,' you said.

'I am sure he will.'

'It will be hard for Maureen. If she doesn't hear from him. His silence, you know. Well, it would break her heart.'

The afternoon before he left for university, David turned up at my flat. He had come to collect my textbooks, he said. He hovered at my door, looking surprisingly nervous. He kept swiping his fringe, although normally he was happy for it to flop all over his face. I assured him he didn't need to come inside, but he said he would like to. The truth is, I was nervous too. We hadn't fixed a definite time, and I hadn't been sure he would turn up. Even though I'd only spent a few evenings with him, I understood he could be unpredictable.

'You'll have to excuse the mess,' I said. My flat wasn't untidy, it never was, but I didn't know what else to say. It is one thing to teach an eighteen-year-old boy to foxtrot in a public place. It is altogether stranger to allow him to enter the place you call your home. He followed me into the sitting room.

I assembled the books quickly into a pile. I had written my name inside each of them. I thought he would leave straight away, but he took one up and began flicking through the pages. And even as he did so, I watched him take in, out of the corner of his eye, the chair by my electric heater, the door to the small kitchen, the two sandwiches I had made for my lunch. It was as though he were observing all these details about my private life and somehow absorbing them for himself.

'I don't have beer to offer you, I'm afraid.' This was me politely saying goodbye.

But David smiled. 'Tea would be nice, Q.'

He dropped down into my chair and continued to read. He didn't take off his coat. When I placed the green teacup at his feet, he reached for it with his long fingers. He drank without seeming to notice, and then he ate my lunch without seeming to notice that either. Afterwards he lifted his legs over the arm of my chair and began to smoke, tipping the ash sometimes into my green cup, sometimes missing and sprinkling it instead on the carpet. 'You must have a lot to do at home,' I said. 'Your parents must be waiting for you.'

'It's fine,' he said. He asked for more tea.

In the end I sat in my kitchen. I wondered if David had told you he was coming to my flat to borrow the textbooks. Once again I resolved that however difficult it was, I must come clean with you. I had failed to set boundaries with David, and it was time to put things straight.

'Hiya.' I hadn't heard him approach, and so when I turned and found David silently watching me, I jumped. I had no idea how long he'd been there. He gave an edgy grin. He'd finished the book, he said.

'All of it?' It was Plato's *Republic*.

'Yeah, it was good.'

He took up the loaf of bread and started ripping bits out of it in an absent-minded way again, as if his body was accustomed to feeding itself without

194

his head noticing. Then he pulled an envelope out of his coat pocket. 'Is this for me, Q?' My stomach turned. *To David.* It was my handwriting.

I'd finished writing the letter just before David turned up. I'd slipped it inside one of the books, intending for him to find it once he got to Cambridge.

I tried to snatch at the letter, but he dangled it high above my head, where I couldn't quite reach. 'It's addressed to me.' He laughed at the way I flapped at his arms, trying to get the letter from him.

'It's nothing,' I said.

'Feels like there's some cash in there.'

'Give it back.'

'It's mine. I want to know what's inside it.'

He ripped open the envelope. He peered inside. I was so embarrassed I had to brush past him in order to leave the kitchen. I paced the little sitting room while he read.

The truth is, I had spent a good deal of time on my letter to David. My father had sent a similar one to me when I left for Oxford, and I still kept it, pressed between the pages of a poetry book. I reminded David what a brilliant young man he was, blessed with phenomenal intelligence and a very bright future. I urged him to think before he spoke, because forgetting to do that was how most people got into difficulty. Like you, I was worried for him, going into the bigger world. I didn't want him to get into trouble; I'd seen the effect he had sometimes. I added that it would be nice for the folks back home to hear from him once in a while. I was referring to you and Maureen. I was trying to help.

Despite my attempt at lightness, it was probably a maudlin message to read as an eighteen-year-old. Shortly after David left, I found the letter discarded, along with the envelope, on my kitchen table. The only thing he had kept was the twenty-pound note folded inside the letter. He had also, as it turned out, helped himself to a further twenty pounds from my purse, a bottle of Gordon's gin from the fridge, and my egg whisk. For reasons I could not understand, it was the theft of my egg whisk that irritated me most.

Every time I wanted to have an omelette and had to make do with a fork I was reminded of what he'd done. Why my egg whisk? What use had he for that? And yet I didn't go out and buy another. Maybe I wanted to mark the ending of that part of my life. I wanted to move on from it. Since David stole my egg whisk all those years ago, I have never been able to buy another. I have lived, as it were, whisk-free.

I should add here that there are things I have tried to lose. A pair of slippers I won on a tombola. A sunflower ornament that clapped its plastic leaves as daylight came and released a refreshing odour of such chemical toxicity that all my bean seedlings died. No matter how hard I tried to lose them, these things stayed. The plastic sunflower, for instance, will still be on my windowsill. The slippers are on my feet as I write.

David didn't refer to my letter. He just walked into the sitting room and picked up the books. He headed for the door. But I was nervous about what I had written so I blurted out, 'Does your father know? That you came here?'

He stopped in his tracks with his back towards me. For a few moments he didn't move, he only stood there. 'Don't worry,' he said. 'Our secret's safe.'

I stammered, 'But I don't want a secret, David.'

Still he remained hidden from me. I was afraid I had hurt him because his shoulders began to shake and he gave a tiny series of nods and sniffs. I reached to touch his coat. 'Are you all right?'

When he turned, he was rubbing his face with his fingers. Tears poured from his eyes and his mouth was swollen. The skin beneath his eyes was so red it was almost blue. 'Yeah, yeah,' he said. He gave a brave nod to show his emotion was over.

'Can I help?'

'I'm just nervous, I guess. About going away and stuff. I'll be fine.'

I gave him a brief polite hug. David seemed tense and uncomfortable. I'd noticed it wasn't easy to get close to him unless he was dancing. I said, 'I'm glad you're going to Cambridge. You need that place. You need somewhere big. It will contain you. I was really happy at Oxford. It was the first time I met people like me who loved books. Are your parents driving you tomorrow?'

David didn't answer that question. Instead he returned to an earlier one. 'Please don't tell the father about the dancing and shit. He'll call me a poof.'

I laughed. The idea seemed so ridiculous. And it was a relief to laugh. It broke the tension. 'He won't. He wouldn't.'

He shoved his face close to mine. His eyes appeared black. 'Just don't tell him, OK?'

I look back to that moment now and try again to understand. I think David wanted to come between us. That's the truth. He saw I respected you, and like a child he wanted to take that away from both of us. He wanted to place himself in the middle. I am sorry to say this, Harold. I don't believe he was deliberately deceptive. But I think he liked danger. It was his instinct. He liked to rub things against each other and set them alight.

I did not see this then.

With my books in his arms, David strode away. 'Good luck!' I called. I waited at the open door, wondering if he would turn to wave, but he didn't. 'Remember to write!' He paced into the dusk with that fast, stooped walk of his, as if he had already forgotten all about me. It was a relief to be alone, although when I returned to my sitting room I saw the empty cup, the cigarette ash and my screwed-up envelope, and I felt trapped again.

It made no sense that I should cry that night,

but a few hours later I could not stop. Even though I had justified my silence, I had no wish to keep deceiving you. It hurt so much.

I ended up telephoning the man with plastic hair from the Royal and accepting dinner. It wasn't because I was hungry. It was because I couldn't bear to be with my head any more. The evening was a disaster. It was the first time I had been out with a man since I'd arrived in Kingsbridge, and instead of being an escape it felt only like another betrayal.

On Monday morning, I asked you how it had been, driving David to Cambridge. I could barely look at you in your driving seat. I felt so ashamed of what I'd done.

'Yes.' You nodded several times as though you were searching in your mind for the right words and could not quite lay your hands on them.

'Was he excited? Did he like his room?'

'Well, you know, he had lots of people to meet. Things to do. Maureen and I waited, but he—You know.'

You didn't tell me any more. Your voice sank into the roll of the engine and you smiled as though the conversation were finished. I assumed that David had given you the slip. A little later you said, 'But no, no. I'm sure everything is fine. I'm sure he'll be OK.' You were answering a question I hadn't even asked.

'Mint?' I asked.

'Don't mind if I do.'

I reached into my handbag and my heart missed a beat. I had to open my bag wide and get a proper look. I pulled out my purse, keys, chequebook, compact mirror, Polo mints. The zipped-up pocket where I kept my love poetry was open.

'What is it?' you said, slowing the car. 'Are you all right?'

My poems were gone.

MIDNIGHT PHONE CALL

Hello? Hello? Do you hear me out there, HAROLD? Do you receive me?

According to the calendar, I have been writing and waiting for 22 days. But yesterday was too much. Another dying. Not Finty or Barb or Mr H or Pearly K, though DOG KNOWS it could be any of us next.

I could not sleep.

Duty nurse brought a fresh pain patch. Morphine shots not ENOUGH.

Dr Shah examined face and neck. He smelt of pressed shirts and vanilla.

DR SHAH (soft hands): *There is further swelling in x gland and an infection in the closed eye.*

A VOICE (cold hands): *Also, problems with—*

I didn't want to hear. HORSE WAS EATING MY PINK SLIPPERS. (HURRAH FOR HORSE.)

NURSE: *Clinishield?*

DR SHAH: *Thank you.*

BLUE BIRDS flying out of the picture frame and <u>TWEET</u> tweeting.

Lady with Grapefruit singing ROCK OF AGES.

Today too tired to lift pencil. Even if I lift, what

is POINT? I will only get to part I don't want to get to. Part where I see DAVID for last time and he—

NO. I can't write it. SOTP. SPOT. STOP.

FURTHER SPIRITUAL ADVICE

'You've got yourself all in a pickle again,' said Sister Mary Inconnue. She sat at the end of my bed with her typewriter, but I had only the page from last night to show her. Sometimes all I need is a sign, Harold. A postcard. A reminder that I am right to wait for you. That is all I need.

Am I going mad?

Sister Mary Inconnue read my message. She smiled. She took my hand.

'I think it is a very hard thing. What you are doing. It's all very well for a man to step out of his front door and tell his friend to wait while he walks the length of England. It's an entirely different kettle of fish when you are the woman at the other end. We take it for granted that the mind is robust and in one piece, but the imagination can take us to all sorts of places. You have to take care.'

I don't want to think about the past any more. It hurts.

'Well, indeed,' she said. 'But I wish you would listen to other people sometimes and take a rest.'

At this point Sister Mary Inconnue slipped her fingers out of mine. 'Would you excuse me?' she said. She lifted her hands and eased off her wimple. It was like watching her remove her head. I almost couldn't look. To my astonishment, her hair was dark, as black and shiny as the wings of a crow. She had braided and coiled it into two pincushion shapes either side of her face. She scratched vigorously behind one ear. 'What are you staring at?' She did her wink. 'Do you think nuns don't get itchy?' She replaced the cornette. She rested her red-raw hands in her lap. I wondered if I had dreamed this last bit.

'Look at the window, Queenie. What do you see?'

I wrote, **Clouds.** I put, **Grey ones.** I added, **This is England. What do you expect?**

She laughed. 'But you also see sky.'

Well, yes.

'And sun.'

I do.

'The sky and the sun are always there. It's the clouds that come and go. Stop holding on to yourself, and look at the world around you.'

I made a grunt. I was still feeling put out.

'You're upset. You're frightened. So what can you do? You can't run any more. Those days are over. You can't make the problem beautiful by dancing. You can't even prune it. Those days are over too. So the only thing left for you to do now is to stop trying to fix the problem.'

She reached out and stroked my tired fingers.

'Don't try to see ahead to the nice bits. Don't try to see ahead to the end. Stay with the present, even if it is not so good. And consider how far you've already come.'

I scrambled to pick up my pencil. I wrote fast: **What do you mean, look how far I've come?**

Reading my message, she smiled. 'When I first met you, you were so afraid. You sat apart from the others in the dayroom. You didn't want to visit the garden. You wouldn't take your nutritional drinks. You certainly didn't think you could wait for Harold Fry or eat a peach. It takes a long time to learn that there are other ways of doing things. It doesn't just happen overnight.'

Sister Mary Inconnue pursed her mouth and blew out her cheeks. 'Would you listen to us now. Getting all philosophical.' She laughed.

We didn't do any writing after that. We just watched the clouds come and go. Sometimes they appeared as big as smoky islands, and sometimes they were only silk ribbons. I forgot about everything else. Then the sun came out and it began to rain. The rain cloud glowed, fat and rosy, and the drops fell slantingly in silver sparklets.

'Look,' she said. 'Look at that. And it doesn't cost you a penny.'

It was so beautiful we had to sit still and not speak, only watch.

Do you think it is a sign?

Sister Mary Inconnue swung her large feet and sucked her pen. I like the way she never replies until she has thoroughly absorbed the question. 'Do you mean a religious sign? A sign to you to keep waiting?'

I gave a shrug. I suppose that is what I mean, though I am loath to call it religious. There was another pause.

'Maybe,' she said at last. 'Maybe it's a sign. But it is also not a sign. It is a cloud and some rain. Do you fancy a banana?'

Yes, I said. I did.

GLAD TIDINGS FROM STROUD

'Good news! Good news!'

Sister Catherine ran into the dayroom so fast I feared she'd shoot straight through and fly out the open doors into the Well-being Garden.

'Harold Fry is heading for Stroud! He is in Nailsworth! He rang from a telephone box! I told him you're waiting! I told him to keep walking!' These sentences did not come out in that order. Words tended to get swallowed and chucked about, but remember, she had run from the reception area. She was excited. 'He will be here in another three weeks!'

'Did you hear that, Babs?' shouted Finty.

'Oh, he's racing along now,' said the Pearly King.

Finty attempted a high five with Sister Catherine, only Sister Catherine misinterpreted it and the high five turned into a painful handshake. Finty flashed a dentured grin. 'Didn't I tell you, Queenie Hennessy? Didn't I tell you not to give up?'

For almost a week I have not written to you. There has been death here, yes. The undertaker's van.

There has been grieving. But there have been other things too. There has been music therapy. Birdsong. The nuns wheeled us outside to watch the first swifts. The small leaves on the tree outside my window have stretched into green hands. In the garden, there are buds on the roses, the first columbines. We have had French manicures, massage, lavender oil and hairdressing. Nutritional drinks and card games. Sister Lucy has read more of *Watership Down* to Barbara and, inspired by Barbara's new glasses case, a volunteer knitted a selection of similar multi-coloured bags for the syringe drivers. This may seem a small thing, a needless one, but it makes you feel human again to keep something so practical in a pretty knitted case. One patient even felt well enough to return home. We waited by the window to wave as her son helped her to his car.

'What a nice young man,' said Finty.

'He has a comb-over,' said Mr Henderson. 'He's probably got a bus pass.'

'Well, you can fucking talk,' said Finty.

I have slept, and the songs have played in my head, and for once I have not sought the words. The thing on my face has been dressed. I have taken medication and pain relief, and every morning I have practised my finger stretches. There have been trips to the garden with the other patients, and I have dozed beside Sister Lucy and her jigsaw. On Wednesday she gave me a tissue-wrapped gift and when I looked surprised she only straightened her sleeves and said:

'Doesn't someone have a birthday?'

It was a new notebook.

I have watched the light at the window as it turns from white to blue to black, with sometimes a pinkening in between. I have lain in the dark and listened to Barbara's songs or the wind in the tree. And we wait, all of us, Harold; the singing, the wind, the night. We wait for you.

It is four and a half weeks since you began your walk. I can get to the end of my letter.

'Good,' says Sister Mary Inconnue. 'This is all good.'

A HAPPY DAY

It's late October. One of those beautiful mellow days when the light is blue-gold and the trees haven't yet lost all their leaves. The greens are tinged with red and brown, and that gives them more definition. Michaelmas daisies make banks of purple along the road. Summer is gone, and yet here is the sun again, and it is a kinder, older version of its August self.

You and I travel with our car windows down. The air is soft and warm and it strokes our faces. It occurs to me to ask how things are going in Cambridge, but I don't want to spoil this late afternoon so I choose to stay silent.

And then the car gives a splutter and you glance at the dashboard and the car gives another shudder. When you pull over and turn off the ignition, the engine emits a heavy hiss, as if it is sighing.

'Bloody hell,' you say. You open the driver's door. Step out of the car. I remember the silence in the country lane. There is nothing but birdsong, the buzzing of insects. The stillness of a warm road. Ahead of us there are only trees. Behind us too.

You rub your hands and lift the bonnet. I close my eyes a moment. Feel the autumn sun on my skin.

'What is it, Harold?'

No reply.

When I step out of the car, you are puzzling over the engine. The light falls gold on your shoulders. You scratch your head. When you stop, a smear of black grease sits above your left eye.

'Is there a problem?' I ask.

It seems there is. We need a garage. But this is South Devon. The nearest one will be in Kingsbridge. Also, you add, there is another more significant problem. You have no idea where we are.

'Do you mean we're lost?'

'I was sort of hoping you wouldn't notice.'

I look at the empty lane ahead and behind us. A watery haze shimmers above the tarmac in both directions. 'What should we do?'

'I need to go and fetch help.'

'But you don't know where we are.'

You grimace. You sigh. 'Ah, no.'

'Do you have a map?'

Ah, yes. A map. You dive into the car and produce the Ordnance Survey. After slamming down the bonnet, you unfold the map very carefully and spread it out. We both bend over it, trying to work out where we are. For a moment I forget about you, I forget about the autumn light, I am completely absorbed in deciphering the map. And so it surprises me to realize that we are almost touching, arm against arm, face against face, the smell of you so close it is on my skin too, and yet I am able to look at the map and see the roads, the contours, the marked farm buildings and churches.

'Here we are,' I say. I point my finger triumphantly at the spot. 'This is where we are.'

To my surprise you begin to laugh. I straighten up, and frankly if anyone should be laughing it is me, because you are the one with oil grease above your left eye. What is so funny? I ask.

Whatever is so funny has robbed you of the ability to communicate. You hold your stomach and laugh, a high *hee hee* noise.

So I pull your sleeve, and you whimper as if I am going to tickle you, and you giggle, 'Get off, will you?' And when again I ask what has been so funny, you pull an altogether straighter face and you say, 'You.'

'Me?'

'Yes. You always have to get there first.'

You are right, of course. I am fastidious. I have an eye for detail. I'm a hard worker. And yes, I am competitive. But here you are laughing at me and I don't mind. In fact I see the funny side. I smile too. 'It's because I'm an only child.'

'*I'm* an only child.'

'Well, I don't know. You're nicer than me.'

'That is true, of course,' you say.

For this I pluck up the map and swat you. You

cower with your arms in a gesture of mock defence, and I can't think why but even that is funny.

I am happy. That's why. I am very happy.

'At least I know where we are,' I say. And it dawns on me that I know this in more than one way. I know where you and I are on the map. But I also see where we are as friends. My love has moved to a deeper place. I can almost touch your arm and swat you with an Ordnance Survey. I can be beside you and still see other things. You don't obliterate the landscape for me any more. In fact, the sight of you makes everything else a little better, a little finer. The faint scent of wood in the air, I get that. The white ribbon of a vapour trail in the sky as it turns to gold and dissipates, I get that too. The way the berries on a honeysuckle shine so red in this light they almost shout. Loving you makes the world more beautiful. I see things now that I didn't see before.

It is my idea that we walk back to Kingsbridge. You suggest that I should sit in the car and wait, and when I ask who you think I am, the Queen? you say no, but you can't resist a joke about my name.

So we set off. Your feet make a steady *pad-pad* noise on the tarmac. Mine are more of a *clip-clip*. Clouds of summer flies swarm around our heads. You walk with a firm stride, and sometimes I have to skip a little to keep up.

'Oo, oo,' you say once or twice.

'I don't know why you wear those things.'

'What exactly is wrong with yachting shoes?'

'Nothing. If you're on a yacht.'

You stop to laugh. 'I can't even swim.' You wipe your eyes.

After that we don't talk so much. We pass beneath the tunnels of green leaves hanging over the lanes. Your face is flushed, and so, I am sure, is mine. We walk without meeting another soul. And sometimes you ask if I am OK, and sometimes I am so deep in thought, about you and me, and what will come of this, that I forget to answer, or at least it takes me a while.

You say, 'I never walk.'

'Me neither,' I say.

We go on for another half-hour. I can feel a warm wetness beneath my armpits. My knees are beginning to feel weak. As we reach Kingsbridge the road opens and a pavement emerges, as do streetlamps, houses, gardens and cars. Only as I see these things does it occur to me that we are walking side by side, my pace in rhythm with yours, almost touching we are so close.

Almost touching and once again you didn't see it.

For the rest of the year, I heard no news from David. No letter. No postcard. I asked you every now and then in the car. 'Any word from your son?'

I tried to gauge from your answers whether or not David had mentioned anything about my poetry. Clearly he hadn't. I asked too how he was getting along. I asked how he liked the town, how he was finding the course. I even said once, 'Does he like punting?'

You stared at the road ahead and repeated the word. 'I am not sure,' you said. 'Maureen has not mentioned any punting.' I don't know why, but we laughed. It suddenly seemed such a daft word.

Even if David had my poems, as I feared, he could have no idea they were for you. There was no mention of your name. No physical description of you. The poems were more about the nature of love than a history of our time together. If David had taken them, they were certainly in a bin by now. Perhaps he'd done me a favour. Perhaps it was time to let go of my poems.

Now that David had left, I was back to dancing with strangers at the Royal. Men with weak hair. Nervous feet. Clammy hands. The woman at the kiosk said to me one night, 'It's a shame your son stopped coming. I enjoyed his dancing.' She wore her dyed black hair in a giant beehive, which appeared to make it difficult for her to move her head. But that is by the by.

'Oh, he's at Cambridge now,' I said. 'He's reading classics.'

'Classics?' She lifted one eyebrow. A doorman came to stand beside her. 'Brainy, then?'

'Very.' This will seem ludicrous to you, but I felt a swell of pride.

'Maybe he'll come again in the holidays.'

'Maybe.'

'Oh, a boy always loves his mammy.' From the way she looked at me, very fixed, and then shared a smile with the doorman, it was clear the conversation was far more complicated than I had first presumed. She saw straight through me. Though what she saw I can only imagine. I avoided the kiosk woman after that.

It was Maureen I felt for. You told me another time that she was still waiting for David to call or write. 'She misses him. She misses him very much. She always talked to him, you see. They were always at it. Whenever I walked into a room. They were just – you know – talking. It was as if I wasn't there.' Somehow this picture had never come to me before. Of David and Maureen talking. Somehow in my mind I'd pictured him silent at home and prowling, like an animal that has outgrown its cage.

'I'm sure he'll be in touch with her very soon,' I said.

Early December, there you were. Back with the empties in the yard. Rain was falling hard, like black pins it came, but you lifted the cans from your coat and placed them carefully in the bins.

I spotted him once or twice that Christmas, though he didn't see me. He was striding down

Fore Street in his greatcoat and also a black fedora with a feather. The hat made me laugh. People stopped to watch him as he passed, and I would say that he knew and liked it. You have outgrown Kingsbridge, I thought. And even though this would be hard on Maureen, I was happy for David. He needed to be free.

So we had known each other over a year, you and I. I had loved you for nearly a year. I had also begun to date a man called Bill. I no longer left the Royal alone at night. I danced with Bill every Thursday, and met him again on Saturday. We'd see a film. Get a bite to eat. But never in Kingsbridge. Bill had been recently widowed and lived with his two grown-up daughters. 'Why can't I come to your place?' he'd say, and I made excuses about the other residents or the smallness of my flat. Once he said, You're ashamed of me, aren't you? And I reassured him quickly that I wasn't. But even as I said it, I felt my shoulders sink, because he was right. I *was* ashamed, and now that it was out in the open there was no pretending. I didn't love him the way I loved you. And I couldn't. I didn't want to. I had room for only one man.

I caught you once staring hard at my bare ring finger.

'Nobody wants me,' I smiled.

You gave a guffaw, but you didn't say, 'I do.'

I wondered if it was a romance that was occupying David because he barely showed his face in

217

the Easter holidays. I remember feeling that must have been another hardship for Maureen. I thought too of my own parents and wished I had been kinder to them when I was David's age. But it was a relief that he was no longer coming between you and me.

My forty-first birthday arrived. I brought you cream puffs from the bakery. We stopped and ate them by the roadside. 'Any special reason?' you asked. 'Not at all,' I told you. This time you didn't say, 'You'll get me fat,' which was an irony because you were a little plumper at the waist and jowls. Those trousers of yours didn't droop any more.

To my surprise, Bill was waiting for me at the gates of the brewery with flowers and a HAPPY BIRTHDAY balloon. He just wanted to see where I worked, he said. I practically frogmarched him down the street in my efforts to hide him – though it is difficult to hide a man with a foil HAPPY BIRTHDAY balloon. He insisted on taking me for dinner in Kingsbridge, and I'm ashamed to say it was a dreadful evening. Over tiramisu, Bill began to get impatient. 'You're bored, aren't you? You have someone else, don't you?'

'Of course not,' I heard myself say.

'You're always looking out of the window.' He produced a small box from his pocket. He tried to put it into my hand. 'Marry me.'

Outside the sky was still light. I remember because I watched the window for a long time, trying to work out what to do. If I married Bill, I could look after him. Look after his daughters. I could make a home. I kept my eye fixed on the pavement outside in order to concentrate, but then it occurred to me I wasn't concentrating, I was only looking for you.

Bill shifted in his chair. 'I knew there was someone else,' he said.

'I'm sorry,' I told him. 'I'm really sorry.'

He sat very still for a moment. Then he finished his tiramisu. He scraped the glass bowl clean. It's strange how, even when the big things in life happen, we attempt to make them small. 'It's OK, though, if you love someone else,' he said. 'I can make do with that.'

'No. You can't.' I reached for my coat. 'It's over.' It was over with the Royal too. As it happens, it was also the end of courtship for me. I didn't date a man again. And don't feel sorry for me, Harold. It was my choice.

I kept up with Bill's daughters, though. When the younger woman married, I sent her a set of wine glasses. The girls wrote to me, once in a while. Even when I lived in Embleton Bay, I sent them cards. I only stopped when my illness came. I stopped all my friendships when my illness came.

That summer you took your annual holiday but you didn't go anywhere. David had told you he'd be InterRailing, and apparently Maureen had decided she'd prefer to stay at home. And when I asked afterwards what you had done – it had been so lonely for me at the brewery without you – you said, 'I mowed the grass.'

We laughed a lot about that.

FURTHER NEWS

We have a new postcard. 'Historic Warwick'. You can't imagine the stir it caused in the dayroom when Sister Catherine arrived with her postbag.

'What does Harold Fry say?' yelled Finty. 'What does he say?' She had a letter asking if she had suffered any accidents recently; she might be entitled to thousands of pounds in compensation. Then she cried out, 'No, no, don't read the postcard yet! Let's get the brown milkshakes first. Let's make it all special, like Christmas on the TV adverts. Come on, Babs. Stick your eye back in.'

'Oh, I love Christmas,' said Barbara.

Sister Lucy put down the copy of *Watership Down* and fetched the trolley of nutritional drinks. She also brought whipped cream, straws and foil cocktail umbrellas. The Pearly King began to open a parcel. Mr Henderson folded away his newspaper.

'Would you allow me to help, sister?' said the Pearly King, all gracious. He placed his parcel on the trolley and took it to the back of the room, steering with his good arm. When Sister Catherine offered help, he replied that he was managing fine, and here he gave a delicious wink that caused Finty to erupt with laughter. 'What a one,' she kept *ha-ha*ing. 'Yeah, you're a right one, you are. I bet you've fixed some drinks in your time.'

The Pearly King grinned and said that yes, he had. 'Once I found myself tied to a tree,' he said.

'I've heard worse,' said Mr Henderson.

'But the tree was in Rotterdam. And the last I knew, I'd been in a pub in the East End of London.'

The Pearly King handed out the drinks, one by one. And even though he was shaking a little with the effort of walking, most of the liquid stayed inside the glasses and only a little hit our laps and the carpet. He kept apologizing and offering to fetch a cloth and Sister Catherine only laughed and said, 'God bless you.'

'Can you manage, Miss Hennessy?' said Mr Henderson, offering me a tissue.

I nodded to show I could.

We were about to lift our glasses when Barbara spoke. 'You know what? I'm going to cry. It's not because I'm sad. It's because you're such nice people. It's sort of all welling up in my feet.'

'I know what you mean,' said Finty. 'I've met a load of shits in my life. You're all right, you lot. Even you, Henny.' She lifted her glass towards Mr Henderson. He looked as if he might smile, then he seemed to realize what he was doing and reorganized his face into a frown.

'To Harold Fry,' growled the Pearly King.

'God bless him,' said Sister Catherine.

Barbara lifted her glass. 'In the end, it makes no difference who you are. It's friends that count.'

We repeated your name and we drank. At first the liquid was thick and warm and sat in my mouth like paste. I had to work very hard to knock it back towards my throat. I never knew until recently that the simple act of swallowing could be so complicated. Then something inside the liquid, something that didn't taste of cardboard but was sweet and fiery instead, prickled my gums and sent my tastebuds zipping. It was like being a whole person again.

I remembered Christmas in my sea garden. I used to thread string around broken shells and hang them on the bare branches of the trees. Every year people came to look. Once I spent the day with a bag lady sipping sloe gin from plastic beakers and watching as the wind came in from the sea and sent the shell ornaments flashing and dancing above our heads. Her face was lit up. 'I have never seen a place like this,' she whispered. I thought she might go and say another thing and spoil it, but she didn't. I fetched blankets and she sat beside me and we kept watching.

'Wowzers.' Finty slammed down her glass on the dayroom table. She swiped her mouth with the back of her hand. 'I haven't had a drink like that since the day I got arrested.'

Mr Henderson choked into his straw.

'Arrested for what?' That was one of the volunteers.

'Let's just say it involved a man from Gloucester and a fire extinguisher.'

'Good grief,' groaned Mr Henderson, catching my eye.

'I don't understand,' said Sister Lucy, looking both delighted and baffled. 'Are you saying that the nutritional drinks are nice today?'

'They are somewhat better than usual,' said the Pearly King, only he had to whisper because two new patients had dropped their glasses and were fast asleep. Consequently the Pearly King sounded less like a tractor and more like an electric toothbrush.

We all turned our attention to your postcard. It rested where Sister Catherine had left it, propped against a bottle of hygienic mouthwash and some gauze swabs. 'I almost can't bear to hear Harold Fry's news,' said Finty, screwing up her eyes and hiding briefly behind her hands. 'Go on, read it out, someone. Quick. Where is the fella now? Is he still walking?'

Sister Lucy picked up the postcard. She scanned it briefly. There was more tense silence.

'Listen to all the places he has passed!' she said at last.

'Hurry, hurry,' said Finty, 'or I'll piss myself, I'm so nervous.'

'He has passed Cheltenham,' said Sister Lucy.

'Cheltenham?' said the Pearly King. 'I was there

once. I went to the races. I went in my Rolls-Royce and came back on a bus.' He laughed for a long time. 'Yes, that was a good day.'

Sister Lucy continued to read. 'He has passed Broadway.'

'Broadway?' said Barbara. 'I was there once. I went with my neighbour. We had a cream tea. She bought coasters for her conservatory.'

Sister Lucy said, 'He has passed Stratford-on-Avon.'

It was Mr Henderson's turn. 'Stratford? I was there once. I saw *King Lear* with Mary. We fed the swans in the interval.'

'And, wait for it,' said Sister Lucy. 'Now he has reached Baginton.'

Sister Lucy paused for an interruption, but there wasn't one.

She read on. 'He says he met a nice young man called Mick who took his photograph and bought him a lemonade. Also, salt and vinegar crisps. He says—' Here she broke off again and peered. 'He has decided to travel without money. From now on he is going to sleep outside and rely on the kindness of strangers.'

There was no time to reply. A noise came. A long and high-pitched sob, like the whistle on a kettle. We all turned as Sister Philomena gathered Barbara in her arms. Gripped as she was to the healthy body of the nun, Barbara was no more than a bundle of little sticks inside a dressing gown. 'What is upsetting you?' said Sister Philomena. 'Is

225

it Harold Fry? But he will be OK. He is making his journey.'

When the words came they were very small.

'I wish I could have another Christmas,' said Barbara. She shook with tears in the nun's embrace.

We heard, but none of us spoke. We only watched her in the way a child watches another child in trouble, or a motorist slows to observe a motor accident, trying to understand without wanting to exchange places.

'You will, Babs,' called Finty. 'You will.'

Behind Barbara, the mid-May sunshine poured through the dayroom windows like a twisting river of light.

THE POET

David began his second year at Cambridge. And then, out of the blue, there came a letter. It arrived at my flat on a Saturday. As letters go, it was brief. David still liked the course, he said, though the reading was sometimes boring. He said he'd had a crazy time in Europe!!!!! (I've never trusted an exclamation mark, especially a whole batch of them.) He added that he missed the Royal and gave me a return address. There was a PS. Could I spare any cash? There was a further PS. He was sorry.

I wrote back that same afternoon. I thought he had a nerve asking for money again but I forgave him, partly because I was touched that he still remembered me and partly because of the remark about the Royal. I sent him a card and a five-pound note, both in the same envelope.

The letters continued. Not regular but every few weeks, and every time he requested money. Sometimes I ignored them. The more insistent messages I replied to. I will admit, Harold, that I felt used. I knew that if I told you, you'd be mortified. In early December, David wrote to ask if he could visit for a weekend. He needed to see me, he said; things were getting heavy!!!!!!! He referred to me as his friend.

Without wanting to cause alarm, I asked if you or Maureen had heard anything, and you may or may not remember, but you gave me your usual reply about David being too busy to get in touch. In his letter, David had given me the coach times and asked if I'd pay for his fare, so I sent the money by return post. (Twenty pounds this time.) I cleaned my flat. I prepared him a bed on the sofa. Once he was in Kingsbridge, it was my intention to suggest that he should pay you and Maureen a visit. On Friday afternoon I left work early. I was careful you didn't see me go.

David didn't show up. I waited three hours at the bus station with my book, and he never came. He didn't write again either. *Stupid woman*, I thought. Of course he was never going to visit. He just wanted the money. He'd probably drunk his grant already. But at least I was spared lying to you.

Mid-December, you were back with the empties. I wondered if David would have the nerve to turn up at my flat, but he didn't. The first time I spotted him in Kingsbridge, I couldn't believe it was him.

The annual St Nicholas Fayre was in full swing down on the quay. I'd asked if you would be going, but you'd said the Christmas market wasn't Maureen's thing. It was a cold night without rain, and the lights from the stalls threw moving patterns on the black of the estuary. There was the spicy smell of mulled wine, I remember, as well as frying onions for hot dogs and burgers. For the younger children there were a few fairground attractions, and people were shouting and whooping over the noise of the engines. At the far end a large crowd had assembled to watch a local band on a temporary stage. I watched them awhile with my plastic cup of mulled wine warming my fingers – the band members were young, maybe David's age – and people in the audience were beginning to dance. I spotted Napier's secretary, Sheila, with her husband and a few of the reps. The warm wine kicked my throat and lifted me. In a way it was like being at the Royal again – a part of things, and not. It was a shame, I remember thinking, it was a shame you'd stopped at home. I moved on because another crowd was forming and I could hear laughter. I wanted to laugh too.

At the back of the crowd it was difficult for me to see, and the band music was so loud it was hard to hear. I edged forward a little, and that was when I had to stop and check that I was really seeing what I thought I was seeing.

David stood in a central pool of bright light with a hand-held microphone. He had lost some weight. His features seemed more pointed, or rather separated; it occurred to me that he had probably used make-up. He'd grown his hair and tied it into a ponytail. He wore a dark baggy suit with wide lapels, teamed up with his old boots and also my mittens. When I picture the scene now, the gloves provide the only real colour. It's like seeing a surprise burst of red in a black-and-white photograph. It's almost shocking.

I was still annoyed with David for wasting my time and taking my money, but mostly I was angry with myself, for being used. I kept hidden in the crowd. I didn't want him to see me. David was reciting poetry. Despite the cold, he had an ease, a charm, a radiance, that made people draw close and want to listen. I could see that. He smoked while he performed, and he had a bottle at his feet; once in a while he stooped to lift it and take a swig. When someone shouted out, 'Pass the bottle round, David!' he laughed and said, 'Buy your own, sir.' It seemed that quite a few people knew him.

David held some pages, but most of the time he didn't refer to them. He performed in a deep and energetic voice that carried. From what I could gather, the poems were satirical pieces. Each time he finished one, the audience applauded rapturously. They clearly liked him and he knew that. At his feet he'd placed his fedora; a woman came forward and threw a few coins into it. I heard him say he would be publishing his work soon, in a pamphlet, and a few people nodded to show they would be interested.

'So this next one,' David said, 'is called "The Love Song of a Maid Who's Never Had It".' People in the crowd laughed, and while they did he paused for another swig. 'It's sort of got a chorus and you can all, you know, join in.' He slipped a silk scarf out of his jacket pocket and tied it in a knot under his chin. I assumed it was one of Maureen's. Someone shouted, 'Bender!' David grinned and said, 'Yeah, right.' I moved closer.

In a high-pitched voice like a pantomime dame's David began to recite words I knew. Words I had kept in my handbag until I lost them. My poems.

('I look at the world and I see only you', that sort of thing. I can hardly bear to repeat them.)

Here came the chorus – this was nothing to do with me, but it had the crowd roaring – 'My love is pure. I am your maid. Oh me, oh my, will I ever get laid?'

The crowd repeated the line in a raucous shout, and my face burned with the shame of it.

David went on to recite four more poems. I stayed only because what I heard hurt and confused me so much, I was unable to move. All of his poems were parodies of mine. All of them had the crowd jeering. By the end of the fifth poem, I couldn't take any more. I turned and pushed my way free.

After that I began to run. Past the stalls, the children's rides. I had my hand to my face so that no one would see. Once I was at the other side of the quay, I had to stop and sit on a bench. I pictured, across the oily black water, the crowd laughing, and I felt stripped of clothes. I couldn't help myself, I cried out loud in pain. Supposing you'd seen the poems? Worse. Supposing your wife had read them? I wanted to be in my flat, but I hadn't the energy even to get up. The crowd began to wolf-whistle and applaud. I guessed David's recital was over. I sat for a long time, watching people make their way home along the quay. Parents were carrying their children. A young woman shrieked when several men, I recognized them as reps, held her over the water as if to chuck her in. A horse dressed as a reindeer was walked to its box. The pubs began to fill. The Fayre was coming to an end.

'Hey, you.' A slim but firm long hand tugged at my shoulder and pulled me round. I got his smell, and I had to steady myself. 'Were you there?'

I got up to go, but David came after me and stood in my path. I saw the black kohl lines around his eyes, the crimson stain on his lips. He'd coated his face in white pancake.

'Do your parents know about this?' I asked coldly.

He laughed and said, Probably not. He didn't mention the letters or the money I'd sent or the visit he'd failed to make. He glanced over his shoulder at the Fayre. 'It was good. People liked me. Got any cash?'

My jaw dropped, and he laughed again. 'I'm joking.' He showed me the hat. It was full of coins; there were notes in there too. 'Do you want a drink? I'll buy you one.'

'No.'

'Suit yourself.' David shrugged and moved away. I watched him stroll up the street towards the off-licence.

That Monday, when I got in your car, I could barely look at you. You asked if I was feeling peaky. Peaky? I snapped. What sort of a word was that? You smiled a little awkwardly and concentrated on the road ahead.

'Doing anything nice for Christmas?' you said. I didn't reply.

We must have driven awhile in silence because I remember you pulling over in a lay-by. 'Wait there,' you said, and you got out to fetch a bag from the boot.

Once you were established back in the driving seat you told me to watch.

You lifted a red bauble out of the bag and tied it carefully over the rear-view mirror. It spun a little as you moved your hands. You pulled down the sun visor on my side and hung it with another bauble, a gold one this time. Then you hung a blue bauble from the indicator, and the last, a silver one, you tied to the jacket hook behind my seat.

'Merry Christmas, Queenie,' you said.

'I don't understand, David.'

It's Boxing Day, and he has decided to pay me a surprise visit. He is standing at the communal door to the flats, offering a half-full bottle of Southern Comfort and a twig of holly. He's shivering with the wet and the cold – he is wearing only a jacket and jeans and it's pouring out there – but there is no way that young man is coming inside my home.

'Peace offering?' he says. He holds out the bottle.

His shirt is so wet the collar sticks like paper to his skin. I am about to shut the door and maybe he senses that, I don't know, because he lifts his face so that I can see. He's been crying.

Beyond him rain hits the street, the pavement, the estuary. Everything is drenched and grey, everything is water. Watching David, his eyes red, his mouth bunched with sorrow, his body too tall for those wet clothes, I relent. 'Come in, then.'

He leaves a wet trail all through the hall, into my flat and across my carpet, straight to the chair, where he sits with his ankles twisted one around the other, his arms pulled tight around his body. His knee is jigging up and down, up and down.

'David, I'm angry with you,' I say.

'Yeah, I know.' He shakes his wet hair, and rain droplets jump out over his clothes. 'And I am sorry, Q. I'm really sorry.'

I make David tea. I fetch towels and a blanket. I keep busy so that I won't have to sit and talk to him. It's different, though, now that he's inside my flat. He seems smaller. He drains the green teacup and refills it with Southern Comfort.

I sit on a cushion on the floor. OK, I tell him: Explain.

He talks all afternoon. He tells me about the

course, the college, his life in Cambridge. He admits he's been struggling with the work. He had a girlfriend, but she left him. Now he finds it's easier to fit in with people if he's drunk; it makes him more fun, less inhibited. But the work is suffering, of course. The parents don't know this, but his tutors are on to him.

Reciting his poetry is a way of showing people who he is, he says, without upsetting them or putting them off. He does it at the student union and on the street. It's like busking for intellectuals. He enjoys the attention it brings, as well as the cash.

'I want people to notice me,' he says. 'The parents haven't a clue.'

'But you stole my poems, David. You made a mockery of them.'

He looks at me gently, with your eyes, and he says, simply, 'I just want someone to see me, Q. See who I really am.'

It is what we all want, in the end; to be seen.

'Those poems you were reciting weren't yours. So how can anyone see you in them? If they're seeing anyone, it's me.'

He laughs briefly, then speaks again, and it is with the same disarming honesty: 'That's it, though. You *are* seeing me, Q. You're seeing I'm a fake.'

The anger I have felt, the sense of betrayal, melts away. I want to help this boy. I really do. 'You have to show your heart, David.' I place my hand on my own and I feel it throb against my palm.

After a moment he asks, 'Is that what you were doing in your poetry? Showing your heart?'

This time I don't answer.

David reaches for his bottle, untwists the cap and refills the green teacup with Southern Comfort. He wipes the bottle's neck very carefully with his sleeve. I end up heating a Christmas pudding (for one) and sharing it with him by the fire. We eat it from plates on our laps. He tells me a little about his summer in Europe, and it's only as the light goes that he asks, 'Who were they for? Your poems?'

'No one you know. I wrote them years ago.'

When I look up, he is watching me very carefully and smiling. He believes me. He does not realize I love his father. David pours me a cup of Southern Comfort, and I drink so fast the alcohol spikes my throat. 'I just wanted to know for sure,' he says.

Over the next few weeks, David rings a few times. He reverses the charges, of course, and tells me how he's getting along at Cambridge. Since our conversation, he assures me, he's been feeling better. More grounded. He's started writing his own poetry, he says, and he's really pleased with what he's done. It's not funny any more; do I think that's OK? I assure him that if he's really expressing who he is, that is good. It's really good. 'Can I send them to you, Q?' he asks.

Apparently there is someone he's met at Cambridge who knows someone else, and the someone else has read the poems and thinks David has a big future. He's got the ability to take a subject and push it to the edge. The first poems arrive the following day: a thick wad of them in a brown envelope.

I am going to be honest with you, Harold. David's poems aren't up to much. They're full of clichés. Mostly unfinished. There is also a darkness to them that makes them appear self-indulgent. I write notes in the margins. Where his imagery is loose, I suggest new ideas. I am trying to do what I can to help. More poems arrive. They are more bleak. They talk about death, the black hole. Often he writes at the bottom, 'For your eyes only!!!!' He urges me not to tell the parents or he'll never trust me again. 'Your secret's safe,' I reassure him. Nevertheless I am concerned, and I don't know how to tell you.

Easter comes and goes. I remember hiding small foil-wrapped chocolate eggs in your car for a surprise Easter egg hunt, but you go and sit on one and so we spend a long time in a café trying to clean off the mess.

David is home very briefly. When he goes back for the summer term, the poems start arriving again. I continue to help with new phrasing, and sometimes, I admit, I use the opportunity to make other suggestions too. Perhaps he should join a poetry group? Is he eating properly? If anyone had asked me what I was doing with David, I would have explained: I was helping you by helping your son. I, too, had been an Oxbridge student. I, too, had parents who were in awe of my intelligence. I hoped David would find his feet; then I would casually drop into our conversation the whole truth about our dancing and my sending him cash, the poems and all the other things I had failed to admit to you. Told in hindsight, none of those things would seem so big because they would be safely in the past and David would be happy.

And so we continued to drive together, you and I. I watched you, brought you chocolate bars, little things to show I was there. And sometimes you took the long road home and pointed to the birds. We stopped once, do you remember, because you said you thought I looked pale. (I was. David had sent me a poem that morning about 'the blue beasts' in his mind.) We sat beneath a fig tree, but I was too miserable to speak. After a while, you began to collect figs and line them carefully along the empty lay-by. Had I ever played fig ball? you asked. When I said that no I hadn't, you expressed surprise and told me it was very simple; it was like bowling, really, only with figs. 'You can play it anywhere. I don't know why it's not an Olympic sport. And if you can't find figs, you can do it with conkers.'

I was unexpectedly good at fig ball. 'You see,' you said. 'You're smiling again now.'

'One day I will come here with my son.'

We are sitting outside the pub at Slapton Sands. I have sherry. You have a pint of lime-and-lemonade.

A packet of crisps sits on the table between us. It must be summer – the end of David's second year at Cambridge. The sea is very still, like polished glass, and the sky shines silver too, broken intermittently by the flash of light from Start Point. 'We'll have a beer,' you say. 'Me and David.'

A beer? I think. Are you sure? As if reading my thoughts, you smile. 'Or maybe a lemonade. We'll talk. You know.' Your blue eyes mist. 'Man to man.'

'That would be good,' I say.

'When you're young it's not so easy to talk with your father. But one day. One day he'll be old like me. It will be easier to talk when we are old.'

I picture David wearing my mittens. I laugh. 'I can't imagine David in driving gloves, Harold.' You look so sad, so unsure, I am trying to make you feel better but even before I get to the end of the remark, I realize what I've said. I wish I could cram the words back into my mouth. Instead I down what is left of my sherry.

'I don't understand,' you say into the silence. 'Have you met David?' Very quietly the sea brushes the shore.

It would be so quick to say yes. Yes, Harold; yes, I have. You give it to me on a plate. We danced a few times, I could say. He telephones. Asks for money. It is not too late to come clean. It's never too late – and then I think of my poems, the poems he lampooned, and I have no idea how to explain that I love you.

'No,' I say. I say it again, just in case the first

one isn't big enough. 'No. I haven't. I've never met him.'

You give a smile with a noise. Not big enough for a laugh, but warmer than a mere smile. 'I think you'd like him. He'd definitely like you.'

It is all becoming too much.

FIRE ALARM

We were woken very late by the fire alarm. One of the new patients was smoking and had caused a minor explosion in his oxygen tank. The night staff and the nuns wheeled us outside into the Well-being Garden and covered us with blankets, though it had been a warm day and the air was surprisingly mellow. I could smell the earthy sweetness of the hawthorn, the cow parsley, and the very first of the elderflowers.

'The idiot could have killed us,' complained one of the night staff. She looked cross and tired, on the verge of tears.

'Yes, but he didn't,' said Sister Philomena, smiling. 'It's all right, Barbara. No need to get up. Sit still now. Hold my hand.'

The patients' faces glimmered against the lights from the dayroom. Nothing had substance in the dark. The people, the trees, the pagoda, the stones of the rockery, the silvery stars of astrantia and the cascades of laburnum. They were pale in the stillness.

'It's like Watership Down out there,' said Sister Lucy. 'All peaceful.'

'Are you joking?' barked Mr Henderson.

Sister Lucy said she wasn't. It didn't matter she had skipped the beginning; she thought it was a lovely story. She had just finished reading it to Barbara.

'All those rabbits? Being run over and traumatized?'

Sister Lucy covered her mouth with her hands. 'Rabbits?' she repeated. 'Where are the rabbits?'

'They're all rabbits,' said Mr Henderson. 'That's the whole point.'

'What? All of them?' Sister Lucy looked devastated. 'But they *talk*. I had no idea they were rabbits. Oh no.' She sat in silence, taking this in, and sometimes her face buckled and she said, 'Oh no,' again. 'That's terribly upsetting,' she murmured.

Why did you have to go and tell her they were fucking rabbits? hissed Finty. And Mr Henderson said he was sorry. He thought everyone knew they were rabbits; there was even a picture of them on the front cover. He wished he'd never mentioned the rabbits. 'Oh no,' sobbed Sister Lucy. Sister Philomena wrapped the young nun in another blanket. I reached for her hand.

A little later someone said, 'Look, Reverend Mother. Look at the moon.' When Sister Philomena saw it, she asked for the staff to wheel us to a place in the garden where we might enjoy it too.

The moon hung low in the sky, the colour of a clementine. All around, the stars flickered and pulsed. Mr Henderson pointed to the Plough and my father's favourite constellation, the little batch of stars called the Seven Sisters. 'Do you see, Sister Lucy?' he asked. 'Miss Hennessy, do you see too?'

I thought of my sea garden. The figures glowing in the moonlight. The chimes calling in the wind. I pictured Embleton Bay in snow and wind and sun; all the different ways I have come to know it. I saw the winter waves rising in slate-black walls, and I saw the sea on a July morning, like a stretch of pink silk. In reality Embleton is not so far away, only thirty miles, but the space between me and my garden feels a light-year.

After all the emotion of the oxygen tank and the rabbits, I didn't want to cry and make a fool of myself. So I said in my head, Think of something else. Think of Harold Fry. He is under the orange moon and these stars too.

WAYS OF LOVING

'People can love in different ways,' I told David. 'You can love full on, with a lot of noise, or you can do it quietly, over the washing-up. You can even love a person without them knowing.' I was careful to turn away.

It was the Christmas of David's third year at Cambridge, and things had got worse. Whenever he came to visit, he sat in my chair by the electric heater, hunched in his black coat, smoking a joint. If I questioned this, he said it helped him to relax. Apparently he was still writing poetry, but he didn't want to show me any more. When I asked about the coursework, his eyes glazed over. It was the same when I enquired about friends. He often complained about the cold, and I was forever fetching him blankets. I asked if he would see a doctor, but David only scoffed. It was the same when I suggested that he should talk to you.

I had promised myself that I would be a bridge between you and your son, and I was out of my depth.

Perhaps in order to distract me, he took me back to the debate we'd been having about love. It was the idea of loving over the washing-up that appalled him. How could I be so trivial?

'Sometimes you have to think in an ordinary way, David,' I said. 'Sometimes life is not what you expect.'

'I'd rather die than be ordinary, Q,' he said. He lifted his head and fixed my eye, and there was so much trouble in his face, I had no reply.

I understood what David meant, though, when he said he wanted to be more than ordinary. When I was a student, I'd felt the same. I fell in love, over and over, with tall, dark, handsome boys. The tall boys took me on dates in order to ask about my tall friends. I wrote love letters, beautiful things, on their behalf. Afterwards the dark, handsome boys and my golden, beautiful friends called me a good sport or a rock but that is the same as saying You are kind, or You have nice feet. It is being supportive. I didn't want support. I had hosiery for that. I wanted love.

When I began to find it, it was only in ways that came to nothing. I chose people who would let me down. And when I didn't choose people who would let me down, I was chosen by people whom I would let down instead. There is no need to say very much about those affairs. It is a hard thing, this learning to love. I knew, for example, that the Shit in Corby was the wrong choice, and so I had to do a lot to distract myself from the truth. When you know a thing is wrong, you have to work very hard to stick with it. And really, I should stop calling him the Shit now. He is probably a good husband. A good father and grandfather. A good neighbour. All that.

Then I met you and I fell in love with you, and for once I would have stayed. I had saved enough money in my bank account to buy a small house. But there followed the terrible tragedy of David, and so it was the same old story. I delivered my message to your wife and the next day I fled. I went north, off to the east, until I met the sea (damn this small island), and once again I had to stop.

What I discovered when I stopped was that it was not so easy to do the same with love. It doesn't finish just because you have run away. It doesn't even stop when you decide to start again. You can look at the North Sea and you see only the English Channel. You can look at the Northumberland sand dunes and you recall those in South Devon. There is no getting away from the fact that your love is still alive and you must do something with it.

I had no plan when I began my garden. No experience of plants. It evolved slowly. Just as love does. Every day I walked alongside the dunes and the shore and observed what grew among the rocks and paths. I took notes. In Craster, I watched how other people dug and planted. I studied the gardens that front the fishing harbour and are made with stones. When I returned to my beach house, I dug and planted my own garden. Every year it grew bigger. Every season it established itself a little more.

Over time, my garden was tested in many ways. There were my own mistakes, plenty of those. There was the weather. There were gulls. People too. Sometimes they offered help and inadvertently their help got in the way. Sometimes they challenged me. How could I give my life to a garden? How could I stay in one place and not travel? I answered them all. It gave me pleasure to talk about my garden. One summer, I was interrupted by three young women on a hen party. I remember because one of them was wearing a BRIDE-TO-BE sash and carrying a giant inflatable plastic penis. It's not the sort of detail you forget.

The women were wearing shorts, bikini tops and silver tiaras. Their skin was plump, their shoulders and chests bitten with sun and salt.

Nice garden, said one.

Nice suntrap, said the second.

But too near the cliff edge, said the bride-to-be.

So I put down my gardening fork and told the usual story. My garden was a tribute to a man I could not have. It was my atonement for a terrible mistake. I showed the young women the rock pools with the anemones and the tiny blue fishes I had carved from mussel shells. I showed them the driftwood figures and the seaweed banners and the garlands of coloured pebbles, each with a hole bored by the sea. I showed them the spires of agapanthus and angelica (I always favoured the taller flowers), the white foxgloves, and my favourites, the blue poppies and irises. The seasons came and went; the plants died back and reappeared. Every part of my garden had a story, I said. It reminded me of what I'd learned or left behind.

But how could a garden make up for a man? asked the bride-to-be.

'Trisha's getting married next week,' said her friend.

'Tonight we're going clubbing in Newcastle,' said the other. 'To celebrate her last days of freedom.' The three young women laughed.

Couldn't she be free and married as well? I asked.

'Not if you know my fiancé,' said the bride-to-be.

I told the young women that in my garden I'd had to learn there were times to intervene, and there were also times when, however much I loved it, I should leave a plant alone. My garden was not about possession, and neither was it about my sublimation.

'I'd still rather have a wedding,' said the bride-to-be.

'You should see her frock and her veil,' said her friend. And the other one said, 'A woman has to have her special day. She has to be a princess.'

I considered my life. There had been no party, no speech about my kindness, no special dress, no confetti. Nobody had sat with me every evening or woken every morning at my side. And even though I told myself it was my choice, that instead

I had a garden and my solitude, I felt cold even in the sun and could not eat.

A year or so later, the bride-to-be returned. She'd lost weight. She told me the marriage had not worked. She asked if I knew any plants that would be nice in her window box, and I gave her cuttings. She'd met someone new, but she was taking it slow this time. 'No wedding,' she said. We watched the sea, and I think we both smiled.

I never heard about David's poems again apart from once at the end of his third year, when he said how hard it was to be told you were something and then dropped as if you had been nothing all along. He was back at home, supposedly preparing for his finals. It would have been better, he said, to live without expectation.

'But what did you expect?' I asked. 'What did people tell you that you were?'

'A poet. They said I could be famous.'

'Why do you need someone else to tell you what you are? Why can't you just write for the sake of writing? You don't have to be famous to do those things.'

He shook his head angrily. He lit another cigarette. 'You don't understand.'

'No,' I agreed. 'But I would like to.'

'It's no good being a fucking poet if no one knows that you are one. I'd rather be a nobody, like Father. I'd rather know I was nothing and get on with it.'

'You're not a nobody, David,' I said. 'And neither is your father.'

With an impatient grunt, he staggered up from my chair, as if I had become unbearable. He left my flat with his coat slung over his shoulder.

Sometimes I remember David wanting to be famous. I remember him saying that he was a failure because the world didn't sit up and notice. I think of the waste, and, I tell you, Harold: I want to hurl things. It is a hard thing, as I said, this learning to love. But it is an even harder thing, I think, to learn to be ordinary.

Several years after I had begun my garden in Embleton Bay and found the tall piece of driftwood that reminded me of you, I found another. I was down on the beach, hoping to spot oyster-catchers on Craggy Reef, when something hard poked my bare foot. I stopped. Cleared the sand away. It was a blackened piece of driftwood, about the length of my arm, but hunched over into a knotty V-shape, and worn into fragile points at both ends. It was so full of sadness it almost knocked my breath away. I could see only David. I carefully carried the driftwood up to my garden and spent the day deciding where to set it. In the end I chose a bed of stones and a creamy burnet rose. I planted cuckoopint around him and when the red berries came I thought of my wool mittens.

I kept working in my garden that night, long after the sun had gone down, long after the moon had come up and cast a silver trail over the waves. I needed to hear the sea and the wind and keep some movement in my hands. I couldn't bear to go inside.

CONCERNING THE FUTURE

L
ast night I dreamed I went to my sea garden again.

In my dream, Harold, I was attempting to secure the wood figures and stake the seed heads, but the wind kept whipping the sea into swirls of black and white, and tossing my hair and thrashing my garden. The plants and figures began to lift and blow in the air, like a shipwreck in the wind, and I tried to chase after them but I couldn't. I saw the storm carry them away.

When Sister Mary Inconnue arrived, I could not think about my letter. All I could write was:

What will happen to my sea garden?

Sister Mary Inconnue sat in front of the window with her red fingers lifted to her mouth, palm to palm. Behind her, the clusters of leaves in the tree were plump hands too, and little spikes of blossom poked from the branches. She was deep in contemplation. 'Is it the first time you have thought of this?' she said at last.

It wasn't. The question has been in me for a while, but it has lurked in the shadows and I have concentrated on other things because I have not wanted to look at it.

As I waited for her answer, I watched Sister Mary Inconnue carefully. I was so afraid of what she would say, and yet so needful of the truth, that I saw nothing but her. The tree disappeared. I even forgot I was me. I saw only Sister Mary Inconnue and her green eyes.

'Have you made a will?'

No. I felt my throat tighten.

'You need to make a will, Queenie. You know that, don't you?'

I began to cry and she held my hand but the emotion was not one of fear any more and neither was it one of sorrow. It was because she was right and I knew she was right. I had only been waiting for someone to say the words.

'It is not so terrible, dear heart, to make a will. It is like cleaning your house before you go on holiday. It is only making things neat. You need to ask Sister Philomena. You need to say you would like to make your will.'

A little later, Sister Lucy washed my hair. She massaged the conditioner into my scalp, and I felt a melting in my toes and hands. Once again I pictured my sea garden, but this time the chaos had gone and the only movement came from the skittering of orange-tipped butterflies. Down in the bay the sea was an unruffled blue, and the waves were lace frills. There was no wind. Sister Lucy wrapped my head in a warm towel. She blow-dried my hair and painted my nails.

'You look happier today,' said Sister Catherine. 'Would you like a spell in the garden?'

I squeezed her hand to say thank you.

'Good,' she smiled. 'Me too. I'll fetch my cardigan.'

THE SPANISH INQUISITION

'Maureen says I need a jacket,' you told me. Do you remember that day? What sort of jacket? I asked. 'The sort of jacket a father would wear for his son's graduation ceremony.'

We were driving back to the brewery. The Devon lanes were hemmed in with growth. It was like driving through thick green canopies. A few miles on, you cleared your throat. You said, 'Have you any idea, Queenie, what sort of jacket that would be?'

'Are you asking for my help, Harold?'

'I am, actually.' A David-ism, if ever I heard one.

We stopped in Kingsbridge at the men's outfitters. You introduced me to the salesman – he'd had a son at school with David. 'This is Miss Hennessy. Funny thing. We met in the—'

'Canteen,' I said.

'Stationery cupboard.' You laughed.

I remember the salesman asking for news of David and you saying he'd sat his finals. The salesman told us that his son had a job on the rubbish trucks. Nobody said this, of course, but side by side, of those two absent boys, it was clearly David who'd excelled. While he fetched a selection of jackets, the salesman continued to speak in reverential terms about David's intelligence. He'd been smarter than the teachers. He taught himself ancient Greek one weekend from a library book, as well as how to dismantle a bicycle. And I remember noticing your face. The way it shone.

'And do you remember that day,' laughed the salesman, 'when they found the bugger on the roof of the science block? What was he doing? Reciting poetry?'

The shine went from you. You glanced in my direction and dropped your eyes towards your feet, as though you were worried what I would think. As far as you were concerned, I still hadn't met David. 'Ah, yes,' you murmured. 'I'd forgotten that.'

'Pardon my French,' said the salesman to me.

'I like this blazer,' I said, pointing at one in a speckled Harris tweed. I hadn't really looked; I was only changing the subject because you seemed so troubled by the memory of David on the roof. The jacket had wide lapels, three buttons and a breast pocket, and it came in a Harold shade of brown. The salesman said it was the new autumn stock, ready for September, and matched it with a plum tie. Oh, no, you said quickly, replacing it with one in fawn. It occurred to me that the reason you were so desperate to avoid attention might have something to do with your childhood, though you had only mentioned your mother twice. Maybe it was because you were struggling to shake your arms free of your sleeves but I saw the lost boy in you and rushed to help.

'Thank you, Queenie. Do you mind looking after my jacket?'

'Not at all.' I had been looking after you for over three years, remember. I folded your jacket carefully over my arm.

Looking back, the Harris tweed was too formal and too thick. I never saw you wear it again. But as you slipped it over your shoulders, a new memory tickled the salesman and he began to laugh. 'Or what about that night the police found David playing hide-and-seek on Fore Street? He could have killed himself, the bugger.'

You looked sick now.

'Pardon my French,' added the salesman.

You gave what you could muster of a smile and said that the jacket would do very nicely, thank you, and so would the tie. We left quickly and you remained distracted all the way back to the brewery. You kept running your hand through your hair and giving shakes of your head, like little shocks.

'How exciting to go to your son's graduation,' I said. And what I meant was, It will be OK, Harold. You are big enough for this. David needs you.

When I asked David about his finals, whether there had been a question about Plato's *Republic*, he laughed down the telephone. 'What is this?' he said. 'The bloody Spanish Inquisition?' At least I think that is what he said. What he came out with was 'Wa is zis? Tha bla-y Spash Inkyzishun?'

There was no hiding he was drinking even more heavily. When he returned home and came to visit me, the smell of spirits was so strong I was afraid of striking a match lest we both shot up in flames. I would make him toast to soak up the alcohol and pour a glass of milk, but he'd stopped eating in front of me. I'd have to leave the plate and the milk at his feet and go off to do something else. He was like a scorched animal. Thin and frightened and unable to join in with the most basic things. I suggested once that we could go dancing if he wanted, and he glanced at me as if I had sworn at him. What about visiting the doctor? 'There's nothing wrong with me,' he snapped. 'I'm tired. That's all. I'm exhausted.'

Other times he would complain of the cold, and I'd fetch a blanket from the bedroom only to find him already asleep in the armchair when I returned. It shocked me how slight David looked in sleep, as if, given a sudden rush of air, he might lift up and blow out of the window. I wanted to pile a thick wool blanket on him just to add ballast. I had to find a way of talking to you.

The opportunity came after David's graduation ceremony. We were in the car and I asked you how it had been. Had the Harris tweed jacket gone down well? I asked. You said the usual, 'Yes. Yes,' and added it was a bit itchy. It had been difficult to bend your arms. Then a little later you admitted

David had been busy. You hadn't seen much of him because he had all his friends to see. What friends? I thought. He doesn't have any. I remembered my own graduation ceremony. My mother, sitting on the grass with her legs wide and eating sandwiches with her pinkie finger raised into a spike. My father, still holding my mother's straw hat and using it now as a plate to catch crumbs. They were out of their depth. They were a burden, and I couldn't wait to get away. But I would never have abandoned them.

I took a deep breath. 'Is David OK?'

You paled. I assume I paled too. The space between us pulsed.

'OK?' you repeated.

'Sometimes students find it hard. After they graduate. I know I felt a bit lost. I couldn't find work.' I was trying to be careful.

You gave a series of sighs. You also pulled a little too sharply at the steering wheel and we took a corner uncharacteristically fast. But I pressed on. 'Does he need—?' I didn't get to the word 'help' because finding this so difficult I paused. Before I could say any more, you rushed straight in with an answer.

'He's going on a walking holiday. The Lake District. Just as a stopgap. Until he gets a job.'

This was news to me. It gave me hope for David. It implied he was thinking about the future. You kept filling the silence as though to prevent me from saying anything further. 'At least he has a degree. At least David has done something with his life.'

You didn't sound like you. You sounded like someone who was angry with you.

I thought the holiday would do David good. But I was also relieved. With your son home, Harold, you looked tired. And you weren't getting rid of beer cans any more. They were empty bottles.

So when David told me about his idea, I too encouraged him. It was the first time he'd looked excited in months. The exercise, the air, the change of scene. I hoped all these things could help. And when he asked me for cash for a pair of walking boots because the money Maureen had given wasn't enough, I gave it. I remember saying with a wry edge that I looked forward to seeing the boots and him laughing and saying, 'Yeah, right.' At least he'd had the decency to ask for the money.

Do you believe he went to the Lake District? I even wonder sometimes if he sat his finals. He hid so much about himself. With David, I look back and so many things don't add up.

But now that David was apparently happy, you seemed happier too. We played fig ball again, I remember. I asked about the holiday and you said he had rung Maureen a few times. I made picnics for our drives. Another afternoon I suggested we should watch the birds at Bolberry Down and I didn't know it then but it would be our last time.

A few days later, David came home early from his holiday.

He seemed to have moved into yet another space. When he spoke, it was faltering as if he couldn't quite get the ideas in his head to match with words. He didn't maintain eye contact and his cheeks were dents in his face. His skin had no colour; even his eyes, his mouth, his hair were blurred to a shade of grey. There were days when he came to visit and he practically fell into the room. Or he'd phone in the middle of the night and tell me he was down by the quay. He always reversed the charges and it was hard to make sense of a lot of what he said, but if I hung up he rang back. He'd accuse me of not listening, of avoiding him. His ranting could go on for hours. Several times I went down to the quay and found him passed out on a bench. I helped him back to Fossebridge Road, but, not wanting to cause you embarrassment, I never went as far as your front door. I opened the garden gate for him and pointed to the path. I always made sure there were lights. Once I even saw you staring out from an upstairs window. You seemed so tired, Harold.

I tried to warn you one more time. It was lunch-time and I ran after you when I saw you leave the canteen in a hurry. I wanted you to know how worried I was. I wanted you to know David needed help. 'Harold?' I called. 'Could I have a word?'

You turned and said, 'Ah hello. Gosh.' You were crying. You tried to hide in a handkerchief.

Reps pushed past us and you had to keep averting your face so that they wouldn't see your eyes. If only I had not made that stupid mistake at the beginning in not telling you I had danced with David. Or perhaps I should just have said, I love you. It had all become so tangled and complicated. My words wouldn't come.

You said, 'I'm sorry, Queenie. I have something, you know, something in my eye. Could this wait for another time?'

'Harold, this is important. It won't wait—'

'I have to go,' you said. You repeated as you rushed away, 'Another time, Queenie. Another time.'

There was no other time. David disappeared for a week. And I look back now and I see that even then we must have believed, you and I, in our way, that it wasn't too late for us to save him. That a part of you, a piece of your flesh, was not beyond our help for the simple reason that he *was* a part of you.

But five days later, David was dead.

POOR BARBARA

'Why is there a Christmas tree in the dayroom?' asked Mr Henderson. 'It's the twentieth of May.'

'And what is that smell?' said Finty, inhaling deeply.

We sat in our wheelchairs at the doorway, breathing in the resinous scent of pine. The curtains of the dayroom were drawn and the room was dim, daylight a weak trickle at the window edges. The only real source of light was a small fir tree speckled with silver bulbs and red baubles. It flickered in the dark. There seemed to be a figure sitting alone in a chair, though it was hard to see.

'Take the patients inside,' said Sister Philomena to the other nuns. 'I will fetch Barbara.'

Sister Lucy was so happy, she kept laughing and bumping my wheelchair into furniture. I lifted my face towards hers and gave a confused look. For the first time she didn't look panicky. She said:

'Wait and see.'

The person I did not know remained apart. Now that my eyes were accustomed to the dark, I could see that she was small, about my height. She wore a light summer coat and sat with a handbag at her feet. From the way she waited, dressed for outside but sitting all clenched tight, she didn't look like a patient and neither did she look like a regular visitor. I thought of myself a few weeks ago, not wanting anyone to speak to me or look at me. I tried to smile at the stranger to show I was friendly, but she gave a little shiver. I forget these days. I forget what I am.

At last Sister Philomena carried Barbara into the room. Barbara was as small as a child. 'What is happening?' she murmured. The words were slow, but that could have been the drugs. 'I can tell something is happening. Have I died? I'm not dead, am I?' Her face was so shrunken that the skin of her neck hung in folds like a blouse.

'No, no,' said Sister Philomena with a smile. 'You are not dead, Barbara.'

We all laughed. Possibly it was with relief. 'Not dead, Babs,' cackled Finty. 'No way, José.'

Catching sight of Barbara, the stranger sat so straight she almost shot out of her chair. Then she froze. She perched on the edge of her seat with both hands high, gripping the collar of her coat close to her ears.

Sister Philomena settled Barbara in a reclining chair right next to the stranger. The stranger pressed her mouth very tight. Then Sister Philomena asked one of the volunteers to fetch a blanket and pillows. They tucked and slipped them around

Barbara, asking if she was comfortable, if she was warm enough, but Barbara didn't reply.

In a soft voice, Sister Philomena said, 'Barbara, you have a visitor.'

The stranger gave a sob. It was like a little burp. She grabbed a tissue from the box and whipped it to her mouth.

'Can you hear me, Barbara?' said Sister Philomena.

Barbara nodded. Her right hand made a little groping passage in the direction of the arm of her reclining seat and then through the air, towards the stranger. Suddenly the stranger clasped Barbara's hand very tight, and I saw that, of course, she was not a stranger. She was the neighbour. Barbara's neighbour. She had come to visit.

'Oh, I'm sorry, I'm sorry,' said the neighbour, all in a rush. 'I've been so busy.'

Her eyes darted from one of us to the next as if she were a condemned person, arguing for her life.

'At least you turned up, darlin',' said the Pearly King. The woman looked startled again. Maybe she mistook his voice for a piece of heavy machinery.

'Better late than never,' said Finty.

Sister Philomena stood and reached for one of the baubles on the tree. She placed it in Barbara's hand. 'Do you feel how shiny it is?' she asked, the words like a lullaby. Barbara nodded to show she did. She still gripped the hand of her neighbour. It looked as if she would never let go.

Sister Philomena lifted down the paper angel from the top of the tree and gave that to Barbara too. She asked if Barbara could smell the pine, then she lifted Barbara's fingers and guided them towards the branches.

Sister Philomena held Barbara's left hand and whispered her name and told her it was Christmas, it was Christmas, and her neighbour was here. Everything would be all right now.

Briefly in the night I heard Barbara sing. 'Away in a Manger', I think it was. The song came and went, so faint I had to lie very still in order to find it. For the first time in a week, I did not hear Barbara get up. I did not hear her roam the corridors.

The undertaker's van was here this morning.

In the dayroom, nobody spoke. Nobody took a nutritional drink. A heavy stillness sat over us, pressing all the life away. It was like the day your first letter arrived, Harold, only this was harder because then we had expected nothing and now we had grown used to something and it was gone again. No matter how we tried to look at life, everything was over. It was hard to see anything except the end.

'I just thought—' said Finty. She gave up.

'Scrabble?' asked Sister Lucy.

'Maybe not, if you don't mind,' said the Pearly King. 'Maybe not any more.'

Behind him, the Harold Fry corner looked tired

and out of date. A drawing pin must have loosened from one of the postcards and it hung at an angle, on the verge of falling.

We closed our eyes. We slept.

MORPHINE MADNESS

Sip. Sip.

'I am concerned about the eye,' said someone. I couldn't tell who. They were all leaning over me. I could only smell the cleanness of them.

'I do not think she can make it,' said Lady with Grapefruit.

DR SHAH: *Sterilized dressing?*

NURSE: *Yes, doctor.*

DR SHAH: *Eyedrops?*

Plip plop.

I heard someone say 'Infection' and someone else said 'Temperature'.

NURSE: *Don't worry, Queenie. It will be OK.* (But it was not OK. She had spiders in her mouth.)

SISTER PHILOMENA: *Queenie is waiting for her friend called Harold Fry.*

Ha ha ha, went the horse.

DR SHAH: *I've heard about this.*

NURSE: *It's quite a story, isn't it?*

Nurse smiles. (More spiders.)

DR SHAH: *Do you think he hopes to get here soon?*

Soon? laughed Lady with Grapefruit.

Soon? laughed the horse.

Where are you, Harold Fry?

SIX WHITE HANDKERCHIEFS

For two days I have not written. I have not felt well enough. Nothing I've seen or remembered has moved me to lift my pencil. Sister Mary Inconnue visited but I only slept and took my medication. Maybe someone forgot to draw the curtains last night, or maybe the night nurse opened them early without my noticing, but when I woke this morning the light at the window was silver.

There remained a small scattering of stars. The dark leaves of the tree hung without moving. Not a breath of wind. It was that time just before you see the sun rising when there is a tiny slip of grey paling the dark but no more than that, no blue. It was my favourite time for working in my garden. I'd watch the dimmed stillness lift from the plants and figures. I'd watch the colour emerge in the lapping of the sea. It was like seeing the day wake up.

The name for this time seemed significant. I wondered about 'predawn', but that sounded such a half-hearted way to describe the magical wash of light at my window.

When the night nurse came to replace my pain patch, I wrote for her in my notebook. **What is this light called?**

The night nurse said it was probably night, though it could be dawn, and she was sorry but she had lots of things to attend to before she finished her shift. I nodded to show that of course I understood. A little later Sister Catherine tapped on my door with a glass of water.

'I hear you want to know about dawn? I looked it up on the computer.' She pulled from her pocket a piece of paper. 'I did some research.'

And I can tell you now that the stage before dawn is not called 'predawn'. It is called 'NIGHT'. But there are three stages of dawn, and they are called 'astronomical dawn' (looks like night), 'nautical dawn' (just light enough to distinguish an object out of the dark), and 'civil dawn' (the time it is light enough for sensible people to get up without bumping into things).

'But some people call it "the silver hour",' said Sister Catherine. 'I like that best.' Sister Catherine moved to the window and looked out over the sky. She touched the glass as if she were reaching for the air beyond. 'Listen to those birds. It must be very fine, to walk on a morning like this. If I ever walked to Santiago de Compostela, I'd do that. I'd walk in the dawn. I guess I'd make friends too. People I don't even know.'

271

Six doves flew past, and they looked like white handkerchiefs coming in to land.

Sister Catherine turned. 'What are you doing, Queenie?' She laughed. 'Have you started writing already?'

THE WAY FORWARD

After your son's death, Harold, the world changed. It did not change for Napier. It did not change for my landlady or your neighbours or people I passed in the street. If it altered for them, the shift was brief, it was a hiccup, it was a missing of a step, the way the sudden removal of a person is a reminder of one's own fragility before we resume the familiar, ordinary things that make us feel untouchable again. But from where I was looking, a seismic shift occurred. And like most seismic shifts, it cut everything open and pulled it apart. Each morning I woke, and for a moment, perhaps, just a moment, life was as it had been, and then, with quiet horror, I would recall what had happened. Remembering what I had done, I had to get up. I had to be busy in order not to think. I had no idea how you would bear your loss or ever recover. No matter how hard I tried, I couldn't see the way forward.

I remember feeling very angry. It shocked me, because of all the emotions attached to pain, anger is the one least spoken of. Loneliness, yes. Remorse, yes. But white fury? It came in a flash, when I wasn't expecting it. One day a woman pushed in front of me on Fore Street with her shopping bags. She caught my ankles, it was nothing really, but I chased after her. I wanted her to know how wrong she had been, I wanted her to feel nothing but shame because that was how it was for me. The anger throbbed in my belly as if it were breathing. 'What's wrong with you?' she said when I demanded an apology. 'Get a life.'

So I tried to resume the way things had been before David's death. I dressed in the mornings and took the bus to work. I bought milk on my way home. I made toast for my supper. I read at night. But no matter how many times I did these things, none of them had substance. They were things I did but they added up to nothing.

Meanwhile you buried your son. You began to drink. Other events occurred. Other terrible events that I will come to later. It was clear to me I was to blame. I had not done enough to rescue David, and the pain I had caused you was unforgivable. It was time to move on but I still couldn't. I couldn't bear to leave you and Kingsbridge.

When I went, in the end, I went in a hurry. I was hurling things into my suitcase. I didn't pack my dance shoes. I didn't pack the ball dress. And the brown wool suit? Yes, I left that too. The record player. No room for that. It was like shedding skin. Apart from clothing, the only things I allowed myself to keep were my favourite books and the

274

green teacups and saucers. I wrapped them in my socks and tights. As dawn rose, I took the first bus to Exeter. I kept scanning the road, looking for you, but it was early. You wouldn't even have arrived at work.

Then I waited in the café opposite Exeter St David's station and I met the lonely gentleman who was not lonely after all. After that I fled to purchase a train ticket. And there I was. On my way to Newcastle.

I wished I had collapsed when I got there, on the station platform. That would have been a form of escape. As it was, I staggered to the ground and bruised my knees and caused a small flurry of unwanted attention. Later that afternoon I took a room in a cheap hotel. One of those new places beside a roundabout where the walls are so insubstantial you might as well be in a bed at the bus stop. A cleaner was pushing a trolley of clean sheets and towels and small toiletry items. When she saw me alone she showed me how to open the door, there was a knack to it, she said. I admit I wasn't watching. I was only wondering what I was going to do with myself when I got into the room. There seemed to be no internal noise, only the traffic and shouts from the street below.

It was still fairly warm outside, but my room was very cold. I remember that. I could feel the flow of chilled air, even at the open door. I stared at the single white bed, the empty cabinet, the bare walls, and I couldn't go any further. I told the cleaner I needed a walk. I didn't even wait for her reply. I left my suitcase by the open door and off I ran.

I walked fast. I was hungry, but I felt I could never slow down or sit at a table or eat. There was a time when I had been able to see only mothers and babies. Now it was mothers and grown-up sons. They were everywhere. Different versions of your wife and son. I'd have given anything to stop remembering, but Maureen's words were fresh in my ears, even in Newcastle, even as I paced alongside the Tyne, and no matter how fast I went, how far, I couldn't get away from them. By the time I returned to the hotel, it was late and I felt weak with the lack of food. The lights were on in reception, but it was empty.

Only when I was standing outside my room did it occur to me that I had not taken the key. There was no sign of my suitcase, and when I tried the door it was locked. I had been dreading my return to that room and now that I was there, now that I had made up my mind to go to bed, I wanted nothing else. I was desperate for the cold white of that bare room, and sleep.

'Does no one work here?' I pressed my hand repeatedly on the bell at reception. No one emerged. In the end, I crept behind the desk and retrieved the key.

You'd think it should be so simple, opening a door. It is supposed to be simple. One of those things you do without thinking while you think instead about other, more interesting things. No matter how many times I twisted the key and felt the lock spring open, that door would not budge. I pushed and pulled. I rattled. I even kicked it. Nothing. Between waves of despair, I tried to compose myself and think carefully, but whatever I did, it made no difference. The stupid door would not open. I ended up sitting on the carpet and trying to doze in the corridor.

It was the cleaner who found me. 'But I showed you, pet,' she said, helping me to my feet. 'I explained about the door.' She took the key from my hand and twisted it gently in the lock. She grasped the handle, and with the smallest effort she moved the door to the left. Of course. A sliding door. 'Will you be OK now?' she asked. I wish I could tell you that I slept that night because I had not slept for weeks, but life is not like that and I didn't.

The following morning, I took an early bus to Alnwick. Another bus. I had it in my head that I must keep moving north. The bus got as far as a village called Embleton, thirty miles south of Berwick-upon-Tweed, and then it broke down. Another bus? Yes, that will come tomorrow. All change, please. Everything, it seemed, was drawing to a close. I tried to move and all I met was blockage.

The village was almost empty. I could have asked in the local hotel or shop for a taxi but I had no desire to meet anyone. No inclination to ask for help because help implies a conversation, an exchange, and all I wanted was to be alone and keep moving. I dragged my suitcase down a road signposted to the golf course. The road leads like an invitation towards the sea. I know every hedge of it now, every gate, every flower. I can see why I followed it because it has a pull, a wide straight road like that. Between me and a thread of blue in the distance rose pale sand dunes and clumps of marram grass. I don't know that I was thinking of David specifically as I walked but endings were very much on my mind.

I passed the clipped greens of the golf course and made my way up and down the soft paths. When I reached the mouth of the estuary, I smelt the salt of the kelp beds in the same moment that the wind began to tug at my clothes and hair.

The bay stretched wide around me, a perfect whitened arc. Across the other side, the decaying profile of Dunstanburgh Castle poked towards the sky. The tide was out, and the sand shone like glass. Far away the waves met the land and were broken. It's Bantham Beach, I thought. I travel more than six hundred miles and I'm back where I started. Where next? What was left?

I trudged forward, past the kelp beds, past the black stone boulders, until the sea lapped my shoes. This time I would keep going. Let the water wash over my feet. Tip my waist, my breasts, my chin. Get it over and done with this time. The waves folded over my shoes, and the water was so sharp it stung my ankles and I almost cried out. I kept pushing forward.

The sea must have been almost at my knees when something tiny and pale glinted beneath the waves and caught my eye. For the first time I peered down. Threads of green seaweed curled at my ankles. Shells and stones patterned the rills of sand. With the passing of every wave, the image distorted a little, was lost, and then returned. A garden in the sea and I could so easily have missed it.

I thought of the hotel door that wouldn't pull or push but only slid from right to left. Sometimes, Harold, the way forward takes you by surprise. You try to force something in the familiar direction and discover that what it needs is to move in a different dimension. The way forward is not forward, but off to one side, in a place you have not noticed before.

I left the sea and dragged my suitcase towards the dunes.

'Jolly nice day for paddling,' I said to a young family wrapped in coats. They watched with open mouths.

I returned to the coastal path.

THE PILGRIMS

When Sister Catherine wheeled me into the dayroom, Finty was not in her reclining seat. My stomach dropped. Not Finty. Please, not her. I couldn't help myself. I felt hollowed.

'What's up with you?' I had no idea where her voice was coming from. Maybe she was already haunting me. It was the sort of thing Finty would get up to.

I scanned the room. All the other seats were occupied, even the one that had belonged to Barbara. The Pearly King dozed with a parcel in his lap. Mr Henderson stared at the newspaper, failing to turn the pages. Sister Lucy sat at the table, bent over her jigsaw, without picking up any pieces. New patients held hands with family and friends, none of them speaking, only waiting. At the window there was also a fisherman with a yellow sou'wester hat and a pair of binoculars trained towards the North Sea. But no Finty. No sign of her. Finty was gone.

'Over here, gal!'

The fisherman turned. He plucked off his sou'wester. He was bald. He was—

'Finty?' The noise came out of my mouth before I could stop it.

'I'm waiting for Harold Fry!' She lifted her binoculars and fixed them once more on the horizon.

No one spoke. Everyone got on with doing nothing as if the yellow hat was not there. I opened my notebook to begin a fresh page but the sound of the pencil scratching at the paper was so loud in that stillness it was enough to make me stop again.

'Where are you, Harold Fry?' muttered Finty.

Mr Henderson put down his newspaper. 'You're looking at the North Sea, woman. I don't know if this has occurred to you but Harold Fry is not coming by boat. And even if he was, I doubt he would make his passage via the Orkneys.'

Finty found this very funny, but it did not seem to deter her. ('Make his passage? Ha ha ha.') Mr Henderson shared a despairing look with me.

Finty said, 'I've been thinking. Since Babs went, it's been no fun at all in this place. Now I may be dying but I'm not fucking dead yet. If Harold Fry is serious about walking, he might as well do it for me as well. All I gotta do is wait. That's easy.'

My throat felt full, as if I would cry, though I didn't know whether the feeling that came with it was one of joy or sadness.

'You are waiting, Finty?' said Sister Catherine slowly. 'For Harold Fry?'

281

'Too right I am, sister.'

Finty proposed an extra round of nutritional drinks, followed by a nap and some afternoon prayers. She has not attended chapel before. From now on, she said, she has to keep up her strength and widen her options. ''Cos I'm not dying till the man gets here. An' that's final.' She returned to her post at the window, complete with the binoculars and sou'wester hat.

The Pearly King began to make a strange rattling noise that had Sister Lucy rushing to his aid with a glass of water. 'Bless you. I'm laughing,' he rumbled. And when she asked if there was anything he needed, he mentioned he would like to join Finty at the window. 'I'm with her,' he said, as he moved slowly beside Sister Lucy. 'I'm waiting too. If you ask me, Harold Fry sounds a diamond geezer.' So now there was a slight fisherman in a yellow hat and also a huge one-armed Pearly King with the air of a pirate on the lookout for you. I sank a little into my chair.

'Henny?' said Finty. 'Are you gonna wait?'

Everyone turned to Mr Henderson. He in turn glanced at me and gave a chivalrous bow of his head. 'If Harold Fry is a friend of Miss Hennessy's, he is a friend of mine.'

'Yay!' shrieked Finty. 'Henny's in too. Come on, you lot. Anyone else waiting for Harold Fry?'

I could barely look. I thought, No one else will say yes. No one will even answer. And I knew they would be right because what am I doing? Waiting for you when death is everywhere, and I don't mean only in a hospice.

One by one, and in silence, the patients raised their hands. Sunken faces. Skeletal wrists. Bandages and tubes. Sunlight poured through the windows, and the air shone with dust motes, billowing like silvered snow. The friends and families of the patients began to raise their hands too, and so did the volunteers and nuns. At last everyone in the dayroom had a hand in the air. Tall, small, young, old, fat ones, thin ones, healthy, dying. They looked from one person to the next with a dawning sense of wonder. Something new was happening. It was palpable.

'That's it, then,' said Finty. 'It's a unanermous yes vote. From now on, no one dies. We're all waiting for Harold Fry.'

WHAT IS GOING ON?

A change has occurred in the last few days. With so much attention, it has been difficult to find the quiet time to write to you.

Tuesday: Mr Henderson took out his pen and said he would attempt the crossword in the newspaper. I was able to help with several cryptic clues. Sister Catherine's postbag contained three greeting cards from well-wishers in St Boswells, Urmston and Peterborough. Sister Lucy pinned them up in the Harold Fry corner. It took me the rest of the day to reply to my Get Well cards.

Wednesday: Mr Henderson waved his newspaper in the air and said, 'Good grief. Harold Fry has even hit the local news today.' Whatever did he mean? asked a volunteer. With a look of confusion, Sister Lucy read out a short article about Harold Fry and the pluck of the Saga generation. Later Sister Catherine showed me a peony in the Well-being Garden. I confess I wept.

★   ★   ★

Thursday: A woman visiting a new patient turned to me, and I swear she smiled. A tattooed man who was visiting his father gave me the thumbs-up and said, 'God bless you, madam.' We also received a gift delivery of a basket of muffins, brownies and cupcakes. ('Bloody hell,' said Finty. 'Can you liquidize those things?') Sister Lucy asked if anyone would like to help with her jigsaw and three patients said they would. They finished Wales and the south of England and are now racing towards the Midlands.

Friday: A woman tried to take a photograph on her mobile phone of Sister Catherine mixing me a milkshake, and Sister Philomena rushed in, calling, 'No, no, not here. Please.' Later, a man with a long-lens camera had to be escorted from the Well-being Garden. I received six further greeting cards from well-wishers, flowers from a cancer unit in Wales, homemade jams donated by the local WI, as well as olive oil, body cream, a head massager and three hot-water bottles. Mr Henderson said to me, 'It will be a partridge in a pear tree next. Eh, Miss Hennessy?'

This morning, when the duty nurse changed my dressing, et cetera, she said, 'The world is a crazy place.'
 I wrote, **What is going on?**
 'Has no one told you?'
 I shook my head.

'Have you heard of Twitter?'

I knew about it, of course, because Simon, the volunteer who used to come to my beach house to help me, had talked about it. Sometimes he played on his phone while I sat in a tent of blankets in my garden. I wrote about the days when there were flowering topiaries and rose bowers, when people came to visit my garden and brought offerings, and sometimes he said, 'Aw, cute,' and sometimes he only nodded to his phone. I spent many hours sitting side by side with Simon in my garden.

The duty nurse dressed my face. She spoke close to my ear so that her voice was a tickle of words. She said, 'Hashtag Harold Fry. Hashtag Queenie Hennessy. Hashtag unlikely pilgrimage. Hashtag hospice. Hashtag respect. Hashtag live forever. I don't know. Your names seem to be all over the place.'

Finty spent the afternoon learning to tweet with one of the volunteers. She now has three hundred followers.

CONCERNING A BEACH HOUSE

This morning I lay very still and thought about my sea garden. I wasn't ready for the dayroom. Instead I thought of the wind chimes, and the longer I pictured them, the more I remembered. When a breeze came outside, the green leaves of the tree all took it up with a rustle and I smiled because I swear I could hear the tinkle of shells and iron keys.

Sister Mary Inconnue sat in her chair, eating a packed lunch from a Tupperware box and reading her new magazine (*Inside the Vatican*. I can't imagine it has many jokes but she seemed to find it hilarious).

'Maybe you should write about your sea garden,' she said at last, mopping her mouth with a paper napkin.

I want to tell you, Harold, how I made my home in Northumberland.

The sky was a turquoise blue with only pufflets of cloud; the sun lay on my neck and arms; far out, a flat sea shimmered like a blue cloth.

There was nothing but the constant shuffle and flip and trickle of the tide lapping the shore.

That day, twenty years ago, when I walked out of the sea and back to land, I had no thought of building a garden. I had no thought of finding a house. I yanked my suitcase up the sand dunes at Embleton Bay and I had no idea where I was heading any more, I only knew I was searching for something, without knowing what that was. A little way out to sea, a stone outcrop made a perch for the birds, and as the waves met it, they threw themselves up in white curls. I could hear only the gulls and the waves.

The beach houses took me by surprise. It was like coming across a party when you think you are alone. They were mainly boarded up, though a few were still open, with deck chairs set out on the grass. No two huts were alike. Some were no more than wooden sheds. Others were painted and had verandas, steps, circular windows. They were set apart from one another, without any sense of pattern or order, or indeed path, as though someone had taken a handful of beach houses and dropped them on a sandy clifftop. Mine was the last I found. A hand-painted sign read FOR SALE.

The exterior was clad in broken timber slats, and the roof, such as it was, was made of corrugated tin. The window frames were rotten and held no glass, so every time the wind came, the torn red curtains of the sea-facing windows spat out like tongues. Shutters hung loose. A stone chimney poked from one side of the beach house and an elder tree grew from the other. The place was surrounded by undergrowth.

I left my suitcase in the sunshine and kicked my way up to the porch, a sheet of plyboard supported by two paint-peeled wooden poles. When I pushed on the front door, I was met with resistance. Not a slider, though. I checked. The door was propped and tied to the frame with bootlaces. I had to loosen them and lift the door to one side.

Even before I entered, I was met with the dark smell of damp and rotting vegetation. Where the rain had come in, the floor joists were rotted away, and in the gaps sprouted clumps of pink-flowered thrift. Paint flaked from the wooden walls. I had to tread carefully. One wrong move and my foot might go straight through. I tried the tap that hung over a stone sink, and the thing snapped straight off in my hand.

The beach house was divided into four equal-size rooms, each with a window. The front two rooms looked towards the sea. The back two – one of which became my bathroom – overlooked the grassy cliffs. I peered out from each broken window, but there were no other beach houses in view. There was only the bed of nettles, which stopped at the edge of the cliff. Below, there was the sea, the ragged black-tipped shoreline fringed with white foam, the distant silhouette of the broken castle. The beach house gave the impression of being rooted neither on land nor at sea. I left my suitcase beside it and returned to the coastal path.

I asked down at the golf course but no one knew anything about the beach house. They suggested I tried the shop. I was halfway to the village when I realized I wasn't walking any more, I was running. No, they told me at the village shop. No one lived there. It had been for sale a long time, both the house and the plot of land (half an acre) it stood on. The owners hadn't spent a summer on the bay for many years. Who could blame them? The house was falling down. It probably wouldn't survive another winter. I took the telephone number of the owners and I also bought a loaf of bread and a bottle of water.

I returned to the beach house. I sat in the sun with my suitcase, and while I ate the bread and drank the water I gazed out over the bay. The sun was high and threw stars at the sea. The air shimmered with heat, like a veil of water. Beyond it, I made out a cruise ship on the horizon and it was so still it seemed to be pasted there, until I looked again and found it had moved. Black-headed gulls circled the shoreline, and dropped hard as stones, for fish. People made their way along the coastal path, tiny specks, en route to the ruins of Dunstanburgh Castle. All of us, going about our lives. The guests on the cruise ship. The weekend walkers. The gulls. The fish. Me, with a suitcase. The nettles swayed.

The Northumberland coast was not like Devon

after all, or if it was, it was a simplified version. The crumples and folds of the southern landscape were flattened here. Where the Devon lanes had been narrow and high with overhanging hedgerows, so that I could not know what was around a corner, in Embleton the land lay wide and open. I looked out over the bay, the golf course, the clifftops, the higgledy-piggledy castle, and it was like breathing again. I could see everything.

I will live here, I thought. I *need* to live here. And already I felt a flutter of tenderness for that broken-down place.

I rang the owners that same evening and offered to buy their beach house.

FURTHER MADNESS

Dear Queenie, There has been an unexpected turn of events. So many people ask after you. Best wishes, Harold Fry
PS A kind woman at the post office has not charged me for the stamp. She also sends her regards.

Your latest postcard has arrived. This time the dayroom was so packed – so many volunteers, nurses, patients, family and friends had assembled to hear your news – that Finty made Sister Lucy stand on a dining chair to read it out. There followed a lively discussion about the kindness of the lady in the post office, the slowness of the postal service and acts of charity performed by various people in the room. One woman, for instance, who is the sister of a patient, told us she runs three marathons every year in aid of the local children's home. Finty said, since the lady was so kind, could she lend her her mobile phone because Finty needed to check her Twitter account? Sister Lucy pinned up your postcard in the Harold Fry corner. I didn't like to make a fuss and ask what the picture was.

'We need to send him a message,' announced Finty. 'So that he knows about the developments here.'

'What developments, exactly?' asked Mr Henderson. He sat still while the duty nurse changed his syringe driver.

'He needs to know that we're all waiting,' said Finty, pointing at the large group in the dayroom. 'If he knows how many of us are waiting, he might get here quicker.'

'If Harold Fry finds out how many of us are waiting,' said Mr Henderson, 'he might go straight home. And how exactly do you propose to send a message to a man who is walking the length of England?'

Finty ignored this. She addressed instead the table of volunteers. 'We need to start making plans. Harold Fry could get here any day. We have to be prepared.' Here she had to pause to cough something into a tissue.

While Sister Philomena and the duty nurse handed out nutritional drinks and pain relief, Finty began to outline her plans. They were surprisingly substantial. 'First up, we need to make a WELCOME, HAROLD FRY banner. Anyone fancy that?'

Sister Catherine was appointed to head a team responsible for the making of a banner. She fetched the sticky shapes, as well as felt, scissors, glue and a long stretch of white canvas.

Finty also proposed that we write a song in music therapy to welcome you. 'Maybe the local paper will take our photograph. Another thing; we need to think about fundraising.'

'Please could I have my phone back now?' whispered the marathon lady.

'Do you mind?' snapped Finty. 'I'm tweeting here. I'm multi-tasking.'

'Why do we need to think about fundraising?' asked a new patient.

'To subsidize a party. He'll need a party when he arrives. He won't just wanna get here and, like, and . . . sit down.'

I looked over the room of chairs. Apart from sitting, I couldn't think what else you were going to do. I glanced to Mr Henderson and he frowned.

'What about a sweepstake?' growled the Pearly King.

'Fab idea,' said Finty. She asked someone to grab the pencil and notebook from my hands. She needed to make a list.

One of the volunteers offered to make gift cards in order to raise funds. Another suggested cupcakes.

'I am not certain that we should be throwing a party,' said Sister Philomena quietly. 'This is a hospice. If you want to prepare for Harold Fry's arrival, we might persuade Sister Lucy to bring out her blow-dryer.'

'If you like,' said Sister Lucy, warming to this theme, 'I could even do haircuts.'

There were murmurs of assent. Finty went quiet briefly and tugged on her hat. (A brightly coloured wool Rastafarian hat. But we needn't go into that now.) A few of the patients' friends said they would like a haircut if Sister Lucy was offering. There had not been time recently, they agreed, to think about things like hairdressers when you're making hospital trips every day and so on.

'How short can you do mine, Sister Lucy?' asked one of the volunteers. Her hair flew out like a static halo.

'Oh, very short,' said Sister Lucy brightly. 'If you like, you can have a Brazilian.'

For the rest of the day, the activities continued. Sister Catherine supervised the banner. Sister Lucy's face went pink from the heat of her blow-dryer. Finty put herself in charge of media relations. The Pearly King said he could contact a few people he knew for contributions to a raffle prize. I sat beside the window with my notebook.

'I gather Finty has a thousand followers,' said a soft voice beside me. I was surprised to discover Mr Henderson. I had been so absorbed in my writing, I had not noticed his approach. 'What do you do with a thousand followers?' He settled in the chair beside mine. 'I had a wife and a best friend. That was all I needed.'

He looked out over the Well-being Garden. Swifts were swooping between the trees and the wooden pagoda threw a long shadow over the grass. Mr

Henderson and I watched. I did not write. The leaves of the garden have become one gentle green.

Finty gave a yelp from the other side of the room. 'Yay!' she squawked. 'I'm fucking trending!' There were cheers and wolf whistles.

Mr Henderson smiled to the swifts. '*How oft,*' he murmured, '*when men are at the point of death, Have they been merry!*'

IN WHICH I MAKE A HOME
AND A GARDEN

I walked out of my new beach house and put my foot straight through a fruitcake.

Placed also among the nettles were a casserole dish, a pint of milk, a packet of Craster smoked kippers and a flask.

When I bought the beach house and the plot of land where nothing much grew, local people watched with curiosity as if I were not quite in my senses and therefore might need looking after. Initially there were rumours that I had bought the plot in order to develop it, and even though no one wished to live in the beach house, neither did anyone want to see it demolished and replaced. A protest meeting was called in the Castle Hotel. Aside from the protester and two of his friends (a plumber and his wife), I was the only person who turned up. We drank cider, and the plumber and his wife ended up offering to help me renovate my beach house. In exchange, I agreed to look at their account books. And although it hurt me, the work, because it took me back to Kingsbridge and you and David, I accepted that sometimes you cannot clear the past completely. You must live alongside your sorrow.

The protester lent me a tent and a tarpaulin until my roof was fixed. He helped me to pitch it inside my beach house. He said there was nothing I could do to pay him except possibly re-word his campaign to save the ozone layer.

I slept on a wooden pallet, an old mattress and a sleeping bag given to me by a neighbour of the plumber and his wife. In exchange the neighbour asked me to coach her son in O-level Latin. So now I had three jobs. The accounts, the teaching and the protest. I slept fully clothed.

The food offerings continued. Sometimes they made a small edible path through the nettles. Cake tins and Tupperware containers and ovenproof dishes wrapped in foil to keep them warm. If I was desperate, I walked down to the golf course and ordered a hot dish in the clubhouse. When I spoke to the kitchen staff our subject was the weather and in time that became our language, just as you and I had a language in your car. Nice day. Rotten day. We described our emotions in terms of the temperature. And sometimes one of them would ask, 'You all right up there, pet? Had enough?'

The plumber and his wife and I made supports for the roof in order to prevent it from collapsing. We had to push them up the path on wheelbarrows. We cleared the roof of moss and debris so that the rainwater would no longer form stagnant pools in the corrugated roof and leak through it down into the rooms. Another friend of the plumber installed gutters and replaced the rotted window frames. Perspex sheets were glued where there had been only broken glass. As payment I agreed to take on the friend's accounts and also to help him once a week in confidence skills. He felt his shyness held him back in life, and even though I had never thought of myself as a particularly forthright woman, I found that my dealings with Napier had a use.

The timber floor was replaced by three builders I met on the golf course. In exchange I barbecued fish and sausages for their families and carried bottles of cider from the pub. The door was rehung with new hinges. I paid for those with what my mother would have called ready money. Just before my first Christmas in the beach house, I was given a second-hand woodburner by a couple I met in the post office. I learned their marriage was on the verge of collapse. In return for the woodburner, I offered them dance lessons every Sunday after-noon in their kitchen. Slow, slow, quick quick slow, slow. I thought of my mother shelling peas, my shoes resting on my father's boots. And I don't know whether it was the dancing or the festive season, but either way that couple stayed together. In later years, they'd come down to my garden and foxtrot on the shingle paths. We'd set up their cassette player by the window and if one of them asked, What about you, Queenie? What happened to your dancing partner? I might light a lamp in the garden and think of you.

I spent most of my first winter trying to work out how to keep a woodburner going. I lay in bed at night shivering, even though I was dressed in fisherman's socks, a knitted jumper and a wool hat (all donated by a woman from the hotel; in exchange I helped her write a weekly letter to her daughter in Australia). The beach house swayed in the wind, and the wooden boards cracked. The sea threw up waves like walls. But I was safe. I had done what no one said I could. I had spent a winter alone on Embleton Bay.

Spring came. The fulmars made nests in the rocks, and so did the kittiwakes. When the weather began to clear, I bought black bitumen paint – my most expensive purchase yet – and redecorated the entire exterior. That was a day of celebration. Other beach-house owners had begun to open up their summer homes. I invited them over, along with all the people who had helped me. My guests brought guitars and picnics and we danced long into the night on the sand. The window frames I painted later in blue and it was the same with the wooden shutters. I made the inside walls a soft grey. The curtains I replaced with silk drapes I'd picked up at a jumble sale.

So now, you see, I had a home and I loved it, my beach house, because I had rescued it from almost nothing and brought it back to life. I also had at least ten weekly engagements with local people, teaching them the skills I had learned along the way. And sometimes I stopped with them and we shared a plate of food, sometimes we walked along the coastal path to the ruined castle. Sometimes I drank with them or we watched the birds at Newton Pools or we sat down by Craster harbour and ate crab. But I never spoke about where I had come from or the terrible thing I believed I'd done. And always, always, there was the absence of you.

With the arrival of summer, I'd expected to feel at peace. Instead I began to dream of David again. I left my windows open at night, hoping to be soothed by the sea but it didn't work and I often woke crying. That was when I decided to clear the nettles and discovered I had inadvertently begun a rockery.

I found a black boulder down on the beach that was big enough to sit on. It took me and several golfers a full morning to push the thing up the coastal path. I placed it in a central position a few feet in front of the house. It marked the centre of the space like the hub in a wheel. I liked to watch it from my window, the way it changed colour in the sun or rain, the way its shadow lengthened and then shrank as the hours passed. It was one of the golfers who suggested I should carve sand steps directly down from my garden to the beach. If you walk along the sand at Embleton Bay towards Craggy Reef, you can still see the skeleton of the path to my garden, though recently I let the sea take it and the steps are no longer so easy to find.

A little later I dug a hole and filled it with compost and planted a dog rose. It was a fragile thing, and I worried that the combination of the poor soil and the wind would be too much for it. Walking on the beach one morning, I picked up a piece of driftwood about the size of a cane. I screwed it into the soil beside the rose to act as a stake. So now there was a rockery, a black boulder and a rose. My garden had begun.

My inspiration came from what I saw. I studied other people's gardens, as I have told you, and the footpaths, but I also studied the patterns in the sand; the rills, the spokes, the ridges, the rows of indentations like vertebrae. I could lose a morning trying to identify the colours and shapes in a rock pool; anemones with long black tentacles, rust-green flowers, silvery barnacles, skittering black crabs and pink-spotted starfish. I watched the sea mists roll over the land as the tide came in or I'd sit on the black boulders that looked like a beach of seals beneath Greymare Rock. I collected seaweeds and hung them to dry on my wooden porch so that when the storms came they danced like plastic ribbons.

In time I began to see that I had been wrong when I said that nothing grew in my garden. Plenty grew in this barren place. I simply didn't know how to value it. I unearthed sea kale and columbines, poppies and gorse, thrift and wild geraniums. I made a place for each of them.

I built my rock pool in my second year at the

beach house. It is about four feet in diameter and composed of whinstone flints. I lined it carefully to protect the water level. Roaming the beach, I found tiny sea-coal stones, the size of beads, and I used them to make an outer rim for the rock pool. Later I made two further rock pools, with black granite slabs and grey pebbles. Sometimes I placed the stones and the setting was right the first time, other times it took many days of placing and looking and placing again. I found out what was right only by getting it wrong. The stone paths followed the rock pools, leading from one part of my garden to the next. I became more ambitious with my planting.

People began to stop and admire my work. They returned with their friends. They'd wander up from the beach or the golf course or they'd drive over on the way home from work. There was a summer I made wind chimes from broken tools and washed-up ironwork. I erected a washing line in lieu of a boundary wall and I hung the chimes so that you could hear them jangling even from the beach. People brought me things – pieces of junk they had no use for. I placed each item in my garden. With every season it grew bigger.

Visitors spoke of my garden as a work of beauty, a piece of magic. And I have to be honest with you, it made me feel good. Sometimes I knelt at the heart of my garden, adjusting a stone, perhaps, angling the white of it towards the sun, but not really doing anything, only waiting for someone to stop. I made tiny blue fish out of shells and sailed them in the rock pools beside the emerald-green limpets.

The figures came when my garden was at its height. The first I made was you, of course. I placed you beside the stone boulder, right at the centre. Then came David and I made him a bed with the spiny burnet rose. Others followed. After all, I had endless time. I roamed the beach, choosing carefully, and if I did not find what I needed, I stopped and resumed my search another day. In the end, Napier was a shiny small piece of sharp flint that made me laugh. Maureen was a fragile piece of driftwood with a hole in her heart. For Sheila I found two plump rocks. My father was a tall spade leaning towards a stout branch that was my mother. (I gave her a beautiful red seaweed hat.) The female artists from Soho were seven feathers that were always blowing away. Even the Shit had a small damp corner of his own. I made a place for each of them because they had been a part of my life, and even though they were gone I would not leave them behind. In the moonlight they shone, those figures, and seemed to come alive.

But it was the tall figure at the very centre of my garden that I loved the most.

WEDDING BELLS

A young male patient was helped into the dayroom by his boyfriend. The patient was wearing jogging trousers and a T-shirt that drooped from his shoulders. His boyfriend wore a crisp blue suit. 'Hello, everyone,' called the boyfriend. 'Do you mind if we sit with you?'

'Go ahead,' said Finty. She moved her cut-out shapes and carefully folded her WELCOME, HAROLD FRY banner.

'Harold Fry?' said the boyfriend. 'I think I've heard of him.'

'Yeah, he's walking for us,' said Finty, indicating everyone in the room. 'We expect him any day.'

The boyfriend helped his partner to sit and asked if he needed anything, like water or a blanket. His partner lifted his hand to say no, I am OK. He rested his head on his boyfriend's shoulder. The boyfriend stroked his partner's cheek and whispered into his ear. They were only small, still words, like There, there. OK. I love you. Here I am.

'Are you gay, or what?' interrupted Finty.

The boyfriend said, 'Do you want us to sit some-where else?'

'Fuck no,' trilled Finty. 'You're the first man I've seen with his own hair in weeks. You stay right there.'

'Peter and I are getting married today,' said the boyfriend. 'You can all come if you like.'

'I don't think we're going to make it to a church, mate,' growled the Pearly King. He pointed to the knitted blue bag on his lap containing his syringe driver.

'Neither will we,' said the boyfriend. 'Sister Philomena held a meeting with the staff. They have agreed we can have a blessing in the dayroom.'

'What about God?' asked Mr Henderson.

'Sister Philomena's view is that God takes a broader view.'

'A wedding?' yelled Finty. 'Does that mean I get to borrow a new hat?'

As it was, there was no time for borrowing hats. There was no time for confetti. An hour later, we sat in a circle, with the new patient and his boyfriend at the centre. The nurses joined us, and so did a few of the nuns. Those who were uncertain about a gay wedding in a Catholic hospice were given the opportunity to do work elsewhere. The boyfriend slipped a ring over Peter's bone-slim finger, and then he supported Peter's hand so that Peter could fix a ring on the finger of the boy-friend. A woman in a fuchsia-coloured trouser suit conducted a brief civil ceremony. She told us how much it meant to Peter that we were there to witness his wedding. 'I wouldn't have missed this for the world,' sobbed Finty. 'You two look so fucking happy.'

'Can you hear me, Peter?' whispered the boyfriend. 'Can you hear that I'm your husband now?'

Peter smiled and closed his eyes.

Finty emptied an entire family-size box of tissues. She said it was a shame they weren't going to have a party and Peter's new husband gave an easy shrug. 'But we're going to have a party for Harold Fry when he gets here,' she said. 'You can come to that instead. Do you know that other gay bloke? Whatshisname? That singer? Maybe he could come an' all.'

The husband kissed Peter's forehead and laughed that no, he didn't know any singers, gay or straight or indeed both ways.

'Ah, well,' said Finty. 'Never mind. You can join us, if you like. You two buggers can wait for Harold Fry.'

Peter's husband flexed his right hand and gazed at his wedding ring with a sort of rapture, as if he had never seen anything so beautiful.

Peter was not in his chair this morning.

I watched while, in the Well-being Garden, Sister Philomena held his husband in her arms. Afterwards she showed him the blossom. She lifted

307

a branch of philadelphus and he stooped to get the orange-sweet smell of it.

The undertaker parked his van and stepped out to meet them.

A SHOCK

'BLOODY HELL! GET HERE QUICK!'
I was in my room with Sister Mary Inconnue, not writing in my notebook, not even remembering anything in particular, only staring at a large pigeon that was trying to maintain its balance in a particularly twiggy part of the tree, when we were interrupted by a caterwauling from the dayroom.

'Harold Fry is on the telly! Quick, everyone! Quick!'

Sister Mary Inconnue gave a weary shake of her head as Sister Lucy hurried through the door. The young nun lifted me out of bed and bundled me into my wheelchair. As she rushed me down the corridor, other doors flew open and patients emerged, helped by family or volunteers.

When I arrived in the room, people turned and made a space for me at the front. Sister Philomena took the remote control and increased the volume.

There seemed to be a party happening on the television. We watched a group of people walking down a country road, some dressed professionally with sticks and boots and so on, others playing bells and drums. At the head of the procession strode a tall man with weather-tanned skin, little hair and a very serious beard.

It was you.

My insides swerved as if I had missed a step and was about to fall.

'The man on the TV said that Harold Fry has some new people with him now,' said Finty. She got up and tapped the television screen with her red fingernail. Several people complained that she was in the way and that they couldn't see without falling out of their wheelchairs, but she ignored them and continued to point at the assembled group of walkers. 'There's a gorilla, right, and a twat in a hat. Then there's this boy who seems a right fucker and another woman who looks like she's sucking a lemon. They've just passed Harrogate. They're all walking to save us.'

My heart took another plunge. It was the boy at your side that undid me. For a moment, I could have sworn you were walking with David.

HRR-HRM. NO ONE MENTION
(DAVID FRY)

I didn't know what to do, Harold, when I heard the news. The reps were talking about you in the corridor. 'Have you heard what's happened to Fry?' They seemed in a hurry to tell one another because it was a story, it was a tragedy, but it didn't really touch them in any way. I listened in frozen stillness. My first impulse was to come straight to your home and find you. I wanted to confess everything. Instead I went to the wash-room and almost fainted. It was shock. I felt as if the world had just had a great big hole punched out of it and that, without anyone knowing, I was directly responsible. I could barely walk in a straight line.

'You look terrible,' said Sheila. She lifted the back of her hand to my forehead and held it there. 'My God,' she whispered. 'You're boiling.' The gesture reminded me of my mother, and thinking of her I was overwhelmed. For the first time in years I missed her desperately, in the same way I had missed her after her death. I wanted her and my father to take me out of this. I wanted his hand around mine. 'You should go home,' said Sheila.

I don't remember my bus journey that afternoon. I don't know if I paid my fare, or if I spoke to anyone. I remember the heat, I do remember that. More than anything, I longed to be alone. But when I got into the flat, I felt even worse.

It was the silence. I saw the chair where David used to sit and bearing witness to the armchair without him in it was like looking right into the loss of him. Outside there were cars, there were seagulls, there were people taking a late afternoon stroll along the estuary. Everything was as it should be. Except there was no David Fry. I thought of you, and him, and I cried for many hours.

In bed that night, I lay fully clothed with my arms clamped round my knees and my feet tucked up high. No matter how many layers I added, I could not stop shuddering. When I closed my eyes, all I could picture was David, blue in the dark, swinging from the central beam of your garden shed. If only I hadn't heard the reps mention that. My head offered further images of him tying the noose, looking for something to stand on, fitting the rope around his neck. Had he wanted to die? Even as he choked? Had he hoped to be saved? How I longed for him to kick at my door, holler my name through the letterbox. When I slept, it was only briefly.

I woke some time in the early hours of the morning, so hot I couldn't move. I felt I'd been swallowed in concrete. Somehow I got up, and all I could do was not be still. Kitchen, bathroom, sitting room, doorway. I hardly paused. I dressed in a hurry. I couldn't bear to be alone another moment. I had to get back to the brewery.

I overheard the reps saying that you would be away for at least two weeks. There'd be an autopsy before the funeral. It didn't bear thinking about, Sheila said. It didn't seem to bear much talking about either because it wasn't mentioned again.

I had no idea how I would ever look you in the eye. I knew that when I confessed the truth, you must hate me. And equally I knew that of all the men I passed on the street, on the bus, in the canteen, the one I most needed to find was you.

It is a blisteringly hot afternoon. A week has passed since David's death. If anything I'm feeling worse. No sleep. No appetite. I can't stop thinking of him. I haven't seen you since before he died.

I take the bus to the funeral parlour. I have to mark his passing in some way because it's unendurable, this pretending I am one thing and knowing I am another. The sun scorches my eyes. Everything – the sky, the pavement, the passing traffic – is too white, too fierce. I push open the door to the funeral parlour. The place has a chilled, sweet smell that I know is to do with embalming. Nevertheless it's like walking into a different universe. My shoes echo on the cold floor. I wish I had a coat.

A man in a suit greets me. Asks how he can help. He wears a black tie, cuff links; there is a professional air of mourning about him, not the chaos of us amateurs. I assume he's the undertaker.

I ask to see David Fry. Hearing David's name, the man's face softens towards me and for the first time it seems possible someone understands the grief I am suffering. There is a place for it here.

'Do you have an appointment?' he asks.

I explain that I don't exactly have an appointment but I am a friend of the family. I repeat that I would like to see David. I need to see him, I add.

My reply is not the right one. The undertaker grows uncomfortable. He steps back from me and reaches for some sort of notepad and fountain pen. My mouth dries up. The undertaker will need to telephone his client, he says. I cannot visit the deceased unless I have an appointment.

'But he's hardly going anywhere,' I answer, raising my voice. By the end of the sentence I'm also beginning to cry. There seem to be no boundaries any more between normal and grief-stricken.

The undertaker's face hardens. Maybe he suspects I am a journalist. I don't know. 'I can't allow you to stay, madam,' he says. Already he's heading for the door, opening it for me, and the rush of heat and light from outside is so intense it is like noise. I want to remain inside. I can't bear to be thrown out, when it has taken so much strength to face coming, and now I am here I've achieved nothing.

Maybe he senses my pain, because the under-taker asks if I have anything for the coffin. He can pass it on to his client; he can do that much for me. I assume he's asking for money, like they do at church when the silver plate gets passed round, and such is my guilt, my pain, I'd give every penny I've saved if I believed it might bring you some sort of comfort. I am opening my handbag when another suited man emerges from a room at the far end of the reception. I see almost nothing of the room; a soft blue wall perhaps, behind the polish of a wooden coffin, the brass handles. I don't even know that it is David's coffin. But it is like being punched.

I hurt all over. Even inside my lungs there is hurting.

I ask the funeral director to give David his red mittens. They are in my handbag. They've been there since the day I found he'd left them behind. Did they belong to the deceased? Yes, they belonged to the deceased. The undertaker will consult his client. Don't bother consulting your client, I say. Just take the things, will you? Just let me get them out of my handbag. Because I am in torture here. This is all too much. I place the mittens in his hands and I leave before he can give them back to me.

I am waiting at the bus stop when I see your car draw up outside the funeral parlour. I see you get out and move to the passenger door, only before you get there the door flies open, almost hitting you, and a small, slight woman, a little taller than me, springs out. Maureen wears a black summer dress and dark sunglasses and she carries a pillow and a teddy bear. Something for the coffin; of course. Her steps are fast, brittle. She is impatient to get inside the funeral parlour. You in contrast move slowly. You walk behind her, carrying nothing in your hands, and you seem unable to lift your head. At the door Maureen pauses and says something to you, because you nod and step aside. Once you are alone, you pull out a cigarette and ask a passer-by for a light. I hear a shriek, a terrible female cry, resound from inside the funeral parlour. I imagine the funeral director has guided her to the room he would not allow me to enter. You rush to the corner and vomit over a litter bin.

From the opposite side of the street, I see it all. But you don't see me.

A few days later we met. This time there was no avoiding you. I was in the chemist's, searching the shelves for something to help me sleep, when you opened the door. Quietly you asked the assistant behind the counter about a prescription for your wife. You were trying to be discreet, but the shop had become so stiff and solemn on your arrival that it was as if you were the only living thing inside it. The sight of you made my heart churn over and over.

The chemist was in a hurry to find Maureen's tablets. When he passed you the bag, he said, 'Please accept my condolences, Mr Fry.' Another woman in the shop, the customer who was the closest to you, repeated in an uncomfortable way that she too was very sorry 'for your loss'. Nobody seemed to have the right words at their disposal and so it was safer to say nothing or at least stick to the well-worn phrases. You, in turn, gave a listless nod, as if you wished everyone would stop all this and let you go.

You were a different man, Harold.

Your shoulders, which you had once held so erect, were hunched over. Your jacket wore a grease stain, and your hair looked uncombed. You had shaved, but a tuft of sharp hairs grew in the hollow of your left cheek. Maybe you hadn't noticed. Or maybe even as you were shaving, you had thought of David and asked, What does it matter? What difference does it make if I am clean-shaven or grow a beard? But it was the stoop in your shoulders that undid me. That, and the golf club tie.

People say sometimes of another person that they have become a shell, or a shadow of their former selves, but you were neither of these things. You were all liquid. It was impossible to imagine you laughing or dancing or doing anything so daft as fig ball. Those parts of you were gone. You appeared smaller, slower, older too, and almost naive. You were stripped back to your very basics.

You collected the prescription and shuffled towards the door.

'Oh, hello,' you said. I must have moved. I may even have made a noise.

You sent me a smile across the chemist's shop. There was I, a guilty woman, the person who had failed both you and your son, the friend who had meddled with your life and lied and lied, and there you stood in your brown jacket and tie, smiling at me.

You asked if I would care to walk down the High Street. At least I think you did. I noticed how people made way for us as we headed for the door. No one spoke. I remember that. You fixed your eyes to the ground, searching for the thing that had gone from your life, while another customer rushed to open the door and set us free.

'How is Maureen?' I asked outside.

'Pardon?'

You tried to smile again, but your face couldn't do it. Your eyes filled with tears. 'My son is dead,' you said. You told me again: 'David is dead.' Those were the only words in your life.

I said I knew. I'd heard. I was so sorry, I said. So sorry—

'Yes.' You stared at the ground. 'Yes.'

'Is there anything I can do?'

'Do?' You repeated the word as if you had temporarily mislaid the meaning of it, and were very sorry about that.

'To help?'

You closed your eyes and slowly opened them again. Then you said gently, 'That's very kind, Queenie, but I think not. Not now.'

You asked me how things were and I said they were only so-so. So-so? you repeated. Yes, I said. And your face crumpled as you said slowly that you were sorry but you couldn't remember what we were talking about. You turned to walk away.

It was because I thought you were about to go that I dared to call out, 'How are you, Harold?'

You were weeping now and didn't want me to see, so I glanced at my feet to facilitate that, but I wish I had done something else, I wish I'd had the gumption to hold you and let you cry. 'It's worse, of course, for Maureen,' you said. 'Always worse for the mother.' You apologized and you began to move away with heavy pulling steps, as if it hurt you to move. In order to avoid a woman with a pushchair, you stepped to one side and staggered a little. The shape of a spirits bottle swung from your coat pocket. You were drinking now.

A few days later I read in the local newspaper that David's funeral would be a private event. Only family. I realized this meant you and Maureen. You had no other family. There was no further mention of David at the brewery. Your son died and the world swallowed that piece of information and moved on. I never heard anyone refer to him after the first week.

So you buried your son. And the only time I

ever saw you not in fawn was the afternoon you came back to work in a black suit.

'Harold?' I asked gently. 'Should you be here?' Reps were steering out of your way.

You cowered like a man who has had a beating and expects another and is trying to be brave.

'Yes,' you said.

That was all.

THANK YOU, THANK YOU, THANK YOU

For three days it has been difficult, Harold, to find time to write my letter to you or think about my sea garden. It has been difficult even to sit in stillness with Sister Mary Inconnue and watch the clouds at my window. There have been too many other things to attend to. The walls of the dayroom are pinned all over with cards from well-wishers. There have been so many deliveries of flowers that several volunteers have hay fever. Already this morning I have composed ten thank-you notes. My eye is sore from straining to see. My hand is tired. Also, I am not sleeping at night. No one is.

'There's gonna be an all-night vigil,' said Finty. (This was on Tuesday, I think. She was working on her banner.)

'A what?' said the Pearly King. He was trying to help but mostly he was asleep.

'One of them new patients told me. It was on the radio. People are gonna bring candles and stuff and pray for us outside.'

As it turned out, the all-night vigil was more of

a party. Whenever the staff came to check on me, they looked short-tempered and tired. As if we haven't got enough to think about, I overheard one of them complain. It didn't help that Finty was up all night singing along with them from her window. The vigil keepers intend to stay until you arrive.

'Haven't they got homes to go to?' said the duty nurse.

After so much excitement, Finty has taken to her bed.

THE LOSS OF A GARDEN

It wasn't that I regretted coming to Embleton Bay or making my home or even creating a sea garden. But it was getting to be too much. All the people. All the fuss. Sometimes I felt I had to change the garden just for the sake of showing something new. It wasn't a garden for love any more. It was an attraction. And it wasn't about me. It was about other people and the things I felt they expected to see.

Now that my garden was so precious, or at least now that it carried the weight of so much expectation, I had to think about protecting it. After all, there was a small harbour at Craster to keep the fishing boats safe. I began collecting stones for walls, large ones to go at the bottom and smaller flints for the middle and shells for the top. It took me another summer to build the wall, not least because people began to help. They took weekends in the sun to search for stones on the beach and they offered assistance with the building. But here was the thing: they did not listen to me when I explained about the large stones at the bottom and the shells on top. Sometimes I'd spend a whole night pulling down what other people had made and throwing out all the crushed shells that someone had stuck through the middle. You see what I am saying. My garden was no longer the thing I'd started.

One night I lay in bed, thinking of a new idea for my garden, and it dawned on me how fragile it still was, despite the stone wall and my efforts to protect it. Supposing the wind got it, or gulls? The following morning I took the bus to Berwick-upon-Tweed and bought squares of tarpaulin from the hardware shop. I used stones to keep the tarpaulins in place and I painted a wooden sign asking people to take care when walking round the garden. Even when I wasn't there, even when I was supposed to be asleep, my mind was caught up in thinking of ways to keep it safe. I was wrong, though, about the threat coming from wind or gulls. Five years ago, something else got it.

A flock of sheep.

Apparently they had escaped from a local farm. They chewed what they could of the golf course and then made their way along the coastal path in single file. They jumped my wall and ate the contents of my garden.

I took in the devastation, the scattered stones, the smashed rock pools, the snapped sticks, the strewn seaweed and broken shells, and it was so painful my mind emptied. There was no sign of my protective tarpaulin. Where there had been a garden there were now only thirty sleepy sheep.

I cried for a long time. I stayed in my beach house, where no one could interrupt me or try to help. For days I couldn't look at my garden. Every time I left the beach house I had to stare at the sky because it hurt too much to see that ruined place – all that work and for nothing. I even wondered about selling up and moving on, though somehow I didn't have the stomach for travel any more. It was about this time that I felt a lump, low in my jaw. Neighbours were kind when they heard I was going to hospital. But after a while, as the news got worse, it was easier to close my door and hide from the world.

I was wandering on the beach a year or so later when I picked up a piece of driftwood. I used it as a walking stick to help me up the path. When I got back to my beach house I shoved it into the ground and left it.

In the morning I opened the shutters and to my surprise, there it was, glowing like a golden mast. My garden had started again. But this time it was a relief to have nothing to maintain, because there was no longer any reason to be afraid of losing it. I didn't need to show other people the beauty of my love any more. I was ill and I only had the energy to keep it in my heart.

MR HENDERSON SURPRISES ME

'There is a photograph of you in the *Berwick Gazette*,' said Mr Henderson.

'Let's see! Let's see!' clamoured Finty. The paper was passed from patient to patient, until it finally reached my hands. The image showed a young woman in her late teens with a mane of thick brown hair. It must have been taken at Oxford.

I can't believe that young woman was me.

Mr Henderson pointed to another photograph. A tall man in a PILGRIM T-shirt, sporting a thick beard. It took a moment to realize it was you, and when I did I felt my pulse race. 'And have you seen?' said Mr Henderson. 'Have you seen what the man is wearing on his feet?'

Not—? I began to smile. Not—?

'Yachting shoes!' He held on to his stomach and hooted.

It is the first time I have seen Mr Henderson look so happy.

So thank you for that.

THE NAMING OF SHOES

Today, Harold, I have been thinking about you in your yachting shoes. You should probably buy walking boots, but as I suppose you've never worn walking boots and you've always worn yachting shoes, you should probably not buy something that you are not.

I spent the afternoon with Sister Mary Inconnue remembering every pair of shoes I've ever had. It's a humbling exercise. You won't remember, but my feet are small and wide. The type of shoe I have wanted has not been the type of shoe that has fitted.

I've already mentioned the shoes I bought in Kingsbridge – my accountant shoes. They had a rounded toe and a stout heel and they made a solid noise as my feet hit the concrete. Remember?

Besides those, I have counted three pairs of black lace-ups worn during my school years, cork wedges that my mother hated, flip-flops, slip-ons, red patent-leather heels (barely worn), the velvet ball-room shoes I left behind, brogues, wellington boots, gardening shoes, tennis shoes, two sets of blue court shoes (why?), and a pair of white trainers that I have worn almost everywhere in the last five years. It is the ballroom shoes I liked most. No question.

I have measured out my life in ladies' shoes.

Once I met a woman beside my sea garden. This was after the sheep. I'd started to re-create it, but it was an altogether plainer and humbler place now. You could walk past and not notice, or see only some stones and sticks. People had forgotten about visiting and I let the sand steps go.

The woman was leaning on my wall to shake something out of her shoe. I didn't see her footwear. I saw only her crisp white jacket with shoulder pads and gold buttons. When I asked if she needed help, she jumped. She hadn't seen me, she exclaimed, laughing. Or rather, she'd mistaken me for one of the stones in my garden. The woman told me she was attending a wedding reception at the golf club and had escaped to smoke in private.

'These bloody heels,' she said. She told me she always changed her shoes if she felt low. It is the noise you make in the world that is the key to happiness, she said. She was wearing tiger-print six-inch heels at the time. When she walked away, her feet went *ping ping ping* as they hit the stones.

A little later I caught sight of her again. This time she was waving to me from farther down the bay. On closer inspection I discovered that her stiletto heel was caught in the crack of a rock. She wasn't merely waving. She was stuck.

We came – barefoot, in her case – for early after-noon tea in my beach house. Though in truth we drank gin in the garden and watched the waves. She was a lecturer in physics, it turned out. Which only goes to show you should never judge a woman by her heel.

HEAT

I have not been so well again. The vigil leaders are outside every night, and I know it is kind of them to pray for us and dance and chant but I wish they would do it in silence.

I struggled today with the heat. The sun fell into the window in a great channel of light that landed right on me here in the bed, and it was so bright, this light, so white and thick, it made my head hurt. The duty nurse opened the window but it made no difference. The air outside was stiff and hung with seed heads. Sister Lucy bathed my head but even the water felt hot.

DR SHAH: *Is she comfortable?*
NURSE: *I can't cool her down.*
DR SHAH: *There is further swelling.*
NURSE: *The pain patch was fresh this morning.*
DR SHAH: *Can she still take liquid?*
NURSE: *A little.*
DR SHAH: *You can increase the oral dose to every four hours.*

No matter which way I turned, the sheets felt too tight, too hard on my skin. The heat was like a force sucking all the energy from me. I spent the morning fighting the heat and the sheets and the frustration inside me. All I wanted was to get away.

'You have to *be* the heat,' said Sister Mary Inconnue.

If I'd had the strength, I'd have thrown a pillow at her.

As if I had said something to this effect, she laughed. 'The heat is there, and nothing you can do is going to stop it.'

So instead I gave in to the fieriness of it. I felt the slippery film on my skin and tight prickliness below and the dryness of my throat and the white at my eyes. I was not an old woman who didn't want to be hot; instead, I was the heat. It is only a small difference but I slept.

'Are you feeling a little better now?' asks Sister Mary Inconnue. The light has gone and a cool wind plays through the curtains. I can hear the leaves of the tree. 'I know it has been very jolly in the last few days,' she says. 'All these greeting cards. All this activity and so on. But perhaps you'd better get back to your own letter, dear heart.'

MURANO CLOWNS

I knew it was you, Harold, who broke into the brewery. I knew it was you who'd smashed Napier's glass clowns. I'd have guessed even if I hadn't been there, but I was. I saw everything.

After David's funeral, I found it hard to leave the brewery at night. More specifically, I found it hard to return to my flat. I invented reasons to stay out: I watched the same film several times on the trot. I took walks along the quay (though I was careful not to look at the bench where David and I had sat together and I had given him my mittens). Anything to delay that moment when I steered the front door open with my key and saw David's empty chair. Even though you were back at work, Napier had not sent us out on any drives. I was relieved. I wasn't ready to be alone with you.

One night I tried to work late. I'd found a box of old account books and even though they were ten years out of date, I told myself I needed to go through them. I'd been alone in the building for a few hours maybe, not even looking at the numbers in front of me, absorbed in thoughts of my own, when something gave a crack downstairs.

The noise brought me to the present and I realized I was sitting in almost-darkness. The only light was a wash of silver coming from a full moon at the window.

I listened but there was no further sound. I tried to concentrate on my work.

It came again. The noise. A dull knocking against an internal door. A tap, tap. Someone was trying to break into a locked room.

I slipped off my shoes and moved in silence. The concrete walls of the corridors were dark and cold against my fingers, almost damp. I continued as rapidly as I could in the direction of the stairs. Every time the building gave a creak or bang, I was startled. As I neared the well of the staircase, a torrent of light from the ground floor poured into the blackness. I was in full view now and it was hard to see anything else. I took the stairs one at a time. I had to swallow my breathing before it hit the silence.

I heard sobs. Your sobs. From the wetness of the sound, and the abandonment and the tiredness too, I could tell you'd been crying a long time. I knew exactly where to find you.

Quickly I moved away from the light of the staircase, towards Napier's locked office. The ground beneath my feet changed from hard tiles to carpet. The walls were now wood-panelled. Turning the corner, I saw you. I stood to one side.

You were rattling at Napier's door handle, beating the panels with your fists, kicking them with your foot. Sometimes you pressed your head to the door and leaned there, worn out with grieving. Other times, you jumped back and only flailed at the door. Then you must have had a new idea, and you took a few backward steps in order to charge at the door with the full weight of your shoulder. The door gave a splitting crack and you flew out of my vision, into Napier's office. I crept closer.

For the first time I could make out your face, though the moon at the window was curtained with cloud.

You were more animal than man in fawn. Your mouth was stretched into a scream, and shadows cast deep gouged-out lines in your forehead. You held your hands above your head in fists and you moved in disjointed swaggers up and down the room. There was no logic to your movement. It was as if your grief didn't know where to put itself. The cloud outside passed away from the full moon and Napier's glass clowns glittered briefly, stirred to life. I caught sight of them the same moment you did. I cried out to stop you but it was too late. You didn't hear.

You lifted two of the glass figures. One in each hand. You held them high, the way a parent pulls up a child on a swing so that the child will get the full swoop, and then you hurled them towards the ground. They smashed at your feet and you picked up another two, another two. You didn't stop until all twenty of them were gone. You stamped on them. You kicked them. And all the while, you roared.

I didn't stop you. How could I? You didn't want to let your son go gently. You wanted to rage.

Besides, you were in a place of your own. After a few moments of this wild thrashing, you stopped very suddenly and took in what you'd done. Caught in the cold flood of moonlight, you buried your head in your hands.

I was about to step forward when you staggered towards the door. You passed right by me. We were almost touching, Harold. Your foot was by my foot. Your hand was by my hand. But you lumbered past me as if I were no more than another part of the wall. I smelt the drink on you. As I heard you crash out of the building, I moved to Napier's window. You passed like a shadow across the brewery yard. You paused once and glanced back up at the window, and, not seeing me there, you got into your car.

I swept the pieces into one place, trying to make the best of things. Then I returned to my office and waited for the morning.

When Napier entered the building and saw the damage, he screamed. I tell you this because you weren't there. You won't have heard him crash through the building. He fired the cleaner before I could get to him. Gangs of reps quickly began to scour the brewery. It was as though you could be safe or innocent only if you were actively on the lookout for the one person who was not. There were whisperings in corners. Whisperings on stairs. At least one suspect was escorted from the canteen for questioning and emerged later from the yard holding his arm.

I kept a lookout for you all morning. As soon as I caught sight of your car, I hurried down to meet you. Do you remember this?

I said, 'Something happened at the brewery. It was in the night.' I pulled at your sleeve because you couldn't even stand straight. I didn't dare go the whole way and hold your hand. You lifted your eyes to mine. They looked like two lychees. They were that raw and that fragile.

I said, 'Are you listening? Because this is serious, Harold. It's very serious. Napier won't let it go.'

Fear whitened your face. Your guilt was stamped all over you. Your tie hung loose round your neck like a necklace. Your top shirt buttons were undone. And your hands. Harold, you hadn't even bothered to wash or plaster them. What were you thinking of? They were covered in nicks and cuts. And it dawned on me that of course you wanted Napier to find you out. You were back because you wanted him to see you and do his worst.

'Go home,' I said. 'Let me deal with this.'

'You don't understand.' Your words were barely audible.

'You shouldn't be here, Harold. It's too soon. Go home.'

Slowly you turned your back on me. I watched

you make your way along the wood panelling, bumping it sometimes with your shoulder as you lost your balance, your knees weak, your head low. You muttered something I didn't hear. I wish I had called out to you as you moved away. Goodbye. Forgive me. I love you. But I didn't know this was the last time. I was certain I would see you again.

You turned the corner and – snap. You were gone from me. I took a deep breath and headed towards Napier's office.

THE MYSTERY MAN

Three days ago, the Pearly King failed to appear. A parcel was delivered but he was not in his chair to open it.

'I have sad news,' said Sister Philomena.

'Aw no,' groaned Finty. She began to cry. 'No, no. Not him. No.'

'A true gentleman,' said Mr Henderson.

This morning we were sitting with several of the volunteers in the dayroom when the sound of hooves clip-clopped into the silence. A horse-drawn glass hearse passed the window and drew up beside the DO NOT PARK HERE sign. The black horses were adorned with purple plumes. The hearse was glass-domed, so clear that it sparkled in the summer sun. It was packed with white wreaths. The undertaker got out and fed the horses something from his pocket.

'Well, I never,' said one of the volunteers.

Finty watched with her hands to her mouth.

During the course of the morning, many mourners arrived to thank Sister Philomena and her team at St Bernadine's. There will be a procession from here to the church, where the Pearly King will be buried. The nuns tried to look after the guests in the garden, but it began to rain, and what with the vigil leaders blocking the pavement outside and all the new patients and their families in the private rooms, there was no space for anyone except in the dayroom.

The nuns brought tea, and the mourners talked loudly. They were dressed in the style of the hearse. Feathers and black veils and top hats and morning suits. The first they knew about the Pearly King's illness was when they got the news he had died.

'Why didn't he say? Why didn't he tell us?' said a woman with a voice like a growl whom we assumed to be one of his daughters.

'He didn't want us to worry,' said one of the men.

It turned out that the Pearly King had told his friends and family he was holidaying in Malta.

'I loved the fool,' said Finty.

She has not worked on her banner.

IT WAS MY FAULT

'You did what?' Napier screams. The veins stick out in his neck like purple rope. I am standing at one end of the room. He stands behind his almost-empty desk. Between us lie thousands of coloured glass pins. He hasn't allowed Sheila to touch them. Until he finds the culprit, no one is going home.

I grip hold of my handbag. My head throbs. I am exhausted with the lack of sleep. 'I am saying it was my fault.'

He screams again. He slams his fist on the desk. 'The clowns? My mother's glass clowns?'

'It was an accident.'

Napier turns the colour of cream cheese. 'It is the only thing I have of hers.' He snatches something from his desk, and a moment later it is shooting towards my head. I duck, and whatever it is smashes into the wall opposite, landing with a thud on the floor, where it spins several times and then falls dead. A heavy glass paperweight. I wonder how you missed that?

There is an onslaught of abuse. He calls me

many names. They froth and spit from his mouth as he takes off and paces the room with his fingers clenched stiff. He can't keep still. When he releases that right arm of his, it will jab out and punch me. I've never been hit by a man. But I will bear this. I will do it. An eye for an eye.

I speak slowly. 'I stayed on late, doing paperwork. I delivered it to your desk before I left the building. But my foot slipped. And I fell. I am sorry. I am so sorry.'

I can't stop saying it. I don't know who I am talking to any more.

Napier pauses. He twists to face me. He remains still, giving the calm smile of the powerful, and flicking dust from the shoulders of his jacket. I have no idea which is more terrifying, his stillness or his fury.

'You slipped?'

'Yes.'

'And you broke every one of my glass clowns?'

'Yes.'

'Then what? You stamped on them? You trod them into the ground?'

I can't look at him. I can only repeat what I've already said. 'It was an accident. I am so sorry.'

Napier advances closer. He reeks of sweat and smoke. He is almost touching me. 'If you weren't a woman, I'd fucking tear you apart.' He speaks through his pointed teeth. 'Get out. I never want to see you again. Do you understand? I don't want to hear you. I don't want to smell you. I don't even want to pass you on the street. Understand me? Leave tonight if you know what's good for you.'

He lifts his hand and I flinch, anticipating a blow, but he bows his head and grips the chair beside me. His knuckles turn bone white as he shakes.

'Harold Fry's job?' I whisper. My pulse is in my mouth. 'Will he keep it?'

Napier gives a sigh like a snarl. I wonder if he's about to throw another heavy object, though in truth there is little left. Not unless he picks up the chair or hurls the table. Then, without moving his head, he grunts, 'Get out.' The words are tight, squeezed from his throat.

As I walk away, the floor cracks and pops beneath my feet. I am reaching for the door when I notice the splintered hole in the doorframe where you ripped the lock open with the force of your shoulder. Just as I touch it, Napier stops me with one last question: 'You didn't do it, Hennessy. Did you?' My spine freezes over.

I close the broken door carefully behind me. It is like marking the end of a sentence with a silent full stop.

I fetch my handbag from my office. I say goodbye to Sheila. What will I do next? she asks. I tell her I need to find Harold Fry.

That is the last time I see the brewery.

★ ★ ★

There was a woman once who visited my sea garden. She was in Northumberland on holiday with her husband and she was taking a walk along the clifftops while he played a round of golf. It turned out the couple lived near Kingsbridge and knew the brewery. She had a kind face, I remember that, very soft eyes, and I believe she thought she'd upset me. 'No, no,' I said, wiping away tears. 'It's just a long time since anyone has talked to me about the brewery. Please, stay.' I served tea in the green cups and we sat on cushions on the stone boulder. She mentioned Napier too. A motoring accident, she said. And it struck me as strange that you must have known all these things, while I didn't.

She sipped her tea. 'Such a kind man,' she murmured.

For a moment I thought she was referring to you. My teacup trembled in my hand.

'I knew his mother, Agnes. He couldn't do enough for her.'

'Are you talking about Napier?'

She smiled. 'Yes, of course.' Apparently he had rung his mother every day until the night she died. Once a year he hired a minibus and drove his mother and her friends for tea in Plymouth. He couldn't have been more charming, my visitor said.

So you see, people are rarely the straightforward thing we think they are. Even the villains in a story can turn round and surprise us.

I liked the woman who stopped by my garden

and told me about Kingsbridge. I gave her a burnet rose cutting to take home. And sometimes, yes, I imagined you passing that small white rose, and getting the sweet scent of it.

A DINNER ENGAGEMENT

A further surprise, Harold, last night at the hospice. It began like this:

'*Bon appétit*, Miss Hennessy,' said Mr Henderson. The dining room was full and the windows open. Several patients were eating with their families. The nuns wore plastic aprons to protect their robes and the volunteers had gone in search of more chairs. I had been watching a soft June rain pattering on the pink roses outside so that they shivered a little and emitted a sweet, clean scent like linen napkins.

At his table next to mine, Mr Henderson lifted his glass of water as a toast but the glass wobbled in his hand, and Sister Catherine had to rescue it. 'Stupid fool,' he grumbled.

'I'm sorry, Mr Henderson.'

'No, no. I am the fool. Thank you, sister.'

Slowly he turned his face towards mine and gave a series of nods, as though he were agreeing to a number of criticisms being levelled against him. I shook my head to say no. No, you are not foolish, Mr Henderson. We all make mistakes.

'I didn't think I'd live to see the roses,' he said.

'Maybe your friend Harold Fry has saved me after all.'

Sister Catherine lit tea lights for the tables, though for health and safety reasons she had to leave out the patient with the oxygen tank. She gave each of us a small vase of sweet williams from the Well-being Garden. She helped me to open my napkin and spread it over my lap. When the starters were carried through, I saw that Mr Henderson managed to swallow down two grapefruit segments. I had half of one.

Over chicken broth, Mr Henderson told me about his career as a teacher. He saw, in hindsight, that he had been too hard on his pupils. He believed he had projected on to them his disappointment in himself. His hand shook with the spoon, and some of the soup splashed his chin. 'Pardon me, pardon me,' he said. I could manage mine only with the help of Sister Lucy. Even so, I swallowed very little. As Mr Henderson spoke, she murmured words like 'Ah' and 'Well, now.'

He said, 'Years ago, I'd have chosen a good steak. Fine-cut chips. I imagine you'd have asked for the fish of the day, Miss Hennessy.'

I smiled. I'd have had kippers from the smokehouse at Craster and a slice of brown bread. We'd have sat in my sea garden with plates on our laps and helped ourselves to a crisp Sauvignon. I might have lit candles in turquoise glass lamps and hung them in the branches, so that everywhere in the garden there were deep blue eyes.

'I don't like fish,' said Sister Lucy. 'It's the faces that get me. I can't look. They give me the shivers.' To prove it, she shuddered and the plastic of her apron gave a rustle.

Mr Henderson told us about his ex-wife, Mary. It had been an unhappy marriage. Their divorce was difficult. Mr Henderson represented himself in court; Mary hired the services of a solicitor in London who was also his best friend. 'It would have been so much easier if she'd picked someone I disliked. As it was, they took me to the cleaners.' Here he paused to take his medication. 'I lost them both. My wife and my best friend. I fear this has made me a bitter man.'

'That's too sad, Mr Henderson,' said Sister Lucy.

'Ah,' he said. 'It's the way life goes.'

'What are you two up to down there?' shouted a ghost in a wide-brimmed straw hat. 'Making plans for Harold Fry?' She pointed to an embarrassed-looking young man beside her with a microphone. 'I'm on local radio tonight!'

'It's all getting a little overwhelming, isn't it?' said Mr Henderson quietly. And I nodded to show that yes, it was. 'I assume Harold Fry meant a great deal to you?'

Before I could answer, Sister Catherine interrupted with her trolley to offer a choice of desserts.

'I will take the green jelly, sister,' said Mr Henderson. 'Miss Hennessy, what can I tempt you to?'

I pointed to a small glass bowl.

'And Miss Hennessy will take the custard.'

'Squeezy cream?' asked Sister Catherine.

'Squeezy cream?' repeated Mr Henderson.

I shook my head.

'Her cup overfloweth,' said Mr Henderson.

'Her cup does what?' said Sister Lucy. She checked hurriedly beneath the table.

Mr Henderson passed me a fresh napkin. 'Years ago,' he said, 'I would have suggested a fine pudding wine, Miss Hennessy, followed by coffee and mints. Afterwards we might have had a walk along the estuary to watch the sunset. Did you do such things with Harold Fry?' Such was the disquiet in my mind, I could not lift my eyes though I felt him study me, long and hard, as if he were seeing right inside my heart. 'Oh I see,' he murmured at last. 'I see. That must have been very hard for you.'

'Desserts!' announced Sister Catherine, passing our bowls. 'Ding-a-ling!'

Mr Henderson managed even less of the final course than I did. He could take his jelly only in small spoonfuls, and he swallowed little. In the end he mashed it with his spoon and draped the bowl with his napkin. Briefly he dozed while I finished what I could of my custard.

'I wish you and I had met years ago,' he said. 'We might have enjoyed ourselves. But such is life. And maybe, years ago, you and I would not have noticed each other. We must be content with this.' He indicated to Sister Catherine that he was ready to leave. He lifted a sweet william out of his vase and placed it on my table.

I wrote in my notebook so that Sister Lucy could show him the message. **Thank you for having dinner with me, Mr Henderson.**

'Please,' he said. 'Call me Neville.' Sister Catherine wheeled him back to his room.

This morning Neville did not sit in his automatic recliner chair in the dayroom. He was not there this afternoon.

The undertaker's van—

Well. You know the rest.

I pressed Neville's flower between the pages of my notebook because I could not look after it, you see, in my garden.

AN IMPORTANT MESSAGE AND A BASKET OF WASHING

I was holding a bunch of flowers in my hand. White chrysanthemums in a plastic wrapping. 'Excuse me,' I called out. I remained at the gate to your garden. On the other side, your wife was hanging out the washing. At first she didn't notice me. She snatched items, one by one, from her basket and pegged them up on the line. She was wearing a housecoat, I remember that, and standing in weak sunlight. Behind her was a wreckage of splintered wooden planks, and smashed glass scattered every which way over the overgrown grass. I understood then that you had torn down your garden shed. I cast a glance at the windows of the house, wondering if you had heard me and were staring out, but they were hung with new net curtains. There was no sign of you.

Had you ripped down your shed before or after you smashed Napier's glass clowns? One act of violence had clearly not been enough. It looked as if you wanted that wreckage in your garden, you and Maureen. Or maybe I should say, it looked as if you needed it. You needed to see the

350

devastation inside you. To look out of your back window and see not a lawn and a fence, but chaos.

I'd known that facing Napier would be hard but I had also known, even at the outset, that the conversation with him could only end in one place, and that would be my resignation. But this was entirely different. Seeing your wife with her washing, the devastation around her, the nets blanking the windows, I had no idea any more what would come next. I turned to go and then I thought again of what I'd done. I had to find you and tell the truth.

'Excuse me,' I repeated. This time Maureen lifted her head. She furrowed her brow against the light and compressed her mouth, as if trying to understand whether or not she was supposed to know me. 'My name is Queenie Hennessy. I work at the brewery.' She made no reply. She pulled a pillowcase from her basket and, as before, she slung it over the line and trapped it beneath two pegs.

Maureen's hair had been cut short, like a boy's, though it looked a hatchet job to me. I wondered if she'd done it herself and I thought of David's hair, the last time I'd seen him. Her face was thin, very pale.

I held out my chrysanthemums. I had no idea whether I intended to leave them for you or give them to her or perhaps they were really in some strange way for David. I still don't know the truth about why I'd bought those flowers on my way to your house.

'Is Harold home?' I called. There was a path of crazy paving between us. I wondered if she would invite me beyond the gate. She didn't.

'Harold?' She repeated your name as though there were something strange about the way I'd said it.

I told her I had something to say to her husband. It was very important, I told her.

'But he isn't here.'

This was not the answer I was expecting. It hadn't occurred to me I would not find you. 'Where is he?'

'I've no idea. Out. At work. I haven't a clue.'

Maureen returned to her washing. She pulled a towel from the basket, and maybe it got stuck in with the other items because her face twisted in annoyance as she gave it a hard yank. She threw it over the line and slipped two pegs from her pocket, snapping them over the towel.

'Do you know when he'll be back?'

'No.' She replied without looking at me. 'I haven't a clue.'

Overhead a flock of gulls soared past, making a racket. One of them had something large in its beak – a heel of bread, I think – and it made a wild noise that sounded like *Go away, go away*. The others spun and twisted around the gull with the bread, shouting, *Haw haw haw*. We both glanced up, Maureen and I. 'Bloody birds,' said Maureen. 'They're vermin, really.' She looked very pointedly at me. The eyes that held mine were wide and fierce, not wearied by grief, as I had expected, but spiked and charged with it. It was late summer, but my spine gave a shiver. I found I couldn't return her gaze. 'What do you want?' she said.

In a rush, I asked if she could give you a message. I told her that you'd been involved in some trouble at the brewery. It was all dealt with now, I said. No need for her concern. I hadn't intended to tell the whole story, but as she was not speaking, as she was only watching me with that detached expression of anger, I blurted out everything. I was hoping to touch her in some way, I was hoping for her sympathy, and the more she didn't say, the more I told her. I explained that you'd shattered Napier's prize possessions and that I had taken the blame and would have to leave Kingsbridge. Grief did terrible things to people, I said. And even as I spoke, I felt ridiculous. Who was I, to offer platitudes about the appalling loss she was suffering?

She kept staring at me, hard-eyed. I noticed her hands were tightly curled in fists.

I held out the flowers. 'Please,' I said. 'They're for you.'

'For me?'

'I'm so sorry.' And saying those words, I began to cry. It was the last thing she needed, I was sure. I tried to blow my nose and make light of my tears but I could feel her watching me and I would say that something in her softened. Maybe she needed a person to cry in order to have any sort of real conversation.

Maureen came forward. She stopped on one side of the gate while I remained on the other. Now that we were close, I could see the red rims of her eyes. Obviously she hadn't slept. 'Why?' she said. 'Why are you sorry? It wasn't your fault.'

I was about ready to scream. 'Please,' I said. 'Take them.'

Maureen took the flowers. Briefly she touched the shaggy white petals. 'Dead man's flowers,' she murmured. She gave a bitter laugh as though the joke were meant only for herself. 'You're Queenie Hennessy, aren't you?'

I wondered if she'd taken in anything of what I'd told her. I said, 'Will you tell your husband I said goodbye?'

She made no reply at first, she only caught me with her moss-green eyes. 'I suppose you're in love with him.' Her voice was quiet, restrained. I felt the opposite: my face was on fire.

Maureen did not flinch or look away from me. 'Does he even know?'

'No. Not at all. I would never—' I didn't get any further. I couldn't say it.

'Oh,' she murmured, as if despite myself I had told her the whole story. 'Well, take him. If you want him. Go inside the house. Pack his bag. Go on.' She threw a look over her shoulder, back at those white-bleached windows. And then she returned to me with her wild, angry eyes. 'Go on,' she spat. 'Just go.'

I was completely thrown. I had a picture of you and me, side by side, you with your driving gloves and me in the passenger seat, and I couldn't help myself, I started to shake. Even though the leaves were beginning to turn, we were standing in sunlight, Maureen and I. Nevertheless I felt nothing but the cold. It was in my hands, my skin, my hair. It shot through and through me. 'Or maybe *I'll* go,' she said with a bitter laugh. 'How about that? Would that suit you better?'

She turned and marched back to her washing. She threw my flowers on top of the basket, then something caught her eye and she stooped and gently eased out a T-shirt. I knew it at once. It was one of David's. For the second time her face softened while she hung it on the line, while she straightened the T-shirt and smoothed it down, as if he were inside it and she was checking him for creases.

I realized, then, that her grief was as boundless as the sky. It was a form of insanity, and yet it wasn't because it was all there was. No matter where Maureen went, what she did, what she said, what she looked at, her loss was everywhere. There could be no getting away from it.

'I don't have any decent photographs of him,' she said. For a stupid moment I thought we were still talking about you, then I understood, of course, that we weren't. David was all that there was in her mind. 'And now I'm beginning to forget what he looked like. It's only a few weeks since I lost him but when I try to see him in my head, little parts of him already sort of blur and I can't get him right. How can my head do that to me?' She spoke with unconcealed bewilderment.

I didn't know what to say. Telling you the story now, I see Maureen didn't expect or even want me to reply. She only needed to voice the words and for someone, anyone, to hear them. She wasn't expecting me to help, because there was no help to be had. It could have been me standing there, it could have been a neighbour; we were all the same because the person we were not was David.

She straightened the T-shirt sleeves. 'My son went to the Lake District. It was OK then. I had a picture of where he was. When it was night, I could say to myself, It's night with him too. The same with the day. But this time I haven't a clue. I've no idea where he is. All I know is that I'll never see him again.' She began to cry. It was small at first but quickly it became angular, furious bursts, like shouts. She stood beneath the pale blue sky, her slight figure giving spasmodic judders. It felt wrong to stay, it was too private. But equally it would be an abandonment to walk away. So I simply stood at your garden gate, trying not to bow my head and weep with her. When she had done with her crying, she wiped her face angrily.

She said, 'So if you think you want my husband, take him. But if you don't, clear out of our lives.'

Maureen stooped to her washing basket. This time she hung out a selection of men's socks. They belonged to you. Gone was the gentleness with which she had hung David's T-shirt. She whipped each sock out and flipped it over the line, leaving a long space between them, so that they looked like a row of separate flattened feet. There was something so barren and solitary about that laundry. She glanced down at what was now presumably an empty washing basket with a bunch of chrysanthemums inside it. And even though she had only just finished hanging her washing out, she began snapping off the pegs and ripping off each sock and chucking them, one by one, back in her washing basket. After a few minutes the line was empty once more. I wondered if she'd explain what she'd done but she didn't, she only narrowed her eyes and stared at that basket of wet washing with my flowers somewhere inside it, as if she hated the whole bloody lot.

'Will you remember? To tell him I said goodbye?' I called. My heart was in my mouth.

She spun her head towards me. Eyes blazing. 'Haven't you gone yet?' she shouted.

I backed away at speed. I walked so fast down Fossebridge Road I could feel my legs trembling and I still wasn't quick enough. Only when I was near the bottom of the hill did I stop and glance back. There she was, up by that washing line, pegging out her washing all over again. It dawned on me that she could have been doing it for hours. She might continue for days. And even though she had told me that in effect she did not love you, that I could take you if I wanted, I saw the heavy weight that clung to her and I knew that no matter what happened, she was right. I did not want to take you away from her. I'd never wanted that.

I had set out to love you quietly, from the sidelines. Instead I had put myself in the middle of your life, and look what terrible damage I had gone and done.

I took one last look at Maureen. She wiped her eyes, and blew her nose. Then she lifted up her empty basket. She carried it on her hip towards the back door of the house, carefully stepping over the wilderness of broken glass and wooden slats. She did not turn back.

I let you go, Harold, because you were not mine and you never would be. You belonged to your wife.

THE LAST ONE TO GO

In the night, my door opened and a needle of light crossed the room. A tiny silhouette emerged, so slight that at first I thought a child was visiting.

'I need to find my bed.'

It was Finty.

She darted into the room like a luminous scrap and I realized she was naked. She kept pacing. She looked in my cupboard and behind my curtains. She didn't seem to know I was there.

'Where has it gone? Where the fuck have they put it?'

No, no, I called. I tried to voice her name, but that didn't stop her. She checked behind the door, and not finding her bed there, she got on all fours and peered under my chair. Her bare buttocks were two pointed knuckles.

Turning, she appeared to notice my bed for the first time. Only she didn't see me in it. She pulled back the covers and jumped in beside me. Her body was white and cold. Her teeth were chattering.

'I'm so fucking hot,' she said. Even though she was lying down now, she couldn't keep still.

She kept flapping at the sheets and batting them with her feet and hands.

'Finty?' I said. 'Be the heat.'

I don't know how, but she heard.

Finty turned her face to mine, and it was as though it were the first time she'd spotted me, because she smiled. She had on no lipstick, no painted eyebrows. Her face had the look of a mask.

'Flames in my head, Queenie,' she said.

'I know, I know. You must be the flames.'

'I don't feel so good.'

I said, 'Don't fight the heat, Finty. Do you hear me? Be a part of it.'

Suddenly she became so still I thought she must have fallen asleep. Perhaps she did briefly. I turned my head to check and the whites of her eyes were shining through the dark as large as ping-pong balls. She gave a smile. No teeth, of course. Even so, I wondered if she was getting better. Certainly her hand no longer felt cold. I could feel the warmth from her feet.

'Hold me, gal,' she said.

I put my arm over her. She was as small as bone.

'Sing, gal,' she said.

I didn't know what else to do so I began to hum. 'Three Blind Mice'. I couldn't think of anything else. There was only the rattling inside her chest.

She said, 'I've had the best time of my life in this place.' She became very still in order to draw up a new breath. It was like something heavy being pulled across the floor. In the silence that followed,

I feared I had heard her last breath and I felt her loss inside me and thought I would howl, but then another breath came from her, as long and heavy as the first. I held her closer.

I listened to the rhythm of her broken breathing until mine followed hers and we were at last the same. After that my mind began to drift. I thought back to the morning when your first letter came and everything changed. I remembered the day Finty made me take the nutritional drink. I thought about the other things we'd done together. The funeral plan and the banner. I thought of all Finty's hats. The green turban, the sou'wester, the pink cowboy hat. She smiled. Did she? I don't know. Maybe it was pain. Whatever it was, she closed her eyes. I kept her hand in mine and I slept too.

When I woke, Sister Lucy was carrying me down the corridor. She didn't need the wheelchair. Morning light fell into the corridor in bright pools. I mustn't take it too hard, she kept saying.

I didn't have to ask why.

It is 22 June.

The undertaker arrived in time for morning coffee.

A POSTCARD

Three days have gone by since I last wrote to you. Even though I was not well enough to leave my room, I gave Finty a good woman's burial in my mind. I pictured bright hollyhocks from my garden on her coffin. There was rosemary for remembrance and gillyflowers too. I gave her a gospel choir, singing 'My Heart Will Go On' by Céline Dion. There were alcopops in glasses with straws, and everyone wore red and yellow and danced in the car park, exactly as she'd wished. A poor state of health has kept me since then from writing to you in a quiet, good way.

My pilgrims have slipped free and gone on without me. I think of Finty dying at my side, and it is not frightening, but there are so many things I wish I had said to her instead of grunting 'Three Blind Mice'. Things don't so much end as disappear. They don't so much begin as turn up. You think there will be a time to say goodbye, but people have often gone before you know about it. And I don't just mean the dying.

I rarely visit the dayroom, and when I do, I sit apart from the others in a chair near the window.

I do not learn the names of the new patients. I do not go to music therapy or allow Sister Lucy to paint my nails. I sit here and I wait, and every day that I sit I wonder where you are and if you will get here and sometimes it is too much, all this looking ahead, all this wondering.

'Harold Fry has sent a postcard,' said Sister Lucy. 'He's left Newcastle. He completed a detour via Hexham. Now he is heading for Cambo. He is almost here, Queenie. Almost here now. Do you want to look at the picture?'

I look, but I confess it is only a blur and I don't see.

I see only the pink of Sister Lucy's hand and it is full of life.

THE DOG LIKE A LEAF

A dog has turned up. It's a scrappy thing, with wiry hair and a curled tail, the colour of an autumn leaf. It keeps bringing me stones. It places them on my bed and waits for me to throw them. Go away, I tell it. I'm not playing. But then I move and the stone tumbles off the bed, drops to the floor and rolls across the room. The dog trots off to fetch it. The dog picks the stone up in its mouth and returns to my bed. It lifts itself on its back legs and places the stone very carefully beside my fingers. It sits again and watches my hand, its mouth panting a little, its head cocked to one side, as if waiting for a stone also requires careful listening.

'You see, you like my game,' says the dog. 'It's so much fun once you get the hang of it.' The dog lifts a paw.

Shoo, I say. Go home. Or play with the horse over there. She's only eating the curtains. I don't want you.

The dog wags its tail.

'I can wait as long as you like,' he says. 'Waiting is such fun, once you get the hang of it. It's all part of the game in the end.'

A LOT OF FUSS AND BOTHER

I was napping in the sun when I was woken by chanting and a brass band. It didn't sound like the nuns and neither did it sound like a music therapy session. Other patients began to notice the noise and they peered in the direction of the gates to the hospice. Their friends and families crossed the grass towards the drive, in order to get a better look. Beyond the gates, there seemed to be a group of people massing on the pavement, with banners, flags and poster boards. There were many bright colours, theatrical costumes and musical instruments. There also seemed to be a hot dog stand and a gorilla dancing with a woman in a swimsuit.

I assumed it must be the drugs again.

'Whatever is going on out there?' asked Sister Philomena, glancing up from her reading book. I lifted my hands to my eye in order to shield it from the sun.

On the pavement outside a man in a hat called into a megaphone for silence. I couldn't hear much of what he said after that because a wind took up in the garden and all the trees rattled. Mostly what

I heard was 'We've done it, folks. We got here.' I heard that several times.

Then, of all the strange things, they began chanting my name. 'Queen-ie. Queen-ie.'

'Excuse me a moment,' said Sister Philomena. She removed her reading glasses and rose from her deck chair.

I watched her walking briskly along the drive to the gates. As the crowd caught sight of her, they turned to her in the way that waiting family members greet a doctor in the anticipation of life-changing news, putting on best smiles as if that will affect the verdict. There was further applause, though she lifted her hand for silence and shook her head in a no-messing way. She buzzed the gates open and stepped through, carefully shutting them behind her. A sudden flash of cameras met her.

I have no idea what she said to the group, but I could see the tall man take her hand in his and give a sombre nod. He led a slow handclap, and I can't think how but it seemed to become a round of applause for himself. There were further camera flashes, further voices in the megaphone, further rounds of applause. The group began to disband, some moving down towards the seafront, others heading in the direction of town. I saw them waving to one another as they left, clapping one another on the shoulders, high-fiving, wishing one another a safe homeward journey. Others drifted with their arms clasped above their heads in a gesture of victory.

When Sister Philomena rejoined us in the garden, she was carrying another gift basket of muffins and a bunch of lilies. Her face was flushed, as if she had just run a long distance.

'What an arrogant shit that man is,' she said. She glanced at me and winked. 'I didn't say that, of course.'

This evening Sister Lucy wheeled me into the dayroom to watch the television news. We all assembled, the patients and their families and friends, the volunteers and nuns. There was a speech to the camera from the man in the hat, followed by footage of Sister Philomena at the gates.

'It's you!' said one of the patients. 'You're famous!'

'I do hope not,' said Sister Philomena quietly.

Behind her the camera showed a view of the garden and a man watering the grass.

'That's me!' shouted a volunteer.

Someone cheered, and an image of you flashed on to the screen. Now there was only silence. You were walking down a busy road but your shoulders were stooped as if you were bearing an invisible heavy load and you seemed so terribly tired. Cars swerved to avoid you.

The man with the hat was back and he was telling the interviewer it was a shame. It was a shame Harold Fry had had to give up, 'due to fatigue and like, complicated emotional reasons.

But Queenie is alive, that's the main thing. It was lucky that me and the guys were there to step in.' Two boys swung from his hands, and the man stooped to lift them into the air like human trophies.

'Oh, enough of this nonsense.' Sister Philomena snapped off the television with the remote control.

No one spoke. We got very busy, studying our hands, the view from the window, that sort of thing. Gradually the patients began to peel away with their loved ones. Even the nuns and volunteers turned their attention to other things. It was only me left in the middle of the room, staring at the black empty screen of the television. I could still see your face, the pained look in your eyes, your cheeks like hollows, your wild sprouting beard.

One of the volunteers moved with weary resignation to the Harold Fry corner and began to remove the drawing pins. One by one he took down the postcards, and began to roll up Finty's WELCOME banner.

Sister Lucy knelt at my side. She wiped the tears from my face.

'Would you like to help me finish my jigsaw?' she said.

We fitted the last pieces along the Scottish borders. She said she wondered what jigsaw she would choose next. And after a little while she said, 'He's still walking, Queenie. I feel it in my bones.'

The vigil keepers have gone. Tonight the only sound I hear is the rustling of leaves and the sea.

It is you and me now. Me waiting. You walking. From the look of things, Harold, we are down to basics.

A LAST-DITCH ATTEMPT TO STOP

'You think you are the only person in this world who is waiting?' said Sister Mary Inconnue. She was pacing. I wished she would stop, because the light was bright at the window and it is hard sometimes to keep up with a pacing nun. I found I kept losing her. She said, 'The world is full of people like you, waiting for change. Waiting for a job. A lover. Waiting for a bite to eat. A drink of water. Waiting for the winning lottery ticket. So don't think about the end. Picture those people instead. Picture their waiting.'

I have to admit I sighed. I shook my head. How does this help? I said with my eye.

She sat. At least there was that. Then she said, 'Because if you picture other people like you, you will no longer be alone. And when you share, you see that your own sorrow is not so big or special. You are only another person feeling sad, and soon it will pass and you will be another person, feeling happy. It takes the sting out of life, I find, when you realize you are not alone.'

Sister Mary Inconnue pulled a bag of red sweets

out of her pocket and sucked on one for a long time. It must have been pleasant, because she kept swinging her feet. Eventually she said, 'It will be a few more days before Harold arrives. It will be a few more days before you finish your letter. But you know what you have to do in order to get there? In order to keep waiting?'

I groaned. I didn't know, but I could already sense I wasn't going to like it.

She leaned a little closer, and her breath smelt of aniseed. 'It is no good looking ahead to the end. It is no good thinking about how life will get better once you have a new television or a new job. You must stop hoping for change. You must simply be it.'

Be the change? It was all too much.

Sister Mary Inconnue picked up her pages and made a few small changes with her correction pen.

'Here I am. Here you are. There is a pigeon in the tree. And yes, today is a hard one.'

The night is still. It listens. A bird cries, maybe an owl. One of the duty nurses says it has been a long night. Anyone want a cuppa? 'I can't wait to put my feet up,' says another.

I picture the nurse who wants to put her feet up. In my mind I fetch her a chair and I go to my beach house to boil the kettle for her cup of tea, just as I would have done once if she had stopped at my sea garden and we had got talking, she and I.

In my mind we sit next to each other, the nurse who is waiting to put her feet up and me, the woman who is waiting for Harold Fry. And then, in my mind, other people join us. A man waiting for good news. A student waiting for exam results. A woman waiting for a child. Take a seat. Take a seat. Look at my sea garden, while we're at it.

We wait. We wait. It is not so hard any more. Sister Mary Inconnue was right.

I WONDER WHO I AM NOW

'Weren't you Queenie Hennessy?' said a woman in the dayroom. 'The one that Harold Fry was walking to save?'

The woman was visiting a patient. She had brought a blue teddy bear.

A POETIC INTERLUDE

There once was a good man called Fry
Who wanted his friend not to die.
He told her to wait,
Walked straight out the gate,
With no bloody map, just a tie.

There was a sweet boy that I knew
Whose friends were incredibly few.
Strange thoughts filled his head
So he went to the shed
And hung till his red lips turned blue.

There once was a nun with a wimple
Who told me that waiting was simple
Just write in your book—

'This is what happens when you take the big drugs,' said Sister Mary Inconnue. 'You make no sense whatsoever.'
She packs away her typewriter and eats an orange instead.

A FLY

I heard a fly buzz.

It travels in short, straight lines, as if it is contained within an invisible box above my head. It buzzes on a line to the north, stops abruptly, and turns to the east, then turns again and travels to the south, at which point it turns again and buzzes along a west-facing line until it reaches its original point of departure. It has been doing this all day. It doesn't seem to tire. It just buzzes in the stillness.

THE LAUGHING TREE

It was a warm morning and Sister Lucy suggested I might like to sit outside. It would do me good, she said, to feel a little sun on my face. She lifted me gently into my wheelchair and took me to the garden. She fetched a chair and sat with me under the shade of a tree. She held my hand.

Sister Lucy began to tell me about her childhood. I tried very hard to listen but sometimes, I admit, I closed my eyes and listened from inside my head. If she hadn't been called to God, she'd have been a beautician. I opened my eyes and smiled and she smiled too.

She said, 'You can love God and have nice hair too.'

Then she told me it will be her birthday on Tuesday, and I thought, I won't be here. I won't be here on Tuesday. I am almost gone already. Tuesday seemed months away. Almost a different season.

When I woke the sun had moved and Sister Mary Inconnue had taken Sister Lucy's place.

We stayed for a while like that. Not saying

anything. Just looking at the garden and sitting beneath the shade of the giant tree.

Suddenly Sister Mary Inconnue let out a hiccup. She slapped her hand to her mouth but another one followed and another. I realized that what she was doing was laughing.

'What is it?' I asked. Something like that.

A further laugh erupted from her with a gigantic splutter. She had to grip her stomach and lift her feet. Rocking this way and that, she pointed upwards. *Hoo hoo hoo*, she went, while still pointing up at the tree. That was all she could manage in the way of communication.

Why was it so funny? The tree? But even as I thought that and glanced upwards, I was beginning to see the funny side.

'Look at the branches. Look at the leaves. When you really look, you see how fantastic it is. It's so perfect you have to laugh!' She guffawed.

Now that she'd said it, I couldn't see how I hadn't noticed before. The tree above us was a canopy of bright lime leaves, each one shaped like an eye and with perfect crinkle-cut edges. Where the sun caught them they shone luminous, while those in shade hung a deeper green. I took in the solid torso of the trunk, the curls and wrinkles in the grey bark, the milky covering of moss where the sun could not reach. I gazed at the exuberant bow of the five central branches, like sturdy shoulders, and then I moved my eye to the entanglement of twigs and leaves. I watched the insects busy in the white clusters of blossom, the birds balancing in the upper branches. Sister Mary Inconnue was right. It was the most marvellous thing, that tree, now that we sat and took notice. It was hilarious.

We sat, weeping with laughter. And then a wind took up and the great branches trembled and the leaves went a-rattling. *Ha ha,* went the tree, look at those funny ladies. One with a cornette. One in a wheelchair. Look at the beauty of them.

Sister Mary Inconnue wiped her eyes with her handkerchief. 'Dear oh dear. We really should sit and laugh at trees more often.'

A BAD NIGHT

I can't sleep. I lie still and stillness is too much and I have to get up. But when I am up, that is not right either. Nothing is the thing I am hunting for.

Last night was confused. I must have risen in the middle of the night, because the duty nurse found me in the corridor. She helped me into bed, and for a moment I thought: Sleep. It will come now.

But I was wrong. Lying still was out of the question. It was like hanging upside down when you should be on your feet, and I was soon up again. I said I had to find Sister Mary Inconnue.

By this time I was already pulling open my cupboard. It surprised me, the strength I had. Maybe I am getting better, I thought, maybe this is an improvement. I couldn't for the life of me remember where we keep Sister Mary Inconnue.

The duty nurse took my arm. She said, 'You need sleep, Queenie. Remember, Harold Fry is almost here. We expect him tomorrow.'

I have to admit I had no idea what she was talking about. I was thinking only about finishing the letter, you see.

The duty nurse guided me back to bed. She redressed my wound with fresh bandages. She bathed my closed eye. She cleaned my mouth and fetched a pain patch.

A little later Sister Mary Inconnue came to help. She lay at my side on the mattress, and when I tried to get up she spread her body over mine and lay on top of me, her face beside my face, her arms and legs outstretched.

I thought, Help, help, help. I am being smothered by a six-foot nun with a pointy cornette.

And then I felt the closeness of her, I smelt her breathing, and I slept.

THE VISITOR

On waking this morning I felt a claw stuck on my arm and then I realized it was my hand. Sister Mary Inconnue rubbed my fingers and blew on the joints, and still it was no good. I tried to write her a message, but it was arduous and I kept losing grip of the pencil. How could I possibly continue with my letter?

I don't want HF to see me like this. After all, I had done what I was supposed to do. I had waited.

'But he has to see you. That is the end of his journey. It won't be complete until he has seen you.'

Can't you tell him I died?

She read my message and laughed. 'No,' she said. 'You funny girl, I can't. Besides, you haven't finished your letter. You have not finished your journey either, Queenie Hennessy.'

I was beginning to cry and I didn't want her to see. All the time I have been writing, a part of me has been calm, because so long as there was something else to tell you, I did not have to write the end. But now there is nothing else left but the last part of my confession, and I thought I wouldn't be frightened any more but I am, Harold. I am sorry.

Sister Mary Inconnue placed the pencil back in my hand, but it rolled straight from my fingers. She tried again. Same thing. I felt a flush of relief. I thought, I am not up to it. I am too weak for the end. She will see that now.

We were interrupted by quick footsteps along the corridor. My door flew open.

'Harold Fry is coming! He's here!' Sister Lucy burst into the room. 'I've just seen him!'

'Well, excuse us,' said Sister Mary Inconnue, a little put out, but the young nun was so excited she ran straight past. She rushed to my window and pulled back the curtains. The rings gave a tiny shriek on the pole. Standing on tiptoes, she peered down towards the drive, her fingers spread wide on the windowsill. 'Yes, Queenie! It's him! He's here at last!'

My skin prickled, as if I were caught in a North Sea wind. No, no, I am not ready, I thought. This is too soon. My letter. My letter is not finished—

From her watchpost at the window, Sister Lucy began to report on your progress: 'He is going slowly. But— He has a beard. And his hair is quite long. His shoes are—' She bundled her eyes into a squint. 'Oh, my goodness. His shoes are— His shoes, they— They are taped to his feet. They are taped on with this blue stuff. Poor man. I wonder why.' With each of these observations her voice grew more quiet. It was like hearing a person run out of batteries. 'Oh, my goodness,' she half whispered. 'He looks terrible.' For a little while, she said no more. We remained in silence, all three of us, waiting for the buzzer at the door, waiting for your arrival.

Sister Mary Inconnue cocked her head. I heard the creaking of old water pipes, the intermittent *peep peep* of a bird in the Well-being Garden. There was even a child's laughter. But no buzz.

Sister Lucy shot her hands to her mouth. 'Oh, no. What's he doing? He's leaving.'

Leaving? I looked to Sister Mary Inconnue, but she merely nodded, as if this came as no surprise and was in fact the right thing to do, or at least to be expected. 'Why?' asked Sister Lucy. 'Why didn't he come inside?'

Sister Lucy shook the folds of her robes, though there was nothing stuck to them. 'Well, he'll be back soon,' she said. 'I'm sure he will. I'll go and investigate. You wait here, Queenie.'

As if I am in danger of going anywhere. Sister Mary Inconnue and I shared a look of understanding.

Because I knew now. I knew why you could not come inside. It is the same for both of us, isn't it? We were each as frightened as the other. And, you know, if I could turn round and walk back the way I've come, I probably would. I have waited so long and you have walked so far that neither of us is in any hurry to arrive. Endings, it seems, are not all they're cracked up to be.

'You are going to have to make the first move, Queenie,' said Sister Mary Inconnue. I frowned as though I didn't understand, but she was having none of it. 'It is time to tell your last story about David.'

When Sister Lucy came to draw my curtains for the evening, she did not mention your visit. She did not mention that you had walked away again. I pointed to my hand. I pointed to the fresh bandages and dressings on the bedside table. I pointed to the pencil.

Sister Lucy frowned. She glanced to the door, as if she were frightened someone would come in. 'No,' she said. 'No, Queenie. I can't do that.'

The duty nurse interrupted to examine my face. She cleaned the lesions and bathed my eye. She asked if I needed morphine or the pain patches, but I shook my head. I need to have a clear mind.

With the duty nurse gone, Sister Lucy sat beside me. Her clean white robes gave a tiny creak. 'OK, Queenie,' she said. 'I'll do it.'

Sister Lucy took my hand and the pencil, and as she unrolled the length of bandage I watched her face. The scraping of dark hair above her ears, the puff of pale skin under her eyes. She looked tired. She wound the bandage round and round my hand and the pencil, carefully smoothing it so that there would not be a fold that might press hard and cause me further pain.

'I wanted to understand you for so long, Queenie,'

she said. 'Tonight I sort of wish I didn't. Do you need your notebook?' She passed it and turned to a fresh page.

I wrote for her: **Happy Birthday.** It took a while to get used to the pencil strapped to my fingers.

Peering at my words, Sister Lucy gave a frown. 'But it isn't today,' she said. 'It's next week, remember?'

I made a sign with my left hand to show her to remove the page. I folded the page and pressed it into her fingers. Sister Lucy gave a gulp and a little shake of her head, as though she were stopping something from coming to her throat.

She asked if I would like anything else, if she could brush my hair to help me rest, but I shook my head. 'Shall I sit with you?' she said. 'I can sit here as long as you like.'

Once again, I shook my head.

The light thickens at the window. Night is almost here. I must keep writing.

THE LAST CONFESSION
OF MISS Q HENNESSY

Twenty years ago, Harold, you buried your son. It is not something a father should have to do. And I was to blame. I am to blame.

Over my life, I have done many things to absolve my guilt. I saved your job. I ran away. I lived alone. I made you a sea garden. And there are times, it is true, when the pain has not been so intense. It has been dimly present, like a low-energy lightbulb in the hall. There have been many other days, other nights, however, when no matter what I do, I cannot get away from the one thing I wish to escape – and I will never get away from it because, of course, that thing is me.

David was with me the night he died.

You don't know this.

If it weren't for me, he might—

I can't even write it.

I have not been able to say it for twenty years. Why should I now? But Sister Mary Inconnue sits at my side, and every time I push away my note-book, my pencil, she smiles and whispers, 'Go on.'

I must give you this last piece of the story, she says. It is time to put my affairs in order and let go of them.

Forgive me, Harold Fry.

THE LAST CONFESSION OF MISS Q HENNESSY (2ND ATTEMPT)

It was late summer. David was twenty-one.

He had made his trip to the Lake District and he had returned.

A week passed, and there was no visit. No calls. I even wondered if he was backpacking again. I asked you once. I said, 'How's David?' and you frowned at your hands and said, 'Good. Good.'

One early evening the phone rang in the hallway. When I answered I heard the pips, as if someone were struggling to slot coins into a public telephone box in time. About half an hour later there was a loud pummelling at the front door. He seemed to be trying to kick his way through it. I have to admit, I didn't want to see David. I'd had a long day at work and I was tired. I am not trying to excuse what I did that evening. I am only trying very hard to explain exactly how it was. The banging came again. I twisted the key in my lock and pulled open the front door.

David had lost more weight, but what shocked me was his hair. He had shaved it so short it looked as if there had been an assault on his head. It looked painful. There were fresh red cuts where the razor had nicked his scalp. I said it was good to see him. I was trying to be polite, trying to keep the conversation in a safe place. He asked if he could come in and talk.

David's hands were shaking. He had a gin bottle, but he could barely keep hold of it. I took the bottle from him. It was half empty.

Only as David reeled into the light of the hall did I notice how bad his eyes were, so raw and sore that the skin round them was like tender bruises. He must have been crying for a long time. 'Can I have my bottle back now?' he said.

He was very quiet for most of that evening, almost inaudible, like a person shuffling through words. He sat in the armchair by the heater, hunched up inside his coat. He didn't take it off. He said he was hoping to join the army, hence the haircut. It seemed unlikely. He could hardly walk in a straight line.

David told me he'd got some pills from the doctor. The doctor? I asked. Yeah, he said. The doctor. And when he told me to stop watching him, it was giving him the creeps, I said I was relieved, that was all. I was glad he'd seen a doctor.

At one point I was talking about music – I had just borrowed the record of Purcell songs from the library – and he said, 'Do you mind if I take my pills now? I get the depression.' And the way he said it, simply like that, made it sound like a cold. He asked if I knew about the depression, and I said yes, I felt low too sometimes. Everyone does, I told him. Did I have pills? he asked.

'No,' I said. 'It isn't like that for me.' I didn't want him coming too close. I was trying to protect myself. And the truth is, I've never needed pills. We are all wired differently. Sometimes I think that depression must be like a dance in your head and anything can trigger it, if you know that dance.

David tugged three pill bottles out of his coat pocket. He read out the labels and told me what they were for. He emptied the pills on to his lap, then swallowed them back with gin.

'Don't you need water?' I said.

He laughed. I was concerned at the number of pills.

'Do your parents know you're taking all these?'

He told me that Maureen had accompanied him to the doctor, though he'd asked her not to go inside. 'Mother likes it when I'm happy,' he said. He tried to slip the pills back into his pocket, but he couldn't seem to find the opening and in the end I did it for him.

A little later he asked again what I knew about depression and how I thought he should deal with it and I said something like, 'Well, you know, it always passes.' I hope I didn't say, What goes up must come down, but I was in that area.

'Yeah,' he said. He had clearly stopped listening. He didn't say anything for a long time. He just sat in the chair while I tidied up and washed the dishes, and every time I went past him, he was drinking from the bottle he'd brought in with him. I put on a record.

David jerked up his head like a dog when it's heard something outside. 'What's that music?'

It was the song 'O Solitude'. He made me play the track again. Then again and again. Until that point I hadn't really listened to it. I'd just had it as a nice, elegant sound in the background.

David pulled up his knees and sank his head. 'How can the guy make loneliness sound so neat?' he said. 'For me, it's just this vacuum. It's everywhere.'

'Do you want anything else?' I asked because I wanted him gone now.

But David rose to his feet. He began to sway to the music. When he asked me to join him, I said no, I didn't know how to dance to that sort of music. It was a Baroque song, I said, not a waltz. Well, you just listen to the tune and you move, he shouted. He had passed from apathy to something more jagged. He wagged his head as if he still had proper long hair and could swing it from side to side. As he moved he drank from the bottle, only now that he was on his feet he was swaying and throwing the alcohol in spills over his coat and my carpet.

'I think you ought to stop drinking,' I said.

I tried to take the bottle but he lifted it over my head and laughed, just as he had done before he left for university when he read my letter and took, among other things, my poems and my egg whisk. Then he stopped laughing and curled his lip. 'Just dance,' he shouted.

I stood back. I was frightened. I did a small waltz on the opposite side of the room. In my confusion, in my need for you, I lifted up my arms, as if you were there. I rested them on your shoulders. I looked into your blue, blue eyes.

When the record stopped, I realized I was still standing like that, looking up at you.

The noise that came from David was a high-pitched yelp. I twisted to face him. He was pointing at me. He was snorting with laughter. His body was all screwed up with it.

'You sad old bitch,' he howled. 'Father will never love you.'

Everything seemed to melt. The floor, the walls. I threw out both my hands to steady myself on the frame of the kitchen door.

'I don't know what you mean.'

'You do. You love him. You always did.' He spat those words.

As I hung there, my heart wild, my head spinning, I tried to work out what I felt. Anger, yes. Betrayed, that too. Stupid. So, so stupid. But most of all what I felt was intense pain. David knew my secret. Of course he knew. He'd known all along. When he'd asked about my poems and I'd replied that they were written for a man from my past, he was only playing with me. He was an intelligent young man. For all his selfishness, he was astute as a knife. Of course he'd guessed the truth. My answer and my discomfort had only confirmed what he suspected. I thought I had seen David for what he was. But David had seen me too.

And he was right. He was right when he said you'd never love me. No matter what I did, no matter how many years I kept silent, I would always be the woman who sat in your car and told riddles from Christmas crackers and sang backwards and offered you mints. I'd told myself for nearly four years that this was enough, that I could live with it. That I could remain at your side and ask for nothing in return, but as your son laughed I saw myself through his eyes, I saw myself through your eyes, the woman in a brown wool suit, and I knew I couldn't keep going. Not any more. It came as a shock. A terrible, painful shock. I had hoped to find safety in loving you, and look at me. I was a joke.

I groped my way through the kitchen door to the sink, where I poured water into a glass. I had to get away from him. Sometimes we reject the people who tell the truth and it is not because they are wrong. It is because we can't bear to hear.

I let the tap run. I watched the water cascade over the rim of my glass and bubble over my hands. The water became colder and colder. Ice. My fingers burned with the cold of it. But nothing topped the pain inside me.

'What are you doing?' David was at the doorway, blocking me in. He pulled out a cigarette. He lit it, and two snorts of tobacco smoke shot from his nose. He was like a storm, pressing in on me. I have watched the storms since, when I worked in my sea garden. I have noticed the rain clouds drawing over the earth like a slate tablecloth and the wind beating at the black sea and tossing the gulls up and down like twists of white paper. I have stood in those storms, drenched, and I have thought of David.

I said, 'Please leave me now, David. I don't feel so good.'

But he didn't. He moved closer. He reached for me and clung on to my shoulder and bowed his head. His fingers squeezed my skin. I did not want him gripping my shoulder and stinking of pain. I had no idea what he would do next.

'David?' I said. 'You're hurting me.'

'I don't feel good either.' His voice was low.

I took a deep breath. I said gently, 'It's because you're drunk. You need to go home. You probably shouldn't drink at all. Not with those pills you're taking.'

'Oh, quit that. You sound like the parents.' David swung away from me, crashing once into the table, then he righted himself and lurched out of the kitchen.

I followed because I was frightened for him. He ran at my wall and thumped it with his hand, then he threw out his booted foot and kicked my chair so violently that it jumped up and fell, its little legs pointing up into the air like a beast on its back. His eyes were dark and wide, as if he were standing on the edge of something and peering down. My handbag was open on the table; he had gone through my purse again.

'I want to stay the night,' he said.

'Here?'

'Can I sleep on that chair?'

I could have said yes. It would have cost me nothing. I could have gone to bed and let him sleep in the chair and then another day would have happened. It's twenty years since he asked that question, and you have no idea how many times I have relived it in my head and played my answer differently. I have seen him asleep in my chair and I have put a blanket over him in case he is cold, and he has grown old like me, but I have kept him safe. Yes, David, I have shouted in my dreams. Yes, yes, yes.

Not knowing all that would follow, however, this is what I did:

I looked at your son, swaying in my sitting room. I looked at my open handbag, my upturned chair. My blood boiled.

I shouted, 'No!' I shouted, 'Go away!' I shouted, 'I've had enough!' My head was thumping. My throat felt cut. The sentences kept coming, all the things I had never said to David. The words were like holes inside me. I couldn't stop.

'You lie. You lie all the time. You take. You take. You only take. You take from me. You take from your father. You drive your mother mad with worry. And what do you do exactly? What are you for?' I could hardly breathe.

I was so shaken, I had to retreat into the kitchen. No glass of water this time. I poured myself a brandy. By the time I returned, the chair was back in its place by the fire. It was empty, save for my red wool mittens, not thrown down, but placed carefully side by side. There was so much stillness, the room roared.

'David?'

He had gone. I hadn't even heard the front door.

And even now I can picture that chair, without him in it, and it is as though he has melted and left me with nothing except the paltry thing that had once been mine.

The following day I was at my desk when I heard one of the secretaries mention your name. Mr Fry had rung in sick was what I heard. You'd never rung in sick in your life.

David had walked from my flat and hanged himself in your garden shed.

FINAL ABSOLUTION

Sip, sip.

    Are you all right, Queenie? Can you hear us? Can you lift your hand if you're in pain?

Sip, sip.

I slept.

The horse is back. So is the lady with the grape-fruit. The dog has his stone but he has given up bringing it to me. The dog just watches the stone, with his head tilted, one ear poised, eternally patient.

    Once I had a pair of ballroom (?) Ballroom (?) What are the things that go on your feet? I can't remember. I had them anyway.

    Little beauties. I loved those things.

Sister Mary Inconnue glances up from her typewriter.

    'You know it was not your fault?'

I have no clue what she is talking about.

    'All those years you blamed yourself, but David's death was not your fault. You couldn't have stopped him. People do as they want.'

    I begin to cry. It is not with pain. It is a sort of

397

relief. Now that I have shaped the songs in my head and placed them on the page, now that my pencil has turned them into lines and tails and curls, I can let them go. My head is silent. The sorrow has not gone but it no longer hurts.

Sister Mary Inconnue smiles. 'Good,' she says. 'That's very good.'

Beyond the window, light flows through the leaves in the tree and sends silver ripples that lap the whitened wall. It is a new day.

EXIT PURSUED BY A NUN

'We have a visitor,' announced Sister Philomena, opening my door wide and appearing to wish to flatten herself against it. 'How exciting.'

Twenty years of waiting. Twelve and a half weeks in a hospice. And when you finally arrive, what do I do? First I almost fall out of the bed and then, just at the climax of the scene, I nod off.

You hovered at the threshold to the room, peering in beside Sister Philomena. Your face was so wind-weathered that your eyes shone. (I was wrong about the irises, Harold. The blue poppies caught you.) No hint of the beard apart from a paler stain to the skin around your mouth, and one or two stray tufts. On your feet there were no yachting shoes, there were only socks, and through one of them your big toe appeared, swollen and bruised. The straps of your rucksack hung loose around your stooped shoulders. There was no sign of my letter in your hands. The sight of you was too much. I had to look away before your eyes found mine.

I kept my head towards the window, hoping you

would not see me. I wondered if Sister Mary Inconnue had showed you my letter. I wondered if you hated me. My heart was banging inside the bone basket of my ribcage.

'But she's not here,' I heard you say. And from the quick, light tone in your voice, I could tell you were relieved. I thought, Go now. It was enough to see you at the door. It was enough to know that you would do this for me.

Sister Philomena laughed. 'Of course she's here.' She said something else but I did not catch it. I heard only the rattle of my breathing.

I remembered the opening words of my letter and the promise to tell you everything. No lies.

As Sister Philomena's footsteps receded down the corridor, you began to creep forward. I could sense your progress even without looking. I was too afraid to move. One soft footstep, another. Then your eyes must have hit my face, and despite yourself, perhaps, you gave a low groan: 'No.'

I turned my face to meet yours but I tried to keep the worst of me away from you.

Oh, and I saw it all, Harold. The look of shock. Horror. Pity too. And the guilt that the sight of me aroused such feelings. You walked all that way and you believed I'd be pretty? I am sorry, Harold, for the way the truth lies. By now you had tugged your rucksack from your back and were holding it against your stomach as if it might protect you. I tried to move my hand to spare you any more, but I'm sorry, with all the writing, I couldn't lift it.

'Hello, Queenie,' you said. All brave.

Hello, Harold, said I. No words.

'It's Harold,' you said. 'Harold Fry. We worked together a long time ago. Do you remember?'

How do I love thee? Let me count the ways. A tear pressed its way from my closed-up eye.

'Did you get my letter?' you said.

Do you have mine?

'Did you get my postcards?'

Can you forgive me?

You got very busy with the contents of your rucksack. 'I have some small souvenirs. I picked them up as I walked. There's a hanging quartz that will look very nice at your window. I just have to find it.' You produced various items, and I think you mentioned honey and pens, but all the time I was thinking: Give me a sign. Tell me you forgive me. You pulled a crumpled paper bag from your rucksack, and when you peered inside your face brightened. You placed the bag a little to the left of my fingers like a small stepping-stone between you and me and then you stood back again. I did not move. Your hand dived forward and you gave the bag a friendly pat, as if to say, Don't be frightened, little paper bag. This is OK, really.

It dawned on me. Maybe you'd not been given my letter? Maybe you'd missed Sister Mary Inconnue? Maybe you still did not know the truth? I felt a terrible throbbing in my head, because that was the deal, remember. That you must know everything.

I tried to point my hand at the suitcase of pages

401

beneath the bed but my stupid body began to slide sideways. I couldn't stop. And the panic on your face. You lifted your hands as if to help, but by now you were pressed right against the window; there was no helping to be done from way over there. And I felt nothing but my love for you, because I saw how hard it is to visit a person and discover you would rather leave. I remembered how you used to glance away when I got into your car as if you were afraid I would embarrass myself. More than anything I wished I could sit upright like any dignified human being.

'Excuse me! She's—'

You called for help, softly at first and then more violently. And here came dear Sister Lucy, only I could tell she was flustered too because she had turned a heavy pink colour and she kept talking nonsense about morgues and visitors. I thought: Any moment, the poor girl will offer to paint your nails. She lifted me up to sitting with her thick arms. I've never heard her talk so loud. In her consternation, a small moustache of wet sweat appeared above her upper lip. She also seemed to have temporarily mislaid your name.

'Apparently Henry has walked. All the way from— Where are you from, Henry?'

(You know this, Sister Lucy, I thought. You do know this.)

You opened your mouth as if to answer and then shut it again because Sister Lucy was already remembering. 'Dorset,' she said with triumph. We really have to hope that no one asks Sister Lucy to lead a walking expedition.

Now you were shouting too. You seemed to be agreeing that yes, you lived in Dorset, and that yes, your name was Henry. By this time Sister Lucy was so frazzled she asked if we should make you a cup of tea. In fact what she suggested was a cuppa. I've never heard her call it a cuppa before. 'There have been so many letters and cards,' she yelled. 'Last week a lady even wrote from Perth.'

(She meant Penge.)

'She can hear you,' said Sister Lucy, pointing at me. She bundled herself out of the room. And we were alone again. You and I. You took Sister Mary Inconnue's chair and sat. You slotted your hands between your knees, tidying yourself into a neat profile.

'Hello,' you began again. 'I must say you're doing very well. My wife – do you remember Maureen? – my wife sends her best regards.'

At the mention of her name, I felt made of air. She forgives me, I thought.

But you were still talking. You glanced back to the door, and I knew you were longing for Sister Lucy and an interruption. After that you got very busy digging something out of the paper bag. Then you sprang to your feet and rushed to the window. For a long time you seemed to remain there, and I watched you lift your hands to the windowsill as if to steady yourself. You looked out over the green-cloaked tree towards the garden and softly, softly you began to cry.

Twenty years of exile slipped away and I saw everything that has brought me here. Something pink spangled at my window. Once again you turned to look at me and I lifted my face to meet yours. I did not hide.

This time there was no snow between us. No street. No window. See me, Harold, I said. And you did. You looked and looked and you saw me. You didn't step away. You didn't gasp. You came closer.

You took your place beside me on the edge of the bed. Without words, you reached out your hand and took up mine. And I would say I felt prickles of electricity but they were not attraction; it was something far deeper now. I closed my fingers around yours.

There you were, sitting to my right and staring ahead, while I sat to your left. You in the driving seat, and me at your side. I could picture the sun through the windscreen. I heard you reach for your driving gloves. I smelt the lemon-coffee scent of you. I tasted mint sweets from my handbag. 'Where to, Miss Hennessy?' As you put your key in the ignition, I felt a swelling in my heart.

All these years, Harold, I have waited to tell you that I loved you. All these years I thought a piece of my life was missing. But it was there all along. It was there when I sat beside you in your car and you began to drive. It was there when I sang backwards and you laughed or I made a picnic and you ate every crumb. It was there when you told me you liked my brown suit, when you opened the door for me, when you asked once if I would like to take the long road home. It came later in my garden. When I looked at the sun and saw it glow on my hands. When a rosebud appeared where there had not been one before. It was in the people who stopped and talked of this and that over the garden wall. And just when I thought my life was done, it came time and time again at the hospice. It has been everywhere, my happiness – when my mother sang for me to dance, when my father took my hand to keep me safe – but it was such a small, plain thing that I mistook it for something ordinary and failed to see. We expect our happiness to come with a sign and bells, but it doesn't. I loved you and you didn't know. I loved you and that was enough.

'It seems a long time since I found you in the stationery cupboard,' you said at last. You gave a Harold Fry laugh.

CANTEEN, I thought. We met in the CANTEEN.

But what did it matter? I wrote at the beginning of my letter that you must know everything. The need to confess the truth has been with me so long it was an illness in itself. But now that I have waited here and told my whole story, I no longer see the waste. I see only the different parts of my life as if I were a child on the banks of a river and setting each one to drift, small as flowers on water.

I pressed my fingers tight around yours and closed my eyes. I smiled. I hope you saw that. I smiled so deeply I was filled with it. Even inside my bones, I smiled. And then all I wanted was sleep. I was not frightened any more.

Rattle, rattle. Here came dear Sister Lucy and her cuppa. I have an awful feeling that she went and called you Henry again. She had difficulties with the tray and the door, so she banged it first with her elbows and afterwards with her behind, and finally with the tray itself.

'Do you mind if I leave the tea?' you said to no one in particular. 'I have to go now.'

I opened my eye long enough to find your tall profile at the door. The room began to melt, and when I looked again, you were gone and so was Sister Lucy.

You have walked far enough. Please, my friend: Go home.

THE HAPPY ENDING

Sister Mary Inconnue sits in my chair. She has not used the door. She has no typewriter.

I make notes but I am slow. I find it hard to lift the? and I keep losing words.

I remember that she is supposed to help and I point to her lap.

'But we've finished now,' she says.

It is hard to find her face because all I can see is the lamp at the window. The walls are gone and I smell the sea. I hear the leaves in the tree and the buzzing of the fly.

Sister Mary Inconnue says, 'Are you in pain, dear Queenie?'

I remember that I have been in pain in the past. But there is none of that now – or if there is, it no longer hurts.

She says, 'I can wait as long as you like. If you want to finish your page.'

I nod. There is a little more to go and it is as small as breathing. The next time I look, she is standing beside the window. I would like to touch her.

'You have done it,' she says. 'People think you have to walk to go on a journey. But you don't,

407

you see. You can lie in bed and make a journey too. What's funny?'

I can't help it. I am listening but I am laugh laugh laugh.

Tree, I say. Do I say that? I am not sure. After all there is no need. She already knows.

'Oh, yes.' Her smile shoots into a happy. 'Tree!' She grips her stomach. She howls.

I see Sister Mary Inconnue and I see other things. The hospice. The Well-being Garden. The water that is the sea. And so many people going about their lives, millions of them, being ordinary, doing ordinary things that no one notices, that no one sings about, but there they are nevertheless, and they are filled with life. I see my father, my mother. I see David. I see Finty, Barbara, the Pearly King, and Mr Henderson. Patients whose names I never knew. On the beach I see you, I see Maureen. I see the dayroom and Sister Lucy rushing down the corridor, towards my door. I see the undertaker fetch his keys for the van and his wife hand him a packed lunch.

See you later, he says.

Have a good day, she replies.

I feel the wind in my sea garden and I hear a thousand shells chime. It is all, all inside me.

Queenie? Where are you? Where is that girl?

Here I am! I'm here! I was here all along. From the very beginning here I was.

A light twists at the window and a shower of stars fills the air. They are many colours. Pink and yellow and blue and green. Oh, so much beauty. In one small thing.

'Are you ready?' says Sister Mary Inconnue, reaching out a hand. It is like touching light.

Put down pencil. Put down notebook. Sleep now.

Well. There it was.

THE THIRD LETTER

ST BERNADINE'S HOSPICE
BERWICK-UPON-TWEED

12 July

Dear Mr Fry,

I enclose pages written by Queenie Hennessy in the last twelve weeks of her life. She began when she first heard about your walk and she finished in the last hour before her death.

You will see that the pages are not written in words, but mainly a series of squiggles, dashes and marks. One of my colleagues believes these hieroglyphics are shorthand, another thinks they are Morse code, but I am afraid that since I can read neither shorthand nor Morse code, I am none the wiser. Only a few words are recognizable and your name is one of them. Our patients often leave cards and messages for family and friends, though this is the first time I have seen such a proliferation of pages.

I want you to know that I believe Queenie died in peace. Moments before her death, Sister Lucy passed Queenie's door and heard a burst of joyful laughter, as if another person was with her and had told her something funny. Sister Lucy is certain she heard the words, *Here I am*. She fetched me. When we entered, minutes later, Queenie was alone and at peace. There was no sign of a visitor.

Sister Lucy told me later that Queenie had asked several times for a volunteer, a nun with a French name, who she said was helping to write her letter. No volunteer with a French name has worked in the hospice.

I reassured Sister Lucy she had misheard. It was hard to understand Queenie. The young woman had also formed a strong attachment to our patient; this can confuse one's objectivity. Sister Lucy is currently taking a break from hospice work in order to explore her skills as a beauty therapist. (She is a gifted young lady.) Her co-worker, Sister Catherine, is making a pilgrimage to Santiago de Compostela.

However, Sister Lucy's observations have stayed with me, as has your unlikely pilgrimage and, indeed, the courage of the woman who sat in silence and waited for you. They have caused me to reflect further on the nature of my belief.

This is the conclusion I have come to: if we work at it, it is always possible to find a rational explanation for what we don't understand. But perhaps it is wiser once in a while to accept that we don't understand, and stop there. To explain is sometimes to diminish. And what does it matter if I believe one thing and you believe another? We share the same end.

Queenie's ashes will be scattered, as she asked, over her sea garden. She bequeathed it, along with her beach house, to the residents of Embleton Bay.

Please send my best wishes to your wife. I don't suppose our paths will cross again, but it was a pleasure to meet you, Harold Fry.

Sister Philomena, Mother Superior, St Bernadine's Hospice

Dear Friend of Harold Fry,

When *The Unlikely Pilgrimage of Harold Fry* was first published, a few people asked if I would be writing a sequel. I quickly assured them that I would not. I felt that I had said everything I needed to say about Harold and Maureen and it was time to let them get on with life, without me watching and taking notes. The person I didn't consider was Queenie Hennessy, Harold's friend: the woman whose first letter inspired a walk that changed Harold Fry's life and, to some extent, mine. She remained very quiet (which is exactly the sort of thing Queenie would do), and then out of the blue one day she shouted, 'Here I am!'

It was not good timing. I was 20,000 words into a new book. I was also working on a radio piece. The last thing I needed was to start writing something else. But then, there I was in the kitchen with my children when Queenie's story arrived. It was one of those ideas that come in a flash, but fully dressed – so that you feel it's been around a long time. I told my children because it was so exciting, this idea, I couldn't keep it to myself. And my children said something along the lines of, 'Yes, very good. Now what's for lunch?'

That night I barely slept. I had Queenie's words, her story, spinning in my head. I didn't know if any of those words made sense, but I did know that I was at the beginning of something and that I would have to stay with it and find the whole story. In the morning, when I looked again at *The Unlikely Pilgrimage of Harold Fry*, it occurred to me that in truth I'd had the idea of writing from Queenie's perspective long ago – I had written one small piece, that taste of her voice, in the *Harold Fry* chapter 'Queenie and the Present'. I'd had the idea and I hadn't quite seen it.

Over the last few years, I have talked a lot about Harold Fry. But sometimes people have asked me about Queenie, too. And there have been a few readers, I admit, who have asked, Why? Why did I have to give Queenie her disfiguring cancer? I always explain – as gently as I can, although it is still an emotional answer for me – that this was how it was for my father and I felt I must be true to that. But it has also bothered me as an answer, because although my father's cancer *was* terrible to look at by the end, it wasn't *him*. When I think of him now, for instance, I think of the man who was my father before the cancer. I think of him laughing or calling, 'Wotcha, Rache!' or walking past the window with a ladder. It is the same with Queenie. She had a voice, a life, before she was the woman we find in a hospice at the end of a book. I wanted to discover all that. When Queenie retells the story from her own perspective, she never uses the word 'cancer' and she barely refers to her appearance. The cancer is not her journey. Her journey is one of reparation. In telling her story, she becomes whole.

My father died at home. He was not in pain. So to write this book, I spent time with several Macmillan nurses and I visited two hospices for the terminally ill. Before I went, I felt fearful. Would I see anything I shouldn't? Would I be frightened? Make a fool of myself and cry? But what struck me about both the hospices and the nurses was the life in them. The joy. The hospices were full of light, full of activity and full of laughter. The nurses I met had endless hilarious stories to tell. And so I set out to write a book about dying that was full of life. It seems to me that you can't really write about one without the other – just as you can't really write about happiness if you don't confront sadness. It's by looking at the whole shape of something, I think, that you see it for what it is.

In the hospices we talked a lot about dying. We talked, too, about my father and his own death. At the end of one meeting, the manager said to me, 'You *need* to write this book.' I probably cried – because it had been an emotional day. But I cried also because he was right.

And so I made my own hospice, St Bernadine's.

Several patients arrived – quite shady in my mind to begin with, but gathering colour and volume as I wrote. They became a sort of chorus for Queenie – her backing vocals, if you like. The nuns who look after these patients are inspired by the community of seven nuns who live in our village in Gloucestershire. I saw one of them the day we first came to see the house – a figure walking the land in a cream robe and black apron – and there was something so serene about that picture that these nuns instantly became part of my experience of where I live. Only yesterday I opened the gate to fetch my car and found a nun pressed against our garden wall. She seemed to be waiting for something or possibly blowing her nose. I have no idea, but whatever it was, she was very good-humoured about it.

In order to find Queenie's home, her beach house, I returned to Berwick-upon-Tweed with my husband and children and we visited the stunning Northumberland coastline. I have been back twice more. It was on our final visit – a trip that we made the weekend before I submitted the typescript – that we found Embleton Bay and the wooden beach houses up on the cliff. Queenie's house is one I made in my head, but if you ever go to Embleton Bay, you will find a set of sand steps carved into the dunes that might once have led to her garden.

Queenie's sea garden began as just that – three words. It was after studying Northumberland gardens and the coastal paths that my imagination planted her sea garden with flowers and driftwood figures. I am glad she has those. She fills her garden with the people in her life in the same way that I fill my writing with the people in mine. And by the way, my children are very glad to see that our old border terrier (Dog) is back.

It has been an extraordinary thing for me to revisit *Harold Fry* and replay some of those chapters with a new twist. It has been something, too, to give Maureen a different voice, and David – and to find the Harold Fry that Queenie and indeed Maureen fell in love with. For me, it isn't just Queenie who feels put back together; it is them, too.

And for the record, I still would say that I have not written a sequel to *The Unlikely Pilgrimage of Harold Fry*. I have not written a prequel either. What I have written is a book that sits alongside *Harold Fry*. They really should come that way – her in the passenger seat, him in the driving seat. Side by side.

I would call this book a companion.

Rachel Joyce
2014